DOLLY
AND
THE
COOKIE
BIRD

DOLLY
AND
THE
COOKIE
BIRD

DOROTHY DUNNETT

Vintage Books
A Division of Random House
New York

First Vintage Books Edition, September 1982
Copyright © 1970 by Dorothy Dunnett
All rights reserved under International and
Pan-American Copyright Conventions. Published
in the United States by Random House, Inc., New
York. Originally published in Great Britain by
Cassell & Company Ltd. and in the United States
by Houghton Mifflin Company under the title
Murder in the Round in 1970.
Library of Congress Cataloging in Publication Data
Dunnett, Dorothy.
Dolly and the cookie bird.
Originally published: Murder in the round.
Boston : Houghton Mifflin, 1970.
I. Title.
PR6054.U56M83   1982   823'.914   82-40043
ISBN 0-394-71164-5 (pbk.)   AACR2
Manufactured in the United States of America

With affection
for Willie Mackinley,
who knows these seas
better than DOLLY

DOLLY
AND
THE
COOKIE
BIRD

CHAPTER 1

BIFOCAL GLASSES are common.

So Janey used to say, before it all happened. Common, like see-through gloves and champagne stoppers and high heels with trousers.

I thought so too, until Janey went on her bender in the last term at St. Tizzy's and Flo and I had to undress her and pop her contact lenses out on the bed. I think contact lenses are common.

St. Theresa's is the pricey establishment at which Flo and Janey and I were all pseudo-educated. You couldn't call it broad-minded on sex, but it was absolute death on religious disparity. Naturally, we went through Zen Buddhists like chaff, and I remember going out for weeks with a Catholic boy, and not only to spite the biology mistress. He was, I recall, to have the interest on £20,000 capital when he was eighteen. He told me the percentage, and I worked it out in my prep book. It sounded all right. Then I found him snogging with Janey, and we had a row to end all rows, and that was the end of the ecumenical urge at St. Tizzy's.

I used to wonder if Daddy would have swallowed the Catholic bit because of the money. I think I worried in case he stopped sending me fivers for birthdays, if I upset him too much. Now of course he doesn't send me fivers, and he couldn't swallow anything anyway, if you want to put it like that, since he was found with his throat cut, that night in Ibiza.

I remember Flo in the flat, waiting to tell me that Daddy had passed on to better things. I'd been out all that day, cooking a conference lunch for sixteen dental surgeons. I suppose you'd call Flo my very best friend. She was fat, and rather well off, and had a mother I thought fairly decent. Not too Red Cross and County, but rather giggly and ineffective and well-meaning, like Flo. After we both left St. T's, Flo and I did our course of Mother Trudi Haute Cuisine together. Three months and eighty-nine guineas, forked up by Daddy. And all the qualifications you need to share a flat with another girl and do freelance cooking in London. That was what they told you, at least.

At any rate, I came back to the flat that afternoon with my pockets full of free dental samples and a bit of greaseproof paper with the telephone number of the one unmarried dentist, and there was Flo, looking pained with her teeth sunk into her lip, which meant she wanted to giggle. Sudden death affects a lot of people that way, and after all, there are more dignified ways of committing suicide than taking a razor at night to a boatyard and climbing onto the back of a horse-winch. I suppose, knowing Spain, Daddy thought the gas oven wouldn't have enough pressure. Or maybe he remembered last time, when Mummy first left him, and Derek came in from cricket and turned the gas off.

Derek was always, so to speak, turning the gas off. He's my brother. There are only the two of us, and I must say my first thought when Flo told me Daddy was dead was, Hell. Where does the money come from now? For since Derek got himself a nice job in electronics in Holland, the fivers from that quarter have pined away to a joke. I asked Derek for a thousand pounds when I left the Mother Trudi to set myself up in a kitchen, and when I got his reply I felt bloody Bolshie, I can tell you. What's a thousand quid to an engineer? He doesn't even have dirty weekends to spend it on: he isn't that sort of boy. And there'd be nothing from Daddy. He got an income from a trust that would end when he died, and the same trust had paid for my education and Derek's. After that, we'd get nothing until we were thirty, and even then hardly more than would pay for an E-type Jag apiece. Everyone says that's a hairdresser's car. All I can say is, I never met a hairdresser who had one.

At any rate, there was Flo and the woman who owns the flat, waiting to tell me the sad tale; and apparently the phone had been ringing all morning, and the trustees had called, and a friend or two of Daddy's, and the press. Flo had given the newspapers the Tatler picture of Daddy and me at the Malaysian banquet. I'd made the dress myself, and it looked it, but Daddy had sprung the cash for a hairdo, and someone he'd had lunch with had lent him the family tiara, and I'd spent half an hour over my eyes. *The United Kingdom High Commissioner shares a joke with Lord Forsey of Pinner, and the Hon. Sarah Cassells, his daughter.* He was never sober enough to be photographed after the Tatler went out of print; although I don't suppose that had anything to do with it.

Derek was flying out, they said, to identify the body. I didn't want to identify the body, but I'd have liked to have gone to Ibiza which is a Spanish island in the Mediterranean, just south of Majorca. I phoned a couple of cousins with the sad tidings, and they both invited me to stay, after a bit, but nobody forked out, and I hadn't even been paid for the dentists yet. About that stage I went into the bedroom and phoned the telephone number on my piece of waxed paper, but he was working late that night and then going away for a fortnight. In March, I ask you.

In the next room the woman who owned the flat was saying in heavy West Kensington . . . "her mother?" . . . and Flo was explaining. Good luck to her. The press could track down Geraldine, Lady Forsey, and tell her: I didn't care. My mother is an American bitch who married poor Daddy for his title and then walked out on him. And on us. She'll be sitting in the Lincoln Center right now, drinking bullshots with Lenny Bernstein. Music, painting, the Dance. Culture. The artistic experience. A far cry, at any rate, from a Spanish boatyard and a bankrupt and permanently sloshed nobleman riding around and around in the dark on a horse-winch. I approved of him, rather. I mean, you talk of them at school as if they were dotty, and he was a drunken old sot. But I did approve of him.

I wished I could have gone to Ibiza.

It was Flo's night for having her George up to the flat, and I was sort of between boyfriends, so I phoned a few more numbers in my book, but they were all busy, or studying for exams, or something, so I had a hot dog and went to the flicks and bought a pizza pie off the proceeds of my special fruit machine on my way home. I can win up to two-and-six on it if I'm careful, but I don't do it too often in case the Fun Parlor switches the lemons, or something.

Anyway, the pizza pie was still warm, and I charged up the stairs to the flat whistling like stink and rapped on the door before I put my key in, for good measure. George usually brings some beer. I like fizzy stone ginger.

The light was out, which was a bit off, as it was after half-past eleven, and I'd got to get back sometime. I said "Flo-o," very politely, and groped for the switch, but the light didn't come on and I forgave them. Flo couldn't cope with a fuse. The torch in the hall drawer was flat. I went on calling Flo-o but no one answered except the old bitch in the flat above, who banged on the ceiling, so I dropped my coat and my scarf on the floor and dragged a chair across to the meter and stood on it. On top of the fuse box were wire, screwdriver, scissors and a Woolworth's torch in full working order. Unlike Flo, I believe in doing things properly. I switched the torch on and looked for the lever to throw the light circuit off. It

7

was thrown up already, and the handle snapped off.

Now that, Flo wouldn't do. And George is a motor car salesman and would do his necking for kicks in Selfridge's window if the bylaws would let him. My legs felt like candles all of a sudden, but I didn't need to think what to do. I jumped down, and galloping through to the bedroom, torch in hand, I picked up the phone and dialed 999

Someone in the flat sniggered. My hot dog came straight back up into my throat and I swung the torch round, still hanging on to the phone, which was perfectly dead. I had time to see Flo with her new culottes all creased, laid out cold on the floor, then something banged my wrist, hard, and the torch fell and went out.

To hell with that. I'm five foot seven stripped, and I was head prefect *and* principal bat at St. T's. I've sat with two medical students in the back of an old Hillman Minx at three in the morning and come away without losing a button. I ducked in the pitch blackness and ran for the door; and as the man, whoever he was, crashed against me, I kicked him hard in the shins, drove my elbow into his middle, and hauling open the bedroom door, rushed through and slammed it, yelling. I got the key turned just as he laid hands on the handle inside. The old idiot upstairs bumped on the ceiling, and I made for the main door to the stairs.

I forgot, blow it, the chair under the meter. As I went flying. I could hear the door panels cracking behind me and horrible thuds as someone shouldered and kicked them.

The bloody thing was warped anyway. It gave with a crash as I picked myself up and something came at me like a steam engine. I seized the chair and stuck it out in his way.

The thud this time brought down the pictures, and for a moment I thought he was winded. I was going to lay him out with the frying pan and tie him up with the nylon line from the bathroom, with Flo's tights still pegged all along it. But he got up in such a whirl of shoes and fists and pieces of chair that I was a bit daunted, to tell you the truth, and before I could do a thing more, he had jerked open the front door and vanished.

By the time I got there, the stairs were empty, and I was shaking anyway like a speedometer needle and my hot dog was giving me trouble. I groped my way into the bathroom and got rid of it, and then got back into the hall, dragged another chair forward and climbed on it. The light switch was still broken and off, but the power circuit hadn't been touched. I got down, and feeling my way past the sagging door, found the bedside lamp and plugged it into the 13-amp socket. Light.

Flo stirred. She looked like her mother, who is all right but doesn't know how to make up. Then she sat up suddenly, and this time she looked really awful. "My God," she said. "Have I fainted?"

I sat down beside her and held her poor old cold hands. "It's all right," I said. "We've been burgled. You were only knocked out, or drugged."

I've never seen such an improvement in anybody. "Oh, thank heavens," said Flo faintly. "I thought I was preggers."

I promise you. Talk about inefficient.

*   *   *

We found George much later, after I'd told all my story and we'd got Flo's culottes fixed and looked at the mess in the room. Every drawer in the place had been hauled out, and even the bedding unscrambled—or at least Flo said it wasn't like that when she last saw it. She'd lost the charm bracelet she got from her last boyfriend but one, and was livid. According to her, the doorbell had rung, and George had left her to answer it. She heard him speaking, and then a silence, and she had just started to the door to find out why he hadn't come back when the lights all went out. The next thing was an ether pad over her face. "Well, look on the bright side. You hadn't had the pizza," I said.

George we discovered humped on the floor in the sitting room, and it was rather plain from the start that the Lotus Elan touch was a bit wanting. He looked a disaster and obviously felt it, and it was clear from the way Flo was shuffling about that she knew that as far as George's associations were concerned, her wagon was fixed. All we ever got out of him, even after we switched from instant coffee to Flo's half-bottle of Japanese whiskey, was that he had been knocked down by a middle-aged man with a stocking over his face. He was also stinking of ether.

I had the pizza pie myself, after we telephoned the police at my suggestion from the flat up above. We got to bed finally at three, after the police had finger-printed the rooms and asked a whole lot of questions. All we'd lost were Flo's bracelet and my American earrings from Mummy, which had been too nice to throw away. I was always getting presents from Mummy which were too nice to throw away.

My three good family pieces were all right because I was wearing them. I always wear them, sometimes under my clothes and sometimes on top. It reminds me, if I needed reminding, that I am the daughter of the fifth Baron Forsey of Pinner . . . Of the late fifth Baron Forsey of Pinner. Hell.

George slept the rest of the night on the sofa, and I cried with my head under my pillow until Flo gave me six aspirins and the rest of the Japanese whiskey, and I had a wonderful night.

My brother Derek flew over for Daddy's funeral. I didn't want to go: I had a hundred and fifty brandy snaps to make for a wedding in Hampshire, and brandy snaps by Flo are simply well-rolled tarmacadam. However the lawyer-trustee, whom I rather go for, came back from his shoot and took me to a nice plushy lunch at the Café Royal in order to jaw me, and then Derek rang up to say he was back from Ibiza and would I take a taxi round to the Dorchester, which he would pay for.

Daddy never stayed at the Dorchester; he couldn't afford it; but of course he'd been there hundreds of times at private parties and functions, and I knew how to swan in and where. I had a goodish cloth coat, which I'd shortened rather a lot, and a super black hat of Flo's like a highwayman, and long black boots.

Derek's room had a high bed with kicked Queen Anne legs, and there was a battery of taps like Bofors guns in the loo. Derek's pad was usually the Hilton, with non-stop taped music and an ice-water tap and big lamps for snogging in strategic places all over the room. Not that Derek would bother with girls. He is just split-level minded and goes for efficiency.

We are not much alike. I'm fair, like the Forseys, but Derek is brown like Mummy was before she had it turned pink. He's not much taller than I am, which he hates, but he bathes a lot oftener. Derek is a great soap-and-shoe-polish man. He even went through a health-regime fad: sauna baths and nut rissoles; the lot, but he grew out of it and isn't a bad cook at that. At least when he takes you out you can be sure of a good meal and a decent bottle of wine, although he won't touch spirits nor smokes. He isn't bad really: he's just anti-Daddy, and I don't suppose you can blame him.

Anyway, he hadn't much to say about Daddy now. It was suicide all right: they'd found the razor dropped from his hand. He was still sitting on the horse, no doubt neck-high with Vat 69. Out of respect for the dead, Derick did manage to keep the disgust out of his voice, but he said the funeral was to be quiet and quick down at Pinner after the Spanish police had done their stuff, and what the hell did brandy snaps have to do with it. In the end, I got thirty quid out of him for a draggy black out-fit I'd spotted in Fenwick's, and agreed to turn up. If I stuck at it all night, I worked out, I could do my baking and Flo's bit as well.

From then until the funeral was a bit of a dead loss, because Derek said parties were out and wouldn't even consider a discothèque, so we had a number of sedate evenings with Purcell and Strind-berg, interspersed with a lot of silences if I stopped talking, which you have to do sometimes. I gathered

Derek was enjoying his job, had a nice company house with housekeeper laid on, and was concerned more than anything with how poor Daddy's death would affect his professional image. He's with Schuytstraat, the people who'd just mislaid their big new experimental aural sensator.

But he wouldn't talk about that. He asked me twice if I knew why Daddy had done it and what he had said in his letter; but of course Daddy never wrote letters, and I hadn't heard from him for months.

He also asked me, as the trustees had, what I was going to do; and I said carry on cooking. I don't mind it; and I don't see how on earth I'm going to find someone decent to marry unless I do. Derek didn't get the point. I think he thought cooks stay in the kitchen, and his pride was offended. At least he did ask me, without enthusiasm, if I'd like to come and keep house for him, but I said no. My God, Holland.

Mummy didn't come to the funeral, and I think Derek was relieved: he was always a little afraid of her. The papers had dug out her theatrical history and added a bit about her being laid low with a virus in her beautiful Billy Baldwin-designed Fifth Avenue home. I rather respected her for it. Whatever she was, she wasn't a hypocrite. Anyway, the Fenwick outfit was pretty stunning, and I was photographed for two different newspapers, and there were four Daimlers and a Rolls-Royce, private ones, in the funeral procession. The owner of the Rolls-Royce had an alpaca overcoat and eyed me a good bit during the service. He was about Daddy's age but much more the spring-grip dumbbells and chinning-bar type: broadly built with dark hair and the kind of suntan you can't get with a sunlamp, but can with a villa in Trinidad. Afterwards, he came across and took both my hands, and said, *"Sarah!"*

He didn't honestly look as if he needed a cook, but the suntan was more than something. I said, "Are you a friend of Daddy's? It was so kind of you to come."

"My dear girl!" he said. He was still holding my hands. "But surely you were at school with my Jane? At St. Theresa's?"

I removed my hands. Some snotty schoolgirl called Jane. This was always happening. Daddy was only the Hon. Eric Cassells while I was at school, so no one connects me with Forsey. I ran my mind without enthusiasm over the ranks of St. T's. Then something made me look at him again. "Janey Lloyd!" I exclaimed. "You're not Janey Lloyd's father? I can't believe it! How is she?"

He smiled and put his hands in his pockets. "She hasn't changed a bit, and neither have you. You were the two most elegant girls in the school. But Sarah . . ."

I had remembered at the same time. "But what are you doing here?"

The power-beam faded, and his expression got back to the funeral. "You see, I had no idea, Sarah, that you were Lord Forsey's daughter, or of course we'd have written. When I saw you standing there . . . You haven't changed. You see . . . Your father was staying with me," said Mr. Lloyd sadly, "when he ended his life."

CHAPTER 2

"THEY'VE GOT a hotel," I said, "in Seville and a flat at Jerez and an office in Gib and in Malaga. They have acres of vineyards and a bullfarm and an interest in a shipping line and three olive oil factories and some business in Spanish Morocco. Janey was finished in Florence and has been round the world twice and has just spent Christmas in Nassau and came back for the skiing. They want me to stay with them."

"That's O.K.," said Flo soothingly. "Business will stand it."

It was after the funeral, and the rush for our services had cooled off at the same time as George, so Flo and I were staying at her mother's nice house in Hampshire. Flo's Mama is a brick, which compels me to weed the garden and paper the maid's room when I stay with her, so I don't go there too often.

"She's got a brother called Gilmore," Flo added. "Clem knows him."

I looked, but she wasn't hiding a smile. I had a crush on Gilmore Lloyd when we were at school. I only saw him once, but that was enough. He was head boy at Harrow. I said, "How on earth does Clem know him?" Clem Sainsbury is Flo's favorite cousin.

Flo said, "Are you imploying that my cousin doesn't move in the right circles to know Giller Lloyd?" and went off into gales of unladylike laughter. I said, "Flo, you're awful," without really thinking. Clem was an absolute pet: on *that* the whole of St. Tizzy's agreed; but so Duke of Edinburgh it just wasn't true. I never met anyone in my life who used up so much energy on totally useless pursuits. By nineteen I should think he had climbed everything and swum everything and played everything there was in the book, and had never done more with a girl than drag her off to a rugby match and then give her a beer in a pub. We'd all had a try at Clem and got no further than a warm-up inside his sheepskin. Flo said, "You know he's nutty on sailing? He spent his hols last year hanging about crewing at Gib, and he's taken six months off this year to do the same thing." Clem had a modest degree in social anthropology and a lot of big silver cups.

"What does he know about Gilmore Lloyd?" I inquired.

"Spoiled, rich and beautiful. What we all know already. Now, Sarah . . ." said Flo.

"Oh, I know," I said. Flo will make out that I'm overeager. But if you don't put yourself across, who'll do it for you? And you might not get a second chance.

At the beginning of Easter week, I flew to Ibiza alone.

I don't mind flying. Except when I'm out with a new boy, I have a very strong stomach, and the *Trident* from London was full of middle-aged businessmen. I opened a magazine and looked up my horoscope.

I'd been in Spain once before, with Mummy during the school holidays. It must have been just before she got fed up with having an alcoholic society husband with no money, for she used occasionally to take out Derek or me to toughen our cultural muscles: the rest of the time we were foisted on aunts, or other parents, or even on decent old helps in the house. Daddy, I believe, wouldn't have minded seeing much more of us, but once he'd got us, he simply didn't know what to do. You can't drag an eleven-year-old schoolboy to impromptu late-night parties full of wags and wits and bunches of brainy sophisticates and expect him to mix. Or if you do, and he is totally silent, or even worse, sick: then you simply don't take him again. Derek never understood that. And later on, when he was grown up, he had missed out on the training: he hadn't the address or the nous to keep in with Daddy's lot.

I might have done. I suppose I could have had a pretty marvelous time, but by then it wasn't my scene. The sort of people who wanted a tame titled jester, and didn't mind if he drank, weren't my sort, and I didn't enjoy watching my father sing for his supper. He was neat and witty and relaxed and so easy-going it just wasn't true. I don't think I ever heard him say an unkind thing in his life: even about Mummy; even about the fat stockbrokers whose villas he stayed in. He sold them his company because they had money, and he needed money to live on. He didn't seem to despise them.

But I wouldn't do it. I wouldn't go to the Lloyds' and expect to live on their handouts. They meant to be kind, but I'd made that quite clear before I left London. If I went to Ibiza, I would earn my board and my ticket, by cooking. And after a lot of pricey phone arguments, Mr. Lloyd had agreed.

I turned over the magazine. The little plastic food trays had come and had gone, and I had the feeling that someone was watching me. I think that's always exciting.

Anyhow, I was wearing my hair up, and this beret, and this little baker-boy suit with long patterned stockings, and sitting in a first-class seat beside a window that wasn't full of dribbling wing, for which Janey's father was entirely to be thanked, when this man came and sat down, thump, beside me; and somehow I knew at once who had been looking.

He smelt American. He was big and broad-shouldered, with that super kind of Swedish suede jacket in Sahara-sand color and a long white polished tie and hair growing downward, like Jacques Tati. He had a big gold watch showing the seconds, the hour, the day, the date, the month, the moon phase, and the telephone number of his stockbroker; and a gold signet ring on his right hand. Nothing on his left. "I'm terribly sorry, ma'am," he said. "I'm afraid you've got half my seat belt."

18

He was from Minnesota, unmarried, and his father had been a senator with big real estate interests. He had three Cadillacs and an antiques and art-dealing business, with branches all over the place. He even had a shop in Ibiza, called Gallery 7. I asked him what he sold.

He said, "Well, Sarah: maybe you think this is just a sleepy little island full of sleepy little peasants selling straw shopping bags and cheap castanets to the hundred-dollar package-deal holiday trade. But I can tell you I don't sell ballpoint pens made up to look like banderillas. Have you heard of St. Paul de Vence? Biot? Rocquebrune?"

"They're all artists' colonies, aren't they?" I said. "On the Riviera." There wasn't any fizzy stone ginger, so he had bought me a large sherry. I bought myself a pack of duty-free cigarettes to give to Janey's father. I had six pounds left in my bag. It wasn't much.

"That's right," said Austin. He was called Austin. I was praying he was also called Rockefeller or even Woolworth, but we hadn't got beyond Christian names. "And that's what's happening right here in Ibiza. The weather's good, the living's cheap, and any guy with talent who's not too fussy can find a hole somewhere to work and a ready-made market in summer. Sure, they're shoving up concrete hotels on the beaches and selling urbanization parcels like peanuts, but the place is still full of snazzy villas in nice discreet corners owned by big names who want to get away from it all. Singers, businessmen, politicians, actors. You name 'em. In a year or two they'll move on, but Ibiza isn't Majorca just yet. That's my market."

I said, "You mean you buy paintings and stuff from the colony and sell it all in your shop?" I wished, for the first time, I had really listened to Mummy laying off on the topic of new advanced art. It gave Daddy hysterics.

"Sure. Or Gregorio, my manager, does. We sell carvings and oils and ceramics and jewelry, and mix it all with antiques from the mainland. We have a workshop of our own for repairs and a bit of repro work, and we tour exhibitions as well. I've got one in the gallery right now of North American Art in the Round that's traveling right across Europe. You know what I mean? Caro? Volten? Philip King?"

"I'd love to see it," I said. The only Art in the Round I'd ever heard of was a strip show in Soho that George had told us about. "But I don't know how long I'll be here. I'm just visiting a girl I was at school with."

"Come tomorrow," said Austin. "Bring your friend. Where are you staying?"

"Near a place called Santa Eulalia," I said. "At the Casa Veñets with the Lloyds."

His big, scrubbed, handsome face glowed with delight. "You know Tony Lloyd? But of course, you'll be the same age as Janey. Well, whadda you know?" He thought of something I ought to know. "Maybe you haven't been to the Casa Veñets before. But when you get there, you'll find half the antiques are from Mandleberg's."

"That's the name of your business?" I said. He seemed awfully simple. But then, I used to think George was simple, and Flo used to get furious.

"Austin Mandleberg, that's me," he said. "Go right up to the city wall and climb through the old town to the Calle de San Guillermo, No. 7. That's my gallery."

"My name's Sarah Cassells," I said. "I'll come tomorrow. I'd adore to see all your things. Are you going to stay long?"

"Oh, a few weeks, maybe. I get around," said Austin Mandleberg. "I've another gallery in Seville. Ever been to Seville?"

"Only once," I said. That had been the term I was Poppy Phillip's best friend. The parents were always keen for me to come with them on holidays. If Mummy arranged it, she usually saw I had decent clothes but forgot to give me enough spending money. If it was Daddy, he didn't do either. I loved the lush hotels and the big cars and the foreign boys fighting to get you out on the beach after midnight, but I hated the pauperdom.

"You must come again," said Austin Mandleberg. "I'd sure like to show you Seville." He didn't seem to have heard of Lord Forsey, sitting on the horse-winch with his throat cut. I wondered what he'd think, when he got to Ibiza and heard the latest sensation. Out of the corner of my eye, I saw the Pyrenees poke through the clouds. They were snowy, like one of Flo's batches of tea cakes whose Royal icing had run. "Where do you stay, when you come to look after business?" I inquired.

It was a pity, rather. There was a house over the shop. I wondered if Gregorio cooked.

I couldn't quite make out his annual income in dollars, but by the time we were circling over Ibiza, I knew quite a lot about Austin Mandleberg, and I'd told him about Daddy, too, in the end. He was very quiet and intense about it and held my hand for the last half hour, and I could feel my head swimming a bit, with the Dry Sack and the chatting up and the fact that we were flying on our ear for ten minutes awaiting permission to land. I like my horizons horizontal. I always have.

Then we came in very low over a litle network of runways set in a waste of flat scrub. A man in a straw hat was bent over weeding or something in the middle, his miniscooter propped on a stump. He didn't look up as we shaped up to land. I was sorry. I always feel if the undercarriage doesn't come down, at least they could jump up and point.

The undercarriage must have come down, for we landed on it.

I was first out of the airplane. It was warm, and there was this super smell I'd forgotten, made up of cigar smoke and palm trees and dry dust and strong scent and olive oil and something I thought must be orange blossom. I'd looked at Lord Luck before we left London, and he said it was a good day for sport, but I must control my impulses toward evening. Celeste on the other hand had said Mars was moving through Scorpio and should give me the energy and determination to carry out my plans. I couldn't see Janey. I turned on the aircraft steps and said to Austin, "When is your birthday?"

He said, "I beg your pardon?" and then we got it worked out that he was Virgo. He didn't seem worried about it, but I wished I'd looked it up before coming. Celeste hadn't said anything about Virgo.

I took a long time to cross to the airport buildings with Austin. If Janey was waiting, which I doubted, there was no point in depriving her of the view. Beyond the other planes and the red-and-white

Campsa tankers rushing between them, the land stretched flat as a pancake to a lot of green woolly hills with Martini hoardings and windmills in front of them. If you turned back, you could see more hills on the other side of the airport, with a sheet of water before them, divided into sort of dikes. There was a long, low white thing, like a thin clip of paper. "Salt," said Austin. "Those are salt flats you see. They ship out thousands of tons from that anchorage. Let me carry your coat." And we walked up the slope beneath a flowery lattice and between paths edged with cacti and small palms and purple bougainvillea and red climbing geraniums, and into the airport.

Janey wasn't there, and there were no messages. That was no surprise: Janey never yet got anywhere on time, and it just meant that something more interesting had turned up, and I would have to wait.

I didn't altogether despair. The place was modern and airy and full of taped music, mother-in-law's tongue in long boxes, and well-set-up soldiers in clean grey-green uniforms, with cross straps and big black leather holsters on their left hips. Or maybe they were just policemen. There was one with a nice smile.

My case took ages: they had to send out and look for it. By the time Austin tracked it down there was still no sign of Janey. Outside on the tarmac was a lineup of bright-colored buses: Lunn-Poly, Global and Fit; and two taxis; and a beaten up Seat 600, and a Cadillac. The red-and-silver Iberia bus had gone off already.

I turned to Austin. "It *has* been fun," I said. "And you've been sweet to help me so much. Janey won't be long now. May I say goodbye until to-morrow?"

He held my hand. "Now what makes you think I'd leave a nice girl like you standing alone at an airport? We'll just leave a message here for your friends, and then I'll run you to Santa Eulalia."

It was a super Cadillac. We swept away from the Muzak and the noise and the long breathy hoot of planes standing waiting, like vacuum cleaners stuck on a carpet. I took my baker-boy hat off and let my hair whip behind, and the spring flowers and lemon trees and green fields and white houses with shutters all flashed by, and the signs for Pastis 51 and Tio Pepe, and the windmills, like spider's webs spinning with fishtails, until Austin said, "Look."

Above the treetops far ahead was a little wedge-shaped pink hill full of houses, with a sort of clock tower on top. In the setting sun it looked like a bride's cake. I crossed my fingers and said, "It looks like a bride's cake," and Austin agreed. To hell with Celeste. "That's Ibiza," he said. "The town Ibiza, I mean. The clock is on the Cathedral tower. My gallery is a couple of lanes further down. You'll love it."

"I know I shall, Austin," I said.

We went through Ibiza to get to Santa Eulalia, but we didn't go up to his gallery. We turned through a sort of boulevard with shops and cafés and trees at the foot of the hill, and then out to a dazzle of ships and blue sea and a long line of boats queuing neatly right along the main road. A square white-masted building showed up on the right, just past a boatyard with someone's old ferryboat high up on the stocks, and Austin nodded his head as we passed.

"The Club Nautico. The yacht marina and boat-yard."

I looked back, just as he said, "My God: Sarah, I'm sorry." It was the boatyard, I suppose, where a week or two back, Daddy was found on the horse-winch. I gave a brave smile at Austin, but it didn't upset me: not then. In fact, in a funny way, it made me feel more at home.

At the next corner there was a notice saying, Santa Eulalia, 13.5, and a long, straight avenue of leafless trees leading north. Austin let out the Cadillac just as the sun disappeared. Ahead of us, the sky had a few litle pink clouds, but all the color had gone from the roadside. I shut my eyes and let the wind carry my hair.

It was a good road. I felt the drag as Austin slowed down and took a bend sharp on the right, and then we picked up speed again in a long rising course. I opened my eyes and saw the new lights of a road café slide behind, and a dark field full of goats. On the right, the road crumbled into a sort of dusty red ditch, overhung by a little wood with a lot of juniper undergrowth and an old car with no wheels at one end. Austin turned into the dirt and drew up. At last.

It wasn't even off the road: not properly, but I'd forgotten how soon it gets dark. My hair settled all over my face, like Brigitte Bardot, and I pushed it back, carefully, with my hands, which cleared the way for Austin's Sahara suede cuffs to go right round my back. "You're so lovable!" he said, the rest of him following, so I put my hands comfortably round his neck and we had a very soft, long-winded kiss. He was good; and I must say I was glad of every bit of practice I'd ever had. Then he took his hands away and sat back a bit and said, "I beg your pardon. You're too lovely a person, and I want you to forgive me. I don't know . . . I just couldn't help myself."

I thought of the last hunt ball I'd been to, and kept my face straight. "It was nice," I said. "But we don't really know each other. I think perhaps we'd better get on."

Either I hadn't managed to keep my face straight, or he was normal after all, for instead of driving on he suddenly grabbed me in quite a definite way and stuck his mouth on mine in a much more advanced method, doing lots of fancy things, on the side, with his tongue. It was super, but I was being slowly shoved back into the side of the car, and I was just thinking of feeling for my shoe when the car door gave way and we both fell, headfirst, backward into the ditch. We landed just as a seedy old Seat came wheezing up round the bend and slowed, its headlights picking out the whole scene like an art clip from Ulysses. *"Perdone-me,"* said an English voice in horrible Spanish. "Does the Señor require assistance?"

I could see a pair of spectacles winking in the Cadillac's dashboard light: Flo would have killed herself laughing. Austin said, "No, sir; I thank you. There's no trouble at all," in a loud, hearty voice and after hesitating, turned and helped me to my feet. I'd busted my tights, which was more than a bit sad. Austin said one or two bright things about tripping and dark nights and fine weather, and handing me in, got seated and started the engine. I gave the other driver a wave. He stood and watched us go in a bemused kind of way, before turning back to the Seat. Austin drove the rest of the way to Santa Eulalia with a hand on my knee, pressing it.

It was just before we got into Santa Eulalia that I missed my handbag. My hair was a mess, and God knows what had happened to my mouth outline. I grubbed all over the floor of the car, and it just wasn't there.

Austin stopped the car, and by the time we'd made a thorough search it was quite certain it must be back in that ditch where the Seat had interrupted us. Austin said, "You go on. I'll drop you at the Lloyds', and then go back for the bag."

There was nothing else I could do. I drove up to meet Gilmore Lloyd after seven years with my tights wrecked and my hair hanging in hanks and my lipstick all over my chin. All right. At least he could tell I was sought-after.

The Casa Veñets is set on a hillside in five acres of tropical garden, which go right down to the sea. Arriving there in the dark, with the palm trees showing against a big yellow moon like an advertisement for coconut candy, and the cicadas making the sound the B.B.C. always makes them make, and the lizards flicking up and down the house walls, it was a bit breathtaking suddenly, and I wished Flo or someone had been there. Then we got round to the front of the house, where there was a great sweep of drive all done in little honeycomb circles and a £6,000 Maserati with this girl just getting into it.

I'd have known those legs anywhere. "Janey!" I yelled.

I saw her take in the Cadillac. Then she turned, giving Austin the whole view of 32-21-34 and looked at me through two bounces of thick auburn hair. "Darling!" she said, and took me by the shoulders as I got out of the car. "It's grown up. Did you ask Aunty's permission?"

"It all happened in the woodshed before I could help it," I said, before I remembered Austin behind me. "Oh. Janey, I think you know . . . ?"

"Austin!" said Janey, and kissed him with absent fondness on one cheek. "Treasure! Was Paris naughty? Tony is looking for ikons: you must come to dinner next week. How did you meet Sarah?"

Austin explained, and refusing a drink with prolonged American courtesy, said goodbye to us both and drove off. He didn't say anything about coming back with a handbag: I supposed he'd just hand it in. It wasn't the easiest thing to explain.

In the hall, which was white carpet on white marble with those cut-glass German wall lamps, Janey looked me over and said, "Austin's coming on. The work I've put in with that boy. How *are* you, She-she? The lineup's pretty average, but I think I've one or two possibles. You're not hooked already or sold on girl friends or whatever, are you?"

"Janey," I said. Warningly. Janey is terrible.

The plucked eyebrows got right up, along with her smile. "Why not, honeychile? I bet you Derek's a poof."

It had never struck me. Janey's like that. Even while I was thinking hard I said indignantly. "He's jolly well not," and of course was caught in midbleat, sophistication minus a hundred, by Gil Lloyd, coming downstairs.

You would say he made Cary Grant entrances

except that he wasn't the kind who would bother. He dressed in silk and cashmere and had thick, dark hair and a tan and a prowl that was second nature, like Janey's. There is something about them that, sooner or later, makes you want to kick their teeth in. Only, so far, their defense has been smarter than anyone else's attack. And Gilmore Lloyd's defense, so help me, is bloody disarming. He swooped smoothly and kissed: it was like being held by packing-case wire, and my lip started to bleed. I opened my mouth to breath, and he stepped back and said, "Poor She-she. Did Austin try some rough American tactics? We must teach you how to handle him."

Good humoredly, Janey used a very off word. "She's not wasting time on Austin Mandleberg. Wait till you meet Lobby du Cann. And if you're bored with Americans, we've Joe Hadley, and Guppy Collins-Smith and Coco Fairley . . ."

Coco Fairley had been a boyfriend of Mummy's. Good old Janey. "Keep it clean, Janey," I said. "Son of Coco, or nothing." Gilmore laughed, genuinely. The touch comes back to you, after a time.

My room had a balcony, and a bathroom off, and wall-to-wall washed Chinese carpeting in quiet shades of money. On my way there, I was introduced to the Couple. The Couple, Anne-Marie and Helmuth, looked after all the Lloyds' houses. Like the wall lights, they were German and efficient: with the help of Concha the chica, they cleaned and cooked and chauffeured and laundered and mended, getting in local staff when the Lloyds had houseguests or a

29

party. That was where I came in, Mr. Lloyd had said. Anne-Marie needed a rest. I was to take over the cooking.

I found I wasn't meant to take over the cooking that evening: or at least Anne-Marie wouldn't hear of it. She was fair and cheerful and pillowy and spoke perfect English. Like Flo, I've had a few dodgy times with backstairs diplomacy, but I could see this was going to be all right. I'd hardly opened my suitcase when there was a tap at the door and Anne-Marie came in carrying a plate of fat, pink langostinas and a half-bottle of champagne sitting in ice. She put them down and ran me a steaming hot bath, chatting softly, while I hauled my things out of my bag. They were in a horrible muddle. From the look of it, I should think the Customs had taken out and chewed every garter. I'm a neat packer, and I resent being made to look untidy. I opened my own champagne, to show I could, and after cracking a joke or two about the mess I was going to make in her kitchen, saw her out of the room. Then I took the champers into the bathroom, undressed, and lay back in the steam, drinking. After a bit I got out and putting off the light, opened the shutters and got back into the bath again.

Outside, the moonlight fell on the sea and the palms and the flowers and this enormous swimming pool, all floodlit with statues of Greek gods, starkers, all round the edge. Inside, the warm water sloshed about over my skin, and the champagne, very cold, made its way down the bottom of my throat and I lay for a long time, feeling very sad and happy, expecting to wake up.

I was just thinking, rather fuzzily, that it was

about time for dinner when this great bang came from the shutters and I slopped half the fizz into the bath. The shutters swung quickly out and a pair of legs swung neatly in, and before you could yell for your chaperone, one of the Greek gods from the garden, without a stitch on so far as I could see in the darkness, was saying in Giller Lloyd's voice, "A little bird tells me you're drinking champers, sweetie. Do tell me there's a drop for a friend."

Janey always told me I react the old-fashioned way. It isn't true. At least, I don't mean to. It's just that you're brought up to act like a lady and it sticks. I said, "Get the bloody hell out of here Gilmore Lloyd," and heaved a towel into the bath just as the door opened, the light came on, and another masculine voice said mildly, "Excuse me, is this your handbag?"

I honked. I couldn't help it. First there was Giller caught knees up on the windowsill in his bare skin and two hundred watts of Phillips' best. And then in the doorway stood this poor, poleaxed Charlie in seventeen-inch bags and woolly sweater and bifocal glasses He ran his eye over Gilmore and then over me and said again, his voice half an octave lower, "Excuse me, is this your handbag? It's got birth pills in it, popped out to Sunday?"

Poor, poleaxed Charlie, hell. I knew him. It was the man with the Seat. The wag who'd found Austin being overkeen in the ditch and had offered to help. It *was* my bag. "Don't you knock," I said freezingly, "when . . ."

"*He* didn't," said Bifocals, surprised, looking at Greek God. "And I'm dressed."

"Not for long," said Gilmore Lloyd coldly. "What

bloody manners." He wasn't jealous, I think. He was just asserting his territory. He launched himself from the sill and adopting a classical and rather beautiful stance, drove to the jaw with his right.

Bifocals sort of didn't wait for it. I saw Giller's jaw crack against the white marble wall, then he fell down it, and Bifocals stepped over him very carefully and said, "If you don't mind . . . I'll need to take the bag back, if it isn't yours, in case someone is looking for it. It may be a regular . . ."

"It's mine," I said. "And thank you for bringing it. Although I really don't see why you had to walk into my room. Mr. Lloyd would be . . ."

"Mr. Lloyd told me to go right up," said Bifocals. He put one foot on Gilmore's rising chest and immobilized him. "Didn't you hear the last bell for dinner? He didn't know you were getting sloshed under the hot tap."

"I'm not!" I said. I nearly sat up.

"Say *cessation*," said Bifocals.

I changed my ground. "That," I said coldly, "is Mr. Lloyd's son."

"He didn't hear the last bell either, did he?" said Bifocals. "Did Mr. Lloyd send him right up too?"

He removed his foot and Gilmore, rising like Cary Grant, said, "Do I have to ask you again to leave this lady's room?"

"You didn't ask me the first time," Bifocals pointed out. "But that's all right. I hear the tiny voices of dry martinis calling." He looked over Giller's shoulder at me. "Why didn't you pop Monday's pill?"

"I forgot," I said.

"Mistakes," said Bifocals firmly, "are expensive. You'll be late for dinner."

Gilmore grabbed both his arms.

"So shall I," said Bifocals. "I shouldn't do anything dashing. I've just rung for Helmuth."

Gilmore dropped his hands and said, "Are you dining with Father?"

"He did ask me," said Bifocals. "He's rather keen. In fact, he's just offered me twelve hundred pounds to do a portrait of Janey. Miss Cassells, you're stoned." He leaned forward and turned on the cold shower; then leaving me under it, walked through my bedroom and got to the door just as Helmuth tapped on the outside. The door closed. By the time I got the tap off and the freezing water out of my eyes, Gilmore also had gone. I dressed and went down to dinner. I'd been in Ibiza two hours and I'd had a near rape and two uninvited men in my bathroom. It was better than cooking for dentists.

CHAPTER 3

THAT WAS THE WAY I first met Johnson Johnson, and after the drinks and the introductions, I had a good look at him, bifocals and all, over the dinner table. He looked the sort of man who kept spaniels and went in for old beams and growing delphiniums, or maybe tropical fish. His hair and his eyebrows were black, but there really wasn't much of his face that wasn't covered with glasses. On Ibiza, the Lloyds don't wear DJ's except for a party, though of course everyone changes. If Johnson had changed, I wouldn't like to have seen what he had on beforehand: I could see Janey eyeing the woolly and the old crumpled bags, and I could guess she was storing the lot inside her Jane Austin hairdo. Janey can imitate anybody. So can I. We used to do a couple of Cockney charwomen in our Thursday free period, when we had to sew for the poor; and we'd have the whole form in hoots. But of course, Johnson hadn't come to dinner, really: only to give over my handbag.

I don't know whether he expected Janey's father to pounce on him, or why he didn't dodge him if he did: he can't have needed the money. If you believe William Hickey, Johnson Johnson makes more money than Annagoni and Kelly and Hutchinson all rolled into one, painting portraits, and he can afford to be choosey. Mind you, Janey is elegant, and over dinner she had decided to fascinate: I could hear her going into her act. It was just as well she did, for Gilmore, beyond her, was sulking. He'd been even later to table than I was and hadn't looked at me once. He had a pink place on his jaw where it had hit the wall of my bathroom. It was a bit of foul luck, for I really had been looking all right, with my hair piled up on top and my eyelashes wet. He was Scorpio: I asked him over a swallowed martini.

We had artichoke hearts, but Mother Trudi wouldn't have been too delighted over the veal. Once, when Janey let go for a minute, I asked Johnson Johnson if he kept tropical fish. The bifocals turned all merry, whether with the recollection of me in my bath or the question, I wouldn't actually know. He shook his head.

"Too sexy," he said.

"Fish?"

"Have you ever *watched* them?" he said. "You can't cure it, either. Friend of mine used to give his guppies a session of group psychotherapy."

"What happened?"

"They were found making suggestions to a small

party of fry," Johnson said. Then Janey got him again.

After dinner we walked in the garden, where the Greek gods had all gone from the swimming pool, although there was still a nymph or two under the bougainvillea, and the fountains were on. I was beside Gil, and it was rather warm and cosy and hopeful when Father Lloyd flicked on a switch and all the floodlighting came on: I swear they had tungsten halogen behind every mosquito. There was also a grotto with fiber-glass stalactites. Gilmore vanished, and I said to Johnson, "What have you done with my letter?"

I thought he'd say, "What letter?" and he did. I said, "The one in my handbag. From my father."

He could have had the bloody pills. When I found the letter was missing, I felt rotten, I can tell you. It was sheer chance I had got it at all. I'd left Flo with her mother and gone back to the London flat to pack for Ibiza, the day after poor Derek went back to Holland. And there it was, with a lot of other stuff on the mat, in Daddy's writing, dated the day he had died.

It didn't say anything about cutting his throat. I telephoned Derek that night to tell him: I thought it might help. He hadn't been brooding or suffering cancer or something: he'd just been so stoned, I think, that he suddenly got fed up and did it. He was stoned when he wrote the letter: there was a bit in the middle that made no sense at all. But it was all I had: the last thing from Daddy; and Johnson had taken it.

Johnson wasn't indignant or offended or even very excited. "I hadn't, you know," he said mildly. "I don't even collect stamps. But your bag was open when I found it."

"The pills didn't fall out," I said coldly.

"Well, they did, sweetie: and I picked them up because they were white. What else is missing?"

"Nothing."

"Well, let's borrow a torch and go look for it," said Johnson. In the son-et-lumière, his face looked just like uncut moquette. It was all right by me, except that Janey insisted on coming. I had a little knitted coat in the bedroom. I let down my hair, which had dried, from its wraparound, squirted Calèche all over, and sprinted off down. He was on the mature side, but he wasn't married, and I didn't see why Janey should have it all her own way. I couldn't pay for a portrait, but maybe Austin Mandleberg could.

It was jolly dark in the ditch, even with a couple of torches, and the old Seat's headlights simply lay over the top. Janey found a dead brown rat, with its four pink feet all pointing upward, which put me off looking for a bit, so I got the storm lantern and went off under the cork trees, in case the letter had bounced or got blown out or something. It was a bit odd, because the lantern made all the tree shadows slide backward and forward, and if you looked back to the road, I swear you could see bats. I kept looking down, for the letter, and then I thought I had found it, but it was only an old blue empty packet of Ducados, largos con filtros. Beyond it, just at the edge of the light, was the battered old wreck of a car. And behind the car, and just visible under the chassis, was a pair of masculine feet, wearing white canvas shoes.

I got the quarter-mile cup at St. Tizzy's. I had dropped the lantern and lit out of that wood before you could draw breath for a sneeze, and I fell into the ditch just as Johnson was shouting, "I've got it! Miss Cassells! We've dug up your letter!"

"There's a man in there," I said, still rolling.

"You surprise me," said Johnson. "They must call this lovers' corkwood. Was it any two people we know?"

"It was a man," I said and sat up. "Alone. Standing. Not speaking. Right inside the wood."

"Austin," said Janey. "You ass."

"No," I said. "They weren't American shoes."

"Well, for heaven's sake, She-she," said Janey. "Run back."

No one was taking me seriously, and so long as we weren't staying in that wood any longer, why should I care. As Johnson said, at least the feet weren't bare. He handed me Daddy's letter as we all got into the Seat. It was a bit crumpled, but quite intact. "My dear She-she," he'd written.

When we got back, I telephoned Austin. He wasn't in, but a voice in a thick Spanish accent promised to tell him that my bag had been found. Gil was still absent, sulking, and Johnson, though polite, clearly wanted to get back to the harbor, where he was staying on board his yacht *Dolly*. He invited me, after a broad hint or two, to visit him for a drink the next afternoon, and then asked Janey as well, which was mean, because that meant I had transport. I suppose he had to . . . No . . . That's just being draggy. Janey really is gorgeous.

I slept like the dead.

The market in Ibiza opens between seven and half-past in the morning. I was up by six-thirty and leaving the house half an hour later with Helmuth in a hefty old Land Rover with a tire on its bonnet and room for a small horse at the back. I had a lunch party of nine to cook for; or I'd volunteered, anyway. I was rather pleased that Janey's father accepted the offer wtihout the least bit of fuss. He was quite the nicest of all the rich men Daddy had ever stayed with: big and athletic and clean with a great, jolly laugh. For instance, for goodness' sake, he'd no need to offer to entertain a minor Russian trade mission, on a brief break from treaty talks in Madrid, even though he'd met the attaché before. He said he owed a favor to the official delegate for Ibiza and Formentera, who was away till tomorrow. I suspected that the reason actually was that the Reds knew they'd get a jolly good tuck-in at the Casa Veñets compared with anywhere else there in Holy Week. At any rate the four Russians were coming, and the chief Balearic mining engineer and the municipal vet had been thrown in for good measure, and between now and half-past two, which was lunch time, Mother Trudi was going to work like a runaway self-propelled two-speed gear lawn mower, between breaks. Such as visiting Gallery 7 with Janey, for instance.

We left Anne-Marie flowing about with the vacuum, but upstairs all the blinds were still drawn. Janey doesn't like getting up early. I didn't know what Gil's habits were. I spread myself over two seats beside Helmuth and prepared to enjoy the calm predawn country run into Ibiza. It was cool in the garden, and a cock was crowing somewhere beside Santa Eulalia, to the right. There was a pink band along the horizon, over the sea, but the tall, concrete hotels beside the village were all dark, and the white-washed church-fort on its hill. We turned our backs on a sky filled with chalky blue clouds with a sort of peach-colored glitter between. After a bit the sun burst through and shadows sprang out on the road in front of the Rover and were promptly mown down by the traffic.

Seven A.M. is rush hour in rural Ibiza. Between the unwalled fir woods and orchards, the scrub, the small farms, the walled crops, and the bony sheep, the goats, the fat hens, the occasional chained cow, and all the busy, undulating fields that spread in the distance to the low, bald, furzy hills—the greater part of the island seemed to be shifting on wheels toward us. They came in Seats and Simcas and whopping great lorries, on push-bikes and every kind of motorized cycle ever produced outside of acetate locknit: Vespas, Mobylettes, Lambrettas, and old vibrating models with old vibrating workmen in black berets, their lunch in a strapped-on reed basket. Once a real motorbike came by with a crouching rider in fur-collared leathers and goggles and big fur-lined gloves, his mouth and chin con-cealed by a scarf, making straight for Toad Hall. Then we passed the famous wood with the ditch and joined the Portinaitx junction where I had felt Austin take the bend yesterday, and from then on the traffic was going more with us, to Ibiza.

I got to know that road far too well. But I never saw it again as busy as I did on market mornings, black-shawled arm, the top two or three skirts with the tile factory steaming and chaps loading gray honeycomb bricks onto a lorry like mice in a Mack Sennett comedy. The cement factory past the San Miguel junction was going a bomb. The Gasolina was open. Even in fields deserted to little round olives and carob trees, or among the orange and fig trees and pink-and-white blossoms, old Spanish grannies in straw hats and pigtails were whizzing to and fro, the bundle of reeds or whatever under one kilted. I taught Helmuth to sing "One Man Went to Mow" in English, and we bowled along in the Rover a bit over the stipulated 80 km's, bawling it out until we got to the long, straight avenue of trees just before Ibiza.

In front of us were two mule carts just negotiating the sharp, right-hand bend, where the Talamanca path joins the main road in a huddle of buildings. Between the upright lath sides of each cart, a woven mat had been slung, like a dipped carpet, and each mat held a bouquet of round, green, dewy lettuces. They nodded before us, and the sweep of the harbor lay blue behind them, and the high town of Ibiza lay behind that, not like a bride's cake this morning, but a hazy stockpile of windows, with old yellow buildings on top and some trimming, like a club sandwich, of green. Somewhere up there was Gallery 7.

The clock on the Cathedral tower said 7:15 A.M., and the seagulls on the quay were warbling seagull flamenco. I sighed and got out Anne-Marie's list and a purseful of paper money like bits of old blanket, while Helmuth trundled behind the lettuces round the bay past the yacht marina and into the sort of thicket of shops and offices and workshops that edged up to the hill of the high town. The high town in Ibiza was called the Dalt Vila and had an old wall right round it, Helmuth said.

We parked by the Philips building in the Mercado Nuevo, and you could see the town wall from there —tall and flat and yellowish-white, with palms and creepers, and the sandy roof tiles of buildings behind. It ran just beside us as we walked through narrow, shadowy streets filled with traffic, scurrying men, women mopping out offices, chaps washing their taxis, and housekeepers, like me, with a big woven basket folded over the arm. A boy passed in patched trousers and sneakers, selling the *Diario* newssheet, and Helmuth gave him three pesetas for it.

I wasn't looking. I'd found a Panateria by following the smell of fresh bread round two corners, and there was the window, piled with crystallized pears and cherries and peaches, and plates of soft, glistening iced cakes and small toffee custards in chocolate papers, and rounds of frilled, sugared shortcake and thick patterned cream in the jaws of golden flaked pastry, and chocolate sponges filled with whole cherries, soggy with rum. Inside there were stacks of long, hot, crunchy loaves, and soft, sugared cushions of bread-cake, limp and warm on the hand. I bought enough to put pounds on Janey, and five chocolate Easter eggs. Helmuth dragged me out.

The market was even better. You could find it by the noise, or by following the high walls of Dalt Vila, for the market square footed the ramp that led up to the Dalt Vila gateway. The square itself had shops on three sides, most hardly open. In the middle was a small Doric erection clobbered with people, like the Temple of Diana of the Ephesians in the middle of the Aldermaston March. The building was set on an island, and patched blinds stretched out from its roof to cover the rickety stalls which surrounded it. Inside, between classic columns, was a landscape of counters, with fat, jolly women in jerseys helping to load them from the jam-up of trucks, lorries and carts in the square round about. Helmuth plunged into the middle, and I followed, my hair stuck to my neck.

If the sun had been on the market, instead of on the high town behind it, I should have needed dark glasses. At Mother Trudi's, the fruit and veg were all washed and graded and delivered in polythene. These would have punched their way out of the bags. The lemons were all Wallace Beery: husky, belligerent brutes with cauliflower rinds. The tomatoes were like pumpkins: green heavy-lobed monsters, all blotched with dark red. The radishes reared in a wet, scarlet pile, the size of young carrots. Instead of the neat bunch of bananas I was used to was a thing like a thick green umbrella stand, with the cringing bananas growing down on the stalk. Heaps of peas in the pod lay on old sacking, knotted like golf balls. There were baskets of muscadel raisins and crates of matt carmine apples and attols of oranges; and onions, like gold Chinese lanterns, hung about in red nets. There were artichokes, common as sprouts, and strings of dirty-white garlic, and crates labeled SANGUINAS full of portly blood oranges. The profusion was stunning. I gaped at Helmuth, and he took my arm and pushed me right in.

I knew, of course, about buying: I'd learned the hard way, through indignant employers. I'd also had a year's Spanish at school. I've forgotten most of it, but I've a good ear for accents, so I'd listened to what Helmuth said and scribbled down the words I knew I'd need to use. He steered me from stall to stall and introduced me. They all knew Helmuth: the women waved their arms and their voices swooped. They grinned, showing white gappy teeth, and laughed at everything I said and gave me twice what I asked for. The young ones were sallow and merry and fat, with old jerseys and skirts and flat shoes, and the old ones all wore long black skirts and shawls, kerchiefs over their hair, and sometimes a straw hat with a big brim on top. When they spoke together it was a long sort of industrial rattle, like a macaw talking quickly. They asked a great many questions, personal questions.

I didn't mind. I was wearing a high necked shift, in a sort of thick orange fibre, my hair loose, and sandals, with a fine chain and Mummy's leaving-school pearl thing tucked in where the neck hid it. I told them the worst, and we all shook our heads over the lack of a husband, and one of the younger ones said I'd need to find a good strong Ibizenco.

I said good and strong didn't matter, only something in trousers; and another óne with a voice like a saw said, "Watch out, you never know what comes in trousers these days." We all shrieked with laughter. It's easy. It makes you go all sweet and old-fashioned, like visiting old ladies in hospital. I don't know why, but I only think of using four-letter words when I'm with people like Janey and Gilmore. And Mummy, of course.

I bought what we needed and got some carnations for Anne-Marie. The Lloyds never seemed to cut what was in the garden. I remembered, too, that I must come back and get something for Flo. I choose nice presents, or so everyone says. If you know anyone as well as I know Flo, you know what they really want. Her mother always gives her long johns. I was going to spend three of my pounds on a sexy mantilla. Two were earmarked for something for Janey later, and a trifle for the woman owning the flat. I stood a minute, counting Anne-Marie's housekeeping and ticking off lists, and wished a bit that I'd waited for breakfast. However. "Fish," I said to Helmuth, and we set off again.

They were jolly nice in the fish market as well. That was a funny round tiled building with a roof like an umbrella with a hole in the middle. Inside, you walked between two rings of stalls: the first few were meat, with long, pale chickens hanging, all thin legs and bunched feet, and a pig's head in solid pale pink, its eyes little closed slits. It seemed to be laughing.

I didn't need meat. Spanish beef isn't to Mr. Lloyd's taste, so he has two 15-cc freezers stocked with chicken, whole butchered lamb, and cuts of Aberdeen Angus flown out from home. Anne-Marie had shown me the freezers, proudly. There were ten pounds of raspberries in one, and American ice cream and asparagus tips. "See? There is no one else on Ibiza has this. Not with food. But the Casa Veñets has its own generating plant, Miss Sarah." I got the point. The light had failed twice that night already. I moved along.

There were trays of crushed ice on the squared

concrete paving, with coral prawns in them, strung like a necklace. Seamen, in faded trousers and big rubber boots, were bringing trolleys loaded with boxes to the stalls as you watched: octopus and squid in grey, sloppy envelopes; heaps of whitebait like needles. Fat silver fish lay interleaved on one counter; on another, eels lay beside a tangle of blue mussel shells. There were nameless fish, purple-blue and bright pink, and big silver fish pinstriped in yellow, and green fish, with yellow-white speckled bellies. The names and prices, in Spanish, were chalked on small blackboards or stuck in a cork float. I looked at Helmuth again, and he grinned and took me by the hand and led me forward. The queues parted and then closed around me. We were in conference.

We got back to the car about an hour and a half later, and heaved in the baskets: compared with me, the fish all looked dynamic. Helmuth dragged out the big wicker-cased wine jug he and Anne-Marie use in the kitchen and went off to fill it, and by the grace of God, I trailed off to watch him.

He went into a little bodega at the edge of the square. After the dazzle of sunshine outside, it was cool and dark, and smelt of wet wood and alcohol and the plant house in Kew Gardens. I looked around while the shopkeeper filled the big bottle from one of the kegs. On the other side was a row of small barrels: crème de menthe, jerez. A red plastic pail was hung from each tap. The walls were shelved high with bottles: wine, gin, whiskey, martini, vodka. Beside the door, a jumble of cards were pinned to a notice board. Half of them were in English: a cinema club advertising a showing of

Gentleman Jim; a list of desirable flatlets to let; someone with a Gerrard stereo record player for sale.

It was then I noticed a half-open door at the back which seemed to lead to some kind of patio. I could see a vine trellis against the clear sky, the edge of a bright peacock table, and a number of feet. It appeared, from the voices, to be a popular spot to repair to when shopping was done. I said to Helmuth, "Come on. Let's have a glass of something before we go back."

He'd been sweet, like a quiet old janitor we once had for a term. He hung back, but I took his arm and marched him up to the back of the shop. Through the door one could now see a white well, a fish tank, and lots of pots in yellow and blue, with cacti and flowers and creepers growing up the white walls out of them. There were more tables and chairs and benches, and more feet, two of which were wearing white canvas sneakers.

Lots of people, of course, wear white canvas sneakers, although not perhaps such stained ones as these. I stopped dead, gripping Helmuth like a boa constrictor, and then started moving slowly again. It had been pitch dark under the cork trees. If it was the man I had spotted last night, he had probably seen as little of me as I had of him. And even if he had seen me, it wasn't to say that he had been there with any evil designs against me personally. As Johnson said, it was possibly just an assignment. And finally, even if he was unfriendly, he couldn't be unfriendly to any harmful degree in a wine shop in the open air at nine in the morning. I went on in.

The man in the canvas shoes got up and said, "Strewth."

It was Flo's cousin, Clem Sainsbury.

I think I said the right things. I know I went scarlet, and then probably green. I forgot about the corkwood. After an absolute four-year famine of men, I now had four in a day. Even Janey couldn't take all of them. Clem came over and kissed me, to the silent fascination of everyone in the wine shop, and I introduced Helmuth, and we sat down.

As I think I mentioned before, Clem is big and rugged and blonde, and instead of wearing a sheepskin, he had on stained cook's trousers and a T-shirt and a tatty old pullover with mistakes in the cable stitch, which I bet was Flo's knitting. He had a string bag of shopping beside him. We ordered: I had fizzy stone ginger. Then he said, "And how's Flo and the cooking? Hard luck about the other thing, Cassells." He always called me Cassells.

"I know," I said. He was just the same. Cleancut, with a rather blunt knife.

Clem said, "Were you coming to see us? We haven't swabbed the decks yet."

I didn't get it. Then, coupled with his excessive lack of surprise, I got it all right. "You're with Johnson on *Dolly?*" I said.

"He didn't tell you," said Clem, without resentment. "Bloody pirate. I've signed on for six months. It's all right."

"Just you and Johnson?"

"There's a working skipper, called Spry. Two can sail her, but if the painter is painting, then time is holy. Not that he bugs himself working, so far as I've noticed."

"Do you like him?" I said.

"Never met him," said Clem. "We converse with the bifocals. If you like glass, it's O.K."

"That's what I thought," I said. "Mr. Lloyd wants him to paint Janey."

"Wo-ow!" said Clem. When I was with Clem, I thought in four-letter words all right. You knew Clem was hog and you were sow, and even if you became chief engineer in the Russian merchant navy, you'd stay sow to him. With other boys I tried to be feminine, but Clem had the opposite effect.

I sat there drinking stone ginger and laying off about my career as God's gift to catering, and he heard me out like a lamb.

"You must get pretty sick of it," said Clem. "Don't you? It's a hell of a life, holed up in other folks' kitchens, thumbing anchovies onto Ritz biscuits. You lose weight, and you don't want to eat, and in a year or two's time you'll have slipped disks and fallen arches and a cat and a real William and Mary card table with bun feet, and that's your bloody lot. You want to marry some nice chap and cook for him and your kids."

"I know I do," I said. Patiently. He just hadn't been listening. I said, "Tell me any other job where I can take the waste caviar home and spoon it into the budgie. At sixteen guineas a whack?"

"I didn't know you had a budgie," said Clem.

"It jumped into the fish bowl and died." I swallowed the last of the pop and got up. "Come on," I said to Helmuth. His eyes were half shut.

"Bye, Cassells," said Clem. He heaved himself up and surveyed me, his face puckered in thought. "You've got guts, coming here after what happened.

Can you really stick it? Do you like it? Are the Lloyd people decent?"

"Oh, they're all right," I said. I swallowed. The great sentimental idiot. "I like it. They're sweet, down in the town here."

"Um," said Clem. He studied me a bit longer, then grinned, and stopped to fish in his net bag. Then he straightened and looped me a double cherry over each ear. "Olé," he said. "O.K., Cassells. Be good."

"Look where it's got you," I said. All right, he was a bore. But a nice one. I left, trailing Helmuth. To work.

Anne-Marie had got breakfast, but no one was down. I had mine and did my stint in the kitchen: by half-past eleven everything was laid out and covered with foil, and I went for a swim. Janey was in the pool, without anything on. I suppose Helmuth was used to it. Afterward we lay in the sun for a short fry before driving to Gallery 7. She has a beautiful body.

We had a lot to catch up on. Janey had had a mink coat at fourteen and a Daimler sports car for her seventeenth birthday: name-dropping and place-dropping didn't occur to her. But she knew all the jet-set gossip all right. We had just got through her love life, which was like the haberdashery at Harrod's and of about the same lasting significance, when Janey said out of the blue, "Will you mind going to *Dolly?* To the yacht marina, I mean? That bloody boat-winch is there."

"I don't mind all that much," I said. "I mean. If you knew Daddy."

"You're a born prig, She-she," said Janey. "That's your whole trouble. He knew how to live. Daddy never had a decent party in his life till old Forsey swanned in and the whole of Cine Citta and the Almanachs de Gotha poured in after."

"You got value for money," I agreed. I added quickly, "It was sporting of your father to ask me. I can imagine what a shake-up it must have been, without taking me on as well."

"Well, don't start groveling," said Janey. "He was probably just afraid of the talk. It was a rather wild party."

"Derek didn't tell me how it happened," I said. It was one way to make her talk.

"God knows how it happened," said Janey. She turned over, her red hair bouncing over her face. "Daddy had to go to the mainland, and Gil and I threw this party. Lobby was there, and Coco Fairley, and Guppy—I told you. They'd come round from St. Tropez, and the Hadleys had flown over from Formentor, and a whole bunch who were sharing a villa at that place in Minorca. You know how it happens. Parlor games in the house and more parlor games in the pool. You couldn't see the water for Ping-Pong balls and bottles next day. So they tell me. Then Coco started handing out sugar."

I am a prig, I suppose, since Janey says so. Certainly, LSD on sugar was one of the trips I hadn't yet tried. "Did Daddy take it?" I said.

"In general? I shouldn't think so," said Janey. She slid a blade of grass, delicately, along a thin trail of ants. The ants swerved. "He used to say his acid content was too high already. In any case, that night he was out of the house."

Of course he would be, I thought. If Lloyd was away, Daddy wouldn't be interested in a romp with a lot of boring teen-agers. "Out to dinner?" I said.

"He didn't say. But he hadn't eaten when he went out at eight."

He had eaten somewhere, though. Or so the Spanish police report had said. But not in any restaurant anyone had been able to trace. Janey was still tactfully pursuing her ants. But, I thought, Daddy didn't make secret assignations. Daddy was a person who had friends, publicly and at the highest possible level, and when he visited them, all the world knew it. Janey said, "He'd popped out before, of an evening. He maybe felt a bit rotten, and just wanted to be alone. Or maybe he was just bored."

"But he'd *eaten*," I said.

"Maybe he had an evening with Derek," said Janey. She moved the grass, and the ants all straightened their lines.

"Oh, hardly," I said. If she had lost interest, I wasn't going to flog the conversation to death. "Derek was in Holland. He didn't come to Ibiza till after the suicide."

"He did, actually," said Janey, and turned her gorgeous made-up green eyes in my quarter. You couldn't see her contact lenses at all. "I saw him up in the Vila the day before your poor old progenitor did himself in."

I finished sitting up. "Today's joke. Janey, you wouldn't know Derek if you fished him out of your face cream."

"I should. I remember him from St. Tizzy's," said

Janey. She got up and slung on her bathrobe. "I'd had drinks in the old town with the Rothas, and we were larking about. I thought he saw me too, but if he did, he dodged away. It was Derek."

"He didn't tell me," I said.

"I thought maybe he put it in the letter," said Janey.

My dear She-she. I don't know what made me say it. I hadn't meant to say it to anybody. I think I was getting a bit frightened. "The letter wasn't from Daddy," I said.

Janey stopped dead and turned. After a bit she said, "Oh, look. Now who's flanneling? I posted that letter myself. He asked me to, the afternoon of the party."

"Daddy asked you to post a letter to me? On the day he . . . hooked it?"

"Right," said Janey. She began walking again up to the house. "For Chrissake, She-she. You had us all raking the ditch for it, last night."

"I know," I said. "It wasn't from him. You say you posted it on the day of the suicide. That letter didn't come until ten days later, the day before I left to come here."

"Spanish correos," said Janey succinctly. We were going up the marble stairs.

"All right. And he was sloshed," I said bitterly. "But that doesn't explain why he wrote me a letter starting, *My dear She-she.* He never called me She-she in his life."

'So?" said Janey. Wisps of red hair coiled about under the pile on her head.

"So I think he was murdered," I said.

I didn't exactly expect the Confederates' Rebel

Yell, but Janey simply leaned on her door handle and said, "I thought maybe that was why you came."

"But who'd want to kill him?"

"I don't know," I said.

"Well, why not find out?" said Janey. "I know what *I'd* do."

On the way into Mandleberg's workshop we did it. We sent a cable saying COME AT ONCE. SARAH to Derek.

CHAPTER 4

Austin mandleberg's gallery was in the Daït Vila, the walled bit of the town on the hill. I'd seen the main gateway, flanked with broken statues at the edge of the fruit market, but I hadn't been into it yet.

Physically, there's no break between the old bit of Ibiza and the new, except for this whopping great wall built around the base of the hill. Actually, it's about a thousand years' difference. Janey edged the Maserati through the raging turmoil of the Mercado and up this long, narrow ramp to the portals, and the moment we crawled in under it we were in quiet and shadow. An old woman in black and two girls with long hair and brown boots flattened against the grey, peach-mortared stone of the buttresses, and then we were turning sharp right into a tall, shadowy room, half arcaded, and roofless to the blue sky, at the other end of which was the only exit: another arched portal giving onto the sunlit cobbled plaza of the old Moorish town of Ibiza, under the lee of the tall white houses lodged in a cliff of dazzling masonry on our left.

I hardly had time to take it in: the round glassy cobbles, the kids playing, the pump, the washing hanging high in the sun; a grocer's, a little, dark wine shop, a café with tables out in the sun; a lot of songbirds in cages. Then Janey swung left in a hairpin bend that rolled me onto her shoulder, and we were going up a perpendicular alley about six inches wide, with the wall of the roofless entry room on our left, and on our right, small shops—I caught a glimpse of antiques—broken by stretches of wall. Suddenly the passage widened, and the cobbles gave way to tarmac, and we were in a small square between more little antique shops and bars, with stepped lanes and paths leading up on the right, and a stony slope on the left which seemed to go up to the ramparts. From the square led a broad, garden-lined avenue, still rising steeply, labeled Avenida General Franco. Beyond the strip of park on our right, you could see a low-level dirt road, lined with crowded four-story houses and bars, with small, low, broken doors and children crying, and flights of steep steps overhung with low trees and bougainvillea and cacti. Strings for washing draped every wall, with plastic clothes-pegs in bunches, like lovebirds. The two roads joined with steps at another hairpin bend, and I lurched to the right as Janey fluted the Maserati's horn and spun the wheel coolly, her dark glasses flashing. She had been here before. She had been to Austin Mandleberg's gallery before, often, but hadn't bothered to mention it until a minute ago.

It wasn't much further. The tarmac road went on, with a pavement, past a patch of garden and a green-shuttered church and up to a flat place facing some broad, grassy steps. There Janey changed gear and swung right. I had a glimpse behind us of a wide, modern square with a lot of trees and a long white building with arches, and even of a sudden flash of blue sea at the end; then the Maserati swung its back to the view and went on climbing, this time past beautiful two- and three-story houses linked together, painted brown or dazzling white. As the convertible crawled slowly onward, I looked from side to side at green double-leafed doors and wrought balconies, spilling over with red potted geraniums and creepers. Some of the windows had elaborate grilles: behind one, somewhere, someone was playing the piano. We passed, on our left, a flight of broad whitewalled steps, and then a long stretch of white wall over which the garden above spilled its treasures: cactus creepers, a trail of white roses, a mat of pink and scarlet geraniums. Above the steps you could see palm trees, purple blossoms, and a lemon tree, its globes like gold disks in the sun.

"It's plastic," said Janey sardonically, and drew in just past the garden and halted.

The antique and art businesses, it was clear, were doing all right. Austin Mandleberg's antique shop and gallery was three stories high, with an open, arched door with a fanlight which gave onto a deep pillared hall, paved with black-and-white marble and dotted with eight-foot jugs, young palm trees in them. Against the wall on the left were two antique chairs flanking a large paneled door and a Spanish lantern that would have floodlit a ship. On the right wall was merely a small painted door, closed. Straight ahead, a palatial set of white marble steps rose up and swirled to the right, showing a lot of elaborate wrought-iron balustrade. A neat notice at the foot of the steps said, simply, GALLERY 7, and another, to one side of the paneled door, said Austin M. Mandleberg. I pulled off my headscarf and got out.

I'd changed to pink slacks and a long-sleeved, chain-store blouse, with a heavy link belt I take everywhere. Janey was in thin, ice-pink suede, sleeveless and fringed at the ends. She had one pale square ring and a pair of thin, twisty gold earrings. It wasn't that she was making a special effort for Austin. Janey makes a special effort all the time.

She walked straight in and opened the door on the left, while I hung about after, catching it as it crashed back behind her. She didn't warn me that there were three sunken steps just inside. I nearly landed in Austin's antique shop on my pink Courtelle pelvis.

The little man with dark crinkly hair who came forward to greet us turned out to be Señor Gregorio. The resident manager wore a tight-fitting suit and white collar. He had a big nose and bushy eyebrows and bags under his eyes you could have kept shoes in. He had hardly finished cooing over Janey when Austin ran down the steps, came across, and kissed both our hands. Continental stuff. Then he took us around.

Actually, I can't tell you a thing about that room,

because I was so sorry for Austin. I mean, he'd be busy talking about an alabaster coffer with the apostles carved inside the lid, or some Punic pottery, or a silk shawl, or a bunch of swords, or a painted Saint Peter, or some old maps and keys and pieces of spidery embroidery, and there was Janey —making challenging statements which had nothing whatever to do with what he was saying and making him laugh when he knew he was supposed to be talking to me. I got in a few shots as well, but Janey nicked the ball whenever I paused to draw breath, and it was such a pain in the neck watching poor Austin's native American courtesy struggling with his commercial desire not to offend the daughter of a confirmed ikon buyer that I dropped out of the game and lingered around, watching him topping his drives.

Anyway, Janey was the expert on antiques. Going about with Daddy, of course I've picked up a bit, and when I'm around cooking in a decent-sized house, I know what to admire. But of course Janey had been finished and trailed all through the Uffizi. The first man she ever went to bed with was a waiter in the Piazza Vittorio Emanuele: she said she didn't want to practice on her friends.

At any rate, we took ages to get to the silver, which was the only bit that seemed faintly interesting, and when we did, Janey and I both did our stuff well enough, anyway, to be presented with two dangling chain earrings apiece. Austin was still standing there, flushed with the success of his great thought, when Gregorio appeared, beaming, and took Austin off to the telephone.

He was away for a while. Janey sniffed around

and after a bit, started opening cupboards and trying things on. I felt in a mood for adventure and walked up the steps and back into the hall again. I tossed up, mentally, between the marble stairs and the little green door in the opposite wall: and in the end picked the door.

I crossed the hall, which was empty, and turned the door handle. It opened. Inside was a dark flight of steps running downward, with a half-landing and a twist at the bottom. I went down, out of curiosity, but it only gave onto a long, dirty corridor leading to rooms where Gregorio or someone probably lived. The door at the foot of the stairs was half-open, but that was a dead loss as well: an empty workroom, full of benches and litter, with one or two bits of jewelry being mended or cleaned or something. An old man, who had been hidden inside a cupboard, moved out, and I scuttled before he could see me. A pity. I felt a view of Austin Mandleberg's bedroom, for instance, would have put me definitely one up in the race. I bet Janey hadn't seen it yet, anyway.

By the time I got back, Austin and Janey were drinking big sherries, and I made out I'd been to the loo. I had a big sherry as well and asked craftily if Austin lived in the basement, but he said, "No, only Gregorio," but if I liked to go down I should meet the company craftsman, Jorge. Dead loss. Then Janey said, "Christ, look at the time. Austin darling, if you're going to show us your balloons, you'll have to do it on wheels." And we got back into the hall and climbed the white marble stairs to the gallery.

The shop on the ground floor had been dark. The shiny landing at the top of the stairs had a door on each side, and when Austin flung open the one on the right, the flood of ripe yellow light was quite blinding. In the first place the room was big, with long windows looking onto the street. And at the far end, standing open, were shuttered doors leading out to the garden: the gorgeous garden we'd spotted below, full of little pineapple-shaped palms, and pink and white roses, and a magnolia tree. And, oh Maurice Woodruff: arum lilies.

This time we got in a rut, Janey and I. We both rushed toward the French windows, emitting girlish expressions of joy, and this damned thing first whacked me hard on the head, and then bounced back to do the same thing for Janey. Janey sat down, and I ducked, and we both glared at Austin, who swooped on us, cawing. I thought he was going to cry. The thing that hit us was still swinging. I got to my feet and examined it.

The label said, "Cumulus Cloud with Tartan Carrying Case," and the label was a hundred percent on the ball. It hung from a string on the ceiling, an irregular, inflated pillow of tartan with handles, maybe eight feet, in all, round its zip. At a distance, I suppose its outline could be regarded as cloudlike, but the tartan was a definite caprice. It stopped swinging, and Janey and I gazed at it without comment.

"People," said Austin, "say the artist today has no sense of humor. On the contrary, while most of his work is sober and sometimes even tragic, he has his moments of gaiety. One may smile, while enjoying the freshness and spontaneity of the idea. I do hope it didn't give you a bruise?"

"No," I said. Janey was speechless. Austin looked at her compellingly. "There are more."

There were, hung along the whole gallery. They weren't all clouds. One had cotton Easter chicks in all sizes inside it, and one a pailful of blue water and a lot of toy plastic ships. There was another thirty feet long. "I like them," said Janey. Austin floated before us in a sort of high-voltage, intellectual euphoria. "I knew you would," he said. "Aren't they just darling? Now come and see these."

The fish for the Russians had to bake for thirty-five minutes. I'd rolled and stuffed it with shrimps, with just a flavor of onion and mushroom, and a little minced celery. There was an American salad to go with it, and a sort of orange cream with curaçao to follow. They were also getting stuffed artichokes and a croquemonsieur as starters. No one was going to go way from the Casa Veñets starving. It was the first meal I'd done for the Lloyds, and I wanted it to be just right. It had been after twelve when we got to the gallery. But in spite of that, I stared at Austin's big, regular, well-shaven face, and his shirt with the button-down collar and a very faint shiny stripe, and the grey nugget cufflinks, and I got the link between Austin, the wolf in the Cadillac, and the traveling exhibition of Art in the Round.

It wasn't the tapestries of goats' hair and feathers. It wasn't the towering lanes of green plastic bosses, the labyrinths of quilted-cloth hangings based, said the card, on recurring genitalian contours, or the rows of nailed wooden disks on which lines of verse, or at any rate original expressions, sober, tragic, or gay, had been stenciled. I walked between "Masculine Presence," made of welded car grilles and bumpers, and "Little Eyes," a board studded with pairs of dolls' eyeballs, and down an avenue of stamped crates and plumbing fixtures, before I found it. ". . . perfectly legitimate," Austin was saying, quoting Apollinaire, "to use numbers and printed letters as pictorial elements . . . soaked with humanity . . ." I passed by "Arteriosclerosis": forks and spoons in a glass-covered box. I turned through an avenue of life-sized cloth figures, and there was Austin's psyche, plain as could be, all among the big hoardings that showed us Op Art.

Op art was just black lines on white: whorls and spirals and fine jagged mesh that did something to the backs of your eyeballs and sent your optical nerves into a frenzy. Or it took the form of fifteen-foot circles of plywood, spiralled in thin bandings of shocking pink, lime green, and orange. Janey stood before one of those with her eyes under the contact lenses so dilated that I thought she was going to faint, and Austin asked her if she was all right.

"Frankly," said Janey, "I think it's procuring."

"Now, this interests me," Austin said. "I consider that this art shows a person his innermost being. Great art is a catharsis."

"All I can say is," said Janey, "if I had that in my bedroom, I'd need Dutch caps for my eyeballs. She-she, we're going to be late."

He saw us into the Maserati, holding Janey's hand, and then mine. "You're coming to dinner," said Janey. "I'll ring you. Who was the boy who did all the quilting?"

Austin told her. He was, as I remember, a male nurse in a Sun Valley health farm.

It had been a tough match. My opinion is, Austin won.

The fish was a howling success. I helped Anne-Marie serve it, and Janey's father introduced me to all his guests—two silent Spaniards and four pasty, rectangular gentlemen with hearty smiles and uncertain English. One of the latter group was the commercial attaché at the Russian Embassy in Madrid, and the three others were straight from Moscow on a trade fair excursion. The attaché, whose Spanish was fluent, finally lapsed into that language and interpreted for the other three. It was a dead groovy lunch, I can tell you.

Janey sat at the head of the table, speaking Spanish as well and looking quite elegant. I suppose she's been her father's hostess half her life: her mother died before I even knew her, and her father seems to have gone on just as if nothing had happened, only assuming Janey would carry on in her place. She's been away a lot, of course, but on every return home she seems to have taken control. She has a good brain. And of course she's had Anne-Marie and Helmuth, and any other help that she wanted.

After lunch I served coffee and cognac, and Mr. Lloyd asked me to stay and have it with Janey. He and the six visitors left almost immediately to talk in his smoking room.

Gilmore hadn't come in. "He's at Coco's," said Janey. She had had two cognacs and hadn't even turned pink. "They've got a living-in tennis professional, and Giller is either going to make Wimbledon or spring a coil in his chesterfield."

"Isn't he keen on the business?" I said. A playboy-sportsman is all right. A middle-aged playboy-sportsman is slightly pathetic, especially to a middle-aged playboy-sportsman's wife.

"You're joking," said Janey dispassionately. "He took a law degree because Daddy wouldn't give him an allowance without it; and he went to Harvard because he was dead keen on baseball and rich American girls' legs. He's got the allowance and had the American girls, so why work?"

I cleared up, and lifted an English newspaper three days old off the hall table on my way up to the siesta. It promised Scorpio a good day and Virgo a slight disappointment. Clem Sainsbury was the same as me, Capricorn. Capricorn, said the paper, should treat foreign interests and matters of law with extreme caution, for they are not in control, and there may be conflict, perhaps disaster.

And, I thought, you can say that again.

I don't think Janey actually wanted to be painted. I mean, she'd cheerfully spend days being photographed, but sitting still being turned inside out by another person was something different again. Janey liked to be in charge, on her own terms.

Anyway, after the siesta when it came time to leave for Johnson's boat *Dolly*, I found that Janey had got herself completely tied up in showing the three red squares round the island, and I had to set off alone. I didn't mind. Maybe Johnson would paint me instead. And Janey had lent me the Maserati.

The road from Santa Eulalia to Ibiza is a good one, as I've said: seldom built up for long and mostly running in long, level stretches, above or below the farm country. At places the speed is controlled, but a good, easy sixty to seventy is generally all right. On empty roads you could pick your own speed. Between six and seven in the evening, as now, it's fairly constantly busy. Workmen in Spain stop at seven.

I set off then, taking it easy, and finding a path among the old battered Seats, the Peugeots, the daisy-painted Renaults and Simcas, and the bashed Ebro lorries with two sides gone from their steamy old bonnets.

I enjoyed it. I took time to look for the orange and lemon trees and the house that was building, with the old woman hobbling in and out with her wicker dish of wood shavings. A man was ploughing, his feet on the share, his fists gripping the big horse's tail. The fig trees were budding at last—pale gray—with their branches outspread like the skirts of an Infanta, a green candle-leaf at each tip. The low sun hit fields edged by warped, whitened branches and turned the soil broken orange and the dry stone walls orange too. As the road rose a little, the hills and foothills showed, patched and streaked with green, tan, and pale sandy color, spotted with dark scrub and patched with low trees. Small white houses with tiled roofs faced the sun, shining, and the white cylinder of a well, or the tall pylons with their spidery windmills. Olives, with their brown twisted barks, and orange trees on their thin, spindly sticks. Poppies. Fir trees like thick furzy cushions of dense yellow-green, and yellow haystacks like mushrooms . . . A flower like a telegraph pole, with yellow blossoms on each short, outflung arm caught the sun, over and over, at the side of the road. I was happy.

I don't know when I first noticed the white Alfa Romeo Giolia Spider behind me: I looked in the mirror and got a glimpse of this great yummy car roaring along at about eighty-five, which was a hell of a rate, I can tell you, on that busy road. Coco Fairley was at the wheel, in dark. glasses, with a gold locket and a lilac shirt open right down to the waist, and Gilmore Lloyd was beside him.

Coco was one of Mummy's first poets. His specialties were rich old cows and advanced concrete verse. When she went back to America he found another soul mate, and his career since hasn't been without incident: he had twice got himself slugged by his own poems. Mummy used to say they were good, and she was probably right. From this, anyway, you will gather that Coco Fairley was one of the world's seven great fragrances. I trod on the accelerator, and a donkey cart sort of flinched out of the way. Behind, Coco did the same, grinning, and beside him Gilmore Lloyd gave a rude kind of cheer. Then I realized that they thought I was Janey. I was wearing a little Chinese coat, with a matching bikini under it, and a headscarf of the same stuff wrapped tight round my hair. It would be a mess when I got on board *Dolly,* but I thought it was worth it. I whipped off the headscarf and flung the car, hard, at the road. Through the driving mirror, I saw Coco's cupid's bow shut under his glasses. Then the locket glittered, and he drew out to pass.

One thing I can do is drive. All the big brothers had cars, and you would be a bit of a clot if you hadn't tried out half a dozen by the time you were fourteen or fifteen. At the price of a bit of smooching in the back seat, it was a good way to learn. Clem Sainsbury had an old Rover which was always full of wet towels and Rugby gear, I remember. He was the best teacher of the lot: a bloody perfectionist and no funny stuff while you were driving. I suppose that was why most girls got fed up with him after a while. I had some final lessons and passed my test on a windfall from Daddy, but neither Derek nor I ever had a car till Flo and I clubbed together last year and got our ten-year-old Morris.

The Maserati Mistral can do 155, the book says. I didn't know what the Alfa Romeo's top was, but I did know that I wasn't going to let that indoor coffee plant pass me. I put my foot down and kept it there. An open-tile wall and a patch of garden—marigolds, antirrhinums—jumped past, and a woman sweeping the dirt with a long-handled broom slid back, a dark blur. The road narrowed, the fields dropping below: there was a grey retaining wall with a line of giant grasses on my right. Ahead, a Barreiras lorry packed full of cartons of Kelvinators, *su seguro servidor,* turned a corner and lumbered toward us, followed by a fat Ibiza-tours bus. Coco held it to the last second, and then moved in behind me.

A black-and-white petrol-pump sign and a workman on an old Vespa, a wicker wine bottle strapped on his pillion. I cut out a second before Coco did an droared past the bike and the petrol station, the Alfa Romeo following, and found myself behind an old, high, scarlet Opel with a cloth roof, doing about twenty-five, with a big Seat 1500, a taxi, coming in the opposite direction.

It was coming fast, but it wasn't here yet. The Bar los Cazadores was coming up on the right, and the *Atencion* sign for the long, wire-netted swoop round to the Portinaitx junction. There we joined the main road, and I'd have to give way. I put my hand on the horn, shoved my signal light on, and drew out and found the red Opel right in the path of the taxi.

He didn't even have time to brake. I saw his face and heard a yell from the Opel as I skimmed past, and then I was bearing round the red-and-white netting and up to the Portinaitx junction. It said Ceda el paso. The road to the right was quite empty. A little distance away on the Ibiza road, a cart was coming toward us, an old man holding the reins. I changed down and looked back.

The Alfa Romeo had got past the Opel and was halfway along the big curve toward me, at the point where it divided in two for incoming and outgoing traffic. As I put my foot down and moved out to turn to the left I saw that Coco wasn't following me. Instead, he was cutting across to the left, hugging the wrong side of the junction, in order to cut the corner and strike the Ibiza road just before me.

He got there just as the cart did. I heard, as I accelerated, an almighty screaming of brakes, half drowned by an outburst of yelling in Spanish. Then the rest was covered by the sound of my own engine as I changed up and roared up the road.

Here, the country was flat: low, green fields dotted with trees on the left with small terraced hills lying behind, and on the right, crops and small trees stretching far out of view. They passed in a blur. I overtook a big cream Mercedes, with forget-me-nots painted all over, and had to slow down to fifty for the Santa Eulalia bus; then I was off again. The white steps of a villa, with bright pots on them. A wood with fir trees and juniper and a snatch of wild thyme. Ahead, the San Miguel road about to come in on the right, with a huddle of buildings on each side. A lorry, stacked high with thin metal pipes, came out of the junction and set off before me, the long pipes swaying gently before and behind. There was traffic coming. I slowed down to a respectful distance and glanced in my driving mirror. Empty. The best bit of the road was just coming: a long, straight, well-surfaced speedway between fields and small farms. And soon, after that, the white buildings of Ibiza should show in the distance. The pipes swayed in front of me, mesmeric as a snake-charmer's dance. On the left, another lorry was crawling out of the yard of a solitary brick factory. *Salida de Camiones*. Hell.

A white blur appeared in my mirror. Coco.

I fumed behind those waggling pipes while the other lorry got itself down to the road. It waited for two cars to pass and then lumbered across into place in front of the pipes. All the time the Alfa Romeo, with nothing in front of it, was doing a bomb down the road right behind me, and when the two lorries finally ground into action again, it was on my tail, with Gil cheering and a snide smile on Coco's lips.

We passed one or two buildings and an isolated block of four-story flats without overtaking, edging in and out and getting our ears flattened for us by oncoming stuff whizzing by. Then there came a sharp turn to the right. I stuck my bonnet right out, with my teeth set, and looked. There was the road clear in front of me: a long avenue of tall, leafless trees as far as the eye could distinguish, with the evening sun, on the right, lighting up the sides of the piled houses up in Ibiza. I drew right out, with a long flute of the Maserati's double-tone horn, overtook the bloody pipes and the lorry before it, and then let her right out.

I did a ton up that road, and probably more. I remember the white walls of farmhouses, a glimpse of some palms, and the junction to Jesus coming up on the left, with a café. The Lloyds had got used to the idea of a village called Jesus. I thought if a lorry came out of that road now, I'd go straight to Jesus all right.

It didn't, but Coco was coming instead. I could see the white car in the mirror, howling along on my tail, and I could see too that he was going to try to get past. It was his last chance. After this there were some low warehouse buildings and a piece of waste ground, and then we were straight into the sharp, right-hand corner which led to the harbor, with the Talamanca path coming in at a clutter of walls on the left, and an old café-bar on the right, its pillared porch sticking out in the road with BAR —STOP on a sign. I disapproved of that bar. It was falling down anyway, and the front yard under the porch was cluttered with oil drums and crates of San Miguel bottles, odd bikes and ironmongery for sale. Someone would stop there when he didn't mean to one day.

It's not that I'm psychic, but I realized right then that someone was going to, right now. Coco, with his dark glasses glaring, drew out to pass as we got to the corner, just as a lorry full of lemonade trundled out from the Talamanca path. I suppose he'd seen it. I know I had and was braking already. I think Coco saw my brake lights go on, went mad, and decided to pass me before the lorry got fully across. I've a good idea that when it happened, Gil was trying to take over the wheel. At any rate, I got a glimpse of this great blue thing with a red-and-white top saying PIÑA, NARANJA, LIMÓN, POMELO, and then of the Alfa Romeo in front of me, skidding wildly as he realized he couldn't pass it and was too late to brake. The lorry slewed back into the middle—fast—tried too quick a turn, and got stalled. Coco stood on his brakes, shot across to the Talamanca buildings, turned at the last minute, and twirling right round, shot in front of me straight under the drunken porch of the bar-café. There was the crash of glass and the rending of bicycles: a shelf of potted geraniums tottered and fell, and a pile of polythene pails shivered and sprayed, like monstrous bouncing confetti, over the whole epic scene.

I changed gear very gently. I drove very gently past the bar and the lorry, along to a spare bit of dirt. I made a lot of hand signals and parked. The lorry was still standing plumb across the road center. On the back it said: SMASH, *es mas zumo*. I walked gently over to the Alfa Romeo.

It did me good just to look at it. You could tell without any trouble that Gil and Coco had both had quite a shaking. A ratty, half-dozen people had spilled out of the bar-café, and the lorry driver soon got down and joined them. A lot of money changed hands rather quickly. I went back and sat in the car.

Men don't like it, Flo says, when you do something better than they can. Except for housewifely things, that's to say. I could never quite see what she meant. Whatever you're most fabby at—swimming, dancing, changing a wheel—it gives you an edge in the race. Me, I'd like to know how to do everything, if I'd only had cash for the classes.

Gil was impressed, anyway, or so he said when he came over eventually, grinning bravely. I knew Coco would be annoyed, but that was only partly because of my driving. When he'd finished looking at the Alfa Romeo's busted headlights, bent bumpers, and dented white paintwork, he strolled up and put his hands on the hips of his very tight slacks and said, "Well, darling: a demon driver, aren't you, dear . . . just like Mummy after her remold . . ."

I looked him up and down too. "The color's just you," I said, giving his shirt a cool stare. "Are they selling tat medals as well?"

"You're a road hog," said Gilmore calmly, before Coco could reply. "What do you drive at home?"

"Anything that's around," I said. "I like a Bentley convertible."

"Oh, my goodness, so do I, darling," said Coco. "Race you who sees one first." He had a glittering smile. He added, "I hear you're a cook."

73

Gil said, "Sarah's here as Dad's guest." He looked pale and cross, and I was thrilled to the core.

"Making up for having mislaid old Forsey?" said Coco. His golden, permed sideburns glistened in the hot sun. "Honestly, Sarah, it wasn't Daddy Lloyd's fault. He wasn't even there when the old bugger walked out on him."

"*You* were," I said.

"At the party? Of course," Coco said. He leaned on the bonnet, found it hot, and transferred the hand to his medallion. He couldn't have got a finger into his pockets. "It makes you think, doesn't it? If he'd stayed and taken a lovely up-trip with us, he'd be here, live and well. But true love beckoned."

Gil said, "Coco, you're high."

"No, I'm not," said Fairley, but I suddenly began to see the point of the dark glasses. He said, "If he wants to do naughty things with the lamp out, it's nothing to do with us youngsters. All I can say is, he was in an indecent hurry."

"Coco, shut up," said Gil, but I stopped him.

"Did you see my father leave the party? Where did he go?"

"I don't know dear, but I can guess. He was in Helmuth's car, and going hell for leather in the usual direction."

"Where?" Gil and I said together, but Coco wouldn't tell. "Lady's honor, darling," he said, and smirked, and when we pressed him, doubled up with soprano laughter that nearly split his white pants. When he finished gasping, he said, "I think Sarah should come to the party tomorrow, sweetie, and see for herself."

"She doesn't know Mrs. van Costa," said Gilmore, drawling, with an edge to his voice. Mrs. van Costa was the owner of the tennis courts and the present sponsor of advanced concrete verse.

"Gilly dear, don't be naïve," said Coco, laughing harder than ever. "Do come. Bring her, Gilly, and your America antique, the Mandleberg. Does she have something to wear? Janey could fix her."

"If not," I said, "I'm sure you could, darling," and let in the clutch. The Maserati shot off with a roar.

Dolly was big and white and beautiful, and tied to the quay at the yacht marina, so that all I had to do was to cross the tarmac yard, crammed with cars next to the boatyard, and walk through the yacht club's aluminum mesh gates. There were a lot of bikes parked inside and some pollarded trees. The club was quite small; gray and white with big yellow shutters and Venetian blinds, with a concrete patio on the other side looking straight onto the sea. I turned right, down the patio steps, and walked along to the end of the quay, the wire mesh wall of the boatyard running high on my right. On my left was the water, hazy blue, dimpled and glassy, and the shining sterns of big, blissful yachts tied to a row of pale concrete bollards. Behind me, they stretched in long rows on the other side of the clubhouse, and more remotely, side by side along the built-up, thin jetties running this way and that in the sea.

It was the innermost heart of the harbor, far from the big ships which lay on the waterfront under Ibiza itself which faced me now, over the water, mirrored pink in the turning pink waves. Air from the sea stirred against my hot face. I took off my dark glasses, turned, and walked to the long varnished gangplank that led up to *Dolly*. On deck a small middle-aged man in a peaked cap was sitting splicing a rope. He jumped up. "Miss Cassells? Come this way. Mr. Johnson and Mr. Clem are just sitting for'ard up there."

We walked round a sort of rooftop, which must be over one of the cabins, and then sidled past a huge cockpit with a natty fringed awning and past a second mast to the front of the boat, which was littered with cushions and air beds and books and binoculars and Clem Sainsbury's red, half-naked torso spread out under the rail where he seemed to be chucking food down to the fish. He squirmed back at my footsteps and said, "Hi, Cassells," and got to his feet without glancing at a square inch of my skin under neck level. "I'll get Johnson. This is Spry, by the way. He's the only man who can sail this tub, so be nice to him." The man in the peaked cap grinned and went aft, and I sat down on one of the air beds. I nearly lay down, and then thought better of it. One thing at a time.

In a minute, two bright reflected beams crawled over the air beds followed by Johnson's bifocals. His legs were all right, but he wouldn't stop a bus in mid-Mayfair: he had on a short-sleeved shirt over beach pants, and everything that would button was buttoned. There was nothing to see on his face but a polite smile, eyebrows, and glasses.

The prospect seemed a bit bourgeois after Gil and Coco and fast Maseratis, but I was prepared to be sweet. Something must have been wrong with my smile, for before I said a word, Johnson came to a halt, his hands full of martinis, and shook his head slowly. "This is the bonzai sex department. Perfect, but teeny. How is Coco?"

I turned my head, the way a Forsey should turn her head. "Telepathy?"

"Binoculars," said Johnson. "Have a martini. There isn't a thing in it except sodium amytal. What was he so mad about, apart from your driving?"

"He was inviting me to a party," I said, sipping the martini. My hair kept getting into it.

"When?" Clem came and sat on the hatch lid, a large beer in his hand.

"Tomorrow night," I said. Janey can toss her hair back, but mine doesn't bounce quite the same. "What's so funny?"

Johnson stopped chortling first. "I fear the skids are under Coco," he said. "Tomorrow night, Mrs. van Costa is entertaining the three members of the Russian trade mission and their attaché to dinner. You haven't met Mrs. van Costa?"

"No," I said. "Tell me about her."

"Well, we can tell you one thing about her," said Clem Sainsbury. "She doesn't know about tomorrow night's party. She'll do a vertical takeoff in four different stages."

"What brought you out here, Miss Cassells?" said Johnson, circling the ice in his tumbler. He took a drink and rested his back on the rail. "A pilgrimage because you cared, or a picnic because you didn't care, or something else altogether?"

"Something else altogether," I said. I had seen out of the corner of my eye an odd erection, behind the high netted fence of the boatyard: a thing like a

77

miniature bullring, built of thick white cement. Chains ran from it into the water.

"That's the winch," said Johnson. He didn't miss much.

"Who found him? My father?" I said. I saw Clem look at Johnson briefly, then turn to me. "The night watchman at the yacht club saw him," he said. "First, that is. Then he roused the rest of us sleeping on board. *Dolly* wasn't here then, of course: I had a temporary job looking after another ketch called *Firefly* while the owner had gone back to London. I slept aboard most times, but that night I was a few boats along, on *Sheila,* whose chargehand was an old pal of mine. We talked so late, I just kipped down on *Sheila* and didn't know a thing till Pepe started howling blue murder."

"It was *Firefly,* you see, that was winched up," said Johnson. The sun was glaring its last above the buildings behind us, and his bifocals had turned each a hot, glittering red. "A bunch of whizz kids from your friend Janey's party came rolling along from Santa Eulalia, saw *Firefly* lying all darkened, and thought they'd give Clem here a call. When they found he wasn't aboard, they had an even brighter idea. They roused the man with the horse, paid him a fortune in British cigarettes and dollars and probably pot, and got him to move *Firefly* round and winch her up to the shore. Based on the old Boy Scout principle of removing your sleeping pal's tent, only not quite so innocuous because when Clem had come back from his presumed bender and finally found his missing boat, he'd have to stump up pretty handsomely to get his boat run down again. At any rate, the freak-out departed, leaving the horse to finish the winching, and Lord Forsey presumably passed by—resolved, it seems, on self-destruction—and with a fine sense of the macabre, climbed aboard. The only thing we don't know, but presumably you do, is his reason for killing himself."

I should have kept my mouth shut. It's one thing being dramatic with Janey, but another letting all the town know. It must have been the martini. "I think he was murdered," I said.

This time, it came off. They sat staring at me, their drinks in their hands, and Clem's mouth had come a little bit open. Then Johnson said, "Why?"

"I don't know."

"Who by?"—Clem.

"I don't know."

"Then why . . ." Johnson broke off, and straightening up off the rail, looked at his watch and said, "Wait. Let's go back to the cockpit and make ourselves comfortable. Clem, see if Spry could cough up more drinks and some tapas, and then come back yourself. Sarah . . ." He stopped, his eyebrows lifted over the glass.

"I don't mind," I said. "I've known Clem for ages."

"My name," said Johnson sorrowfully, "is Johnson Johnson. Fore and aft exactly the same. All my life it has prevented an intimate atmosphere. Try and ignore it. Americans call me J.J."

We walked back along deck to the cockpit, which had its awning drawn back. The cushions were stunning. "I don't see you as J.J.," I said, settling. "I don't see you as Johnny either."

"Nor does anyone else," said Johnson. "It worries me sometimes." He didn't look worried. "Now, what made you suspect that your father was murdered?"

As the sun sank, I told the story of the letter Janey posted from Daddy, the letter which turned up so late and which I didn't believe was from Daddy at all.

Clem said, "But why send you a fake letter?"

"Well, to set my mind at rest, I suppose. To stop me thinking any further. There was certainly nothing worrying in it. It couldn't have been more harmless."

"You'll need to think again about that," Johnson said. "If the murderer sent you a letter to stop you investigating a murder, he'd have made your father hint about suicide."

"Unless he wasn't sure," said Clem, "that he was going to be able to fake it as suicide."

"Then why write at all?" Johnson said.

We brooded. The sun disappeared. The sky was quite empty, and where it should meet the water there was no horizon at all. The yachts and the boatyard went dim.

"Unless the mistake in the letter was deliberate," said Clem suddenly. "To bring Sarah out."

"But why?" I said. The bikini was no longer warm enough, and shivering, I buttoned the mandarin jacket right up. "Why should anyone kill Daddy? Why should anyone want me out here?"

"If you don't know, no one does," Johnson said. "But I think you ought to be careful. For example, who could have written that letter, of the people still on the island? Who would know your address, or how to get a letter to you? Who knows you're sometimes called She-she? Who could copy Lord Forsey's hand and be reasonably sure of imitating his style? Not many, surely."

"Mr. Lloyd," I said, thinking hard. "And Janey and Gil, I suppose. Not Austin Mandleberg: he hadn't come yet, and he didn't know Daddy. A good few of the boys at Janey's party, I expect. Anyone who knew Janey would be apt to meet Daddy, and perhaps get a thanker or something from him that would do . . . I can't think of anyone else. There must be friends we don't know." And Derek, my brain said; but my mouth didn't blab it. If, as Janey says, Derek was here.

"I think we can leave unknown friends out of it, Sarah," said Johnson. "If you were induced back here for some reason, the person who wants you is probably in touch with you now. All the same, it's a fairly long list . . . Wait." A match, burning unregarded in his tanned fingers made me realize how quickly the dark falls in Spain. Johnson relit the pipe he had taken from the jacket lying behind him, and took it out of his mouth. "It couldn't have been Tony Lloyd. He'd gone to Barcelona the day of the party."

"He didn't go to Barcelona," said Clem.

There was a little silence. Far across the still waters, from the black piling of houses which was the old town of Ibiza, a throbbing had started: a pulse, hardly discernible, stirring the warm evening air. "How do you know?" Johnson said.

"I heard at the yacht club. Alec Brewer had expected to run into him: he had business on the mainland the same day. Lloyd went to the airport and took the plane to Barcelona all right, but he didn't stay there. He took the next plane to Palma, Majorca."

"From which he could have flown back in half an hour any time in the day," Johnson said. "Without running into so many business friends, either."

Janey's father, who had suggested that I should come to Ibiza. And I had to cook supper for him tonight. The evening air, stirring the rigging, groaned and whined faintly over our heads, and almost under the threshold of hearing, the throbbing from the old town continued . . . *Thud,* quiet. *Thud,* quiet. *Thud. Thud. Thud.*

"The drums," said Johnson. I stared at the town. And as I stared, I saw something moving against the dark houses: a sinuous, barely discernible thing made of insensible prickings of light. It moved. It crawled all over the town. It crept, wherever one looked, among the dark Arab houses and spread down to the quayside, where it lay reflected in the far water, pinpoints of light upon light. "Look," said Johnson, and put the binoculars into my hands.

*Dolly'*s bows and calm, rippling water. The shapes of many yachts and fishing boats, edging the sweep of the harbor. Then, across the width of the bay, the trading ships and the ferries, lying at the foot of the town. And above the ships and the ferries, and moving down from the Dalt Vila, slowly, lazily, to the thudding roll of the drums, a file of endless black figures, faceless figures who moved chained like a black trickle through street after street, torch in hand, limbs swaying like robots' below the black spires of their hoods.

"Easter is coming," said Johnson. "And the processions of penitents. The natives won't like Coco's party."

I had a pain in my middle. I said, "Should I go back to London?"

"Do you want to?" said Johnson.

"Yes," I said. "But I don't think I should. Maybe we should tell the police?"

"There isn't really anything to tell, is there?" said Johnson. "And even if they promised to protect you, two Guardia Civiles in the kitchen aren't going to stop the man who comes in through your bedroom window . . ."

I must have squeaked, because he said, "Or has someone already? Oh, Gilmore. I remember. Sarah, has anything else odd happened?"

The only other odd thing I could think of was the burglary before I left London, but that couldn't have had anything to do with Ibiza. There was nothing to get hold of: no sense in anything at all. And then I remembered. I said, "Coco Fairley says he knows where Daddy was going. He hinted at something pretty dirty. If I go to the party tomorrow, I might get him to tell me."

"Take me with you," said Clem. Strong arm stuff always brought out the best in him. I was jolly grateful, but it was giving me a headache working out how also to avoid spoiling my chances with Gil. And then I'd think of the drums, and of Daddy. I wished, suddenly, that I was happily married to an absent millionaire and had a nurse and an undernurse and five children by Cesarean section. "Or I could stick in the background," added Clem, more realistically. I could see Clem helping hand round the hypos.

"That would be super," I said, and shivering again got to my feet.

"Clem can tell me what happens," said Johnson. "And if you want us, we're here. And—don't tell anyone else what you suspect. Who else knows at the moment? Janey?"

"Only Janey," I said. "She doesn't talk. Not about that kind of thing."

"All right. No one else," Johnson said. As we walked aft to the gangplank, the yacht-club lights glittered briefly on his bifocals. "If you've been brought out here, it's because someone thinks you're important. Stay important, and the chances are he'll do nothing drastic. Become a danger, and the chances are that he will."

Clem drove me home. I hadn't said anything about Derek. If Derek was in it, I'd have to cope somehow myself.

I was too late to put on the potatoes. I'd made a lobster in aspic that afternoon, and I shoved it on the table to follow grilled grapefruit with sherry. Since there were no guests, Mr. Lloyd asked me to sit at the table myself. I ate a bread stick—it was all I could manage—while Gilmore Lloyd amused himself and Janey, speculating on how I had spent the evening on *Dolly*.

The new papers had come in: I had a look at them as I was going upstairs. Lord Luck was sort of noncommittal about Virgo and Scorpio, but said that Capricornians would find that a discussion this evening had restored all their confidence. Of course, he might have been thinking of Clem.

CHAPTER 5

NEXT MORNING, Derek arrived.

Janey, who had obviously just finished a thing with Guppy Collins-Smith and was looking for new material, elected to come shopping before breakfast with me, although she called me an extraordinary lot of different names when I tried to wake her. I memorized the ones I didn't know already and got her some coffee, while she climbed into a trouser suit and popped in her lenses. She had a sort of thin, shiny makeup she got from America which filled in all the bags, although actually today the Russians hadn't left any bags, as she'd dropped them at the Hotel Mediterránea at half-past six to read through stacks of papers about the castle, the Cathedral, the salt mines, and the excavations at Es Puig des Molins before having dinner with the director of the Museum of Archeology.

On the way to Ibiza, I told her about the discussion on *Dolly,* missing out the bit about her father not going to Barcelona and stressing the bit about not saying anything to anyone. I don't know what Gil had said about that night in my bathroom, but she was definitely unexcited on the subject of Johnson. On the other hand, Gil had certainly told her about Coco Fairley's party. She didn't bat an eyelid about his offer to take me, and when I probed tentatively about doing them a quick meal that evening, she told me impatiently not to be draggy. I was only being boring anyway because I always liked being a martyr.

I don't. I like doing things for people. I like cooking for them and planning treats and surprises. The trouble is you can't do anything for Janey, for she has it all, and is tired of it anyway. We talked like Guppy Collins-Smith's grandmother, who was a friend of the dear, late Queen, all the way from there into Ibiza. Janey and Guppy said the old creep had been given the plush loos from Marlborough House as a keepsake, but I didn't really believe it.

It was nice in Ibiza: fresh and warm, with no sign of all the "Night on Bald Mountain" stuff of the evening before. According to Mr. Lloyd, that kind of thing was going to go on all week, with the really big thing tomorrow night, when the whole town climbed into robes and dragged floats all the way down from the Cathedral, like students' charity week, only you didn't throw pennies. He quelled Janey's levity by reminding her that in this country these were rites sacred to the Church and that anyone treating them offensively would find it rather hard to do business here in the future. Then Janey got tired of the subject anyway, although Mr. Lloyd started planning with Gil how best to see the Friday night thing. I didn't fancy it much. Not from what I'd seen of it. Not with a killer maybe around.

We parked the car on the quay. The *Juan March* was in from Valencia, unloading furniture and motor scooters and pastas para Sopa and people. On the quay, already unloaded from other ships, lay stacks of pink tiles, rusty gray radiators, telegraph poles, and bed frames and mattresses. I never ever saw so many mattresses going backward and forward at one time as I did on Ibiza. On one ship they were sending red boxes of Henniger down a chute, and then sliding them from hand to hand down a long chain of men over the polished stone flags of the quay. We passed some kids practicing jumping with a roundel of rope trapped between two sets of legs, a wall that said Prohibido lugar a la Pelota, and long trails of stunning blue fishnets, with men, bent over, mending them. Then we dived into the little streets of the town.

This time Janey hustled me on, and I didn't have time to stop at the little shops that could be closed over entirely by shutting two unpainted doors, or at the walls studded with blue and yellow repro Majolica, or at the snazzy boutiques with shifts hanging out on a pole. If you looked up, above all the shoe shops and tiled farmacias, you saw the high living quarters: the balconies hanging with washing—clothes, sheets, embroidery under a polythene cover—the plastic pails, the geraniums. It was blazing hot. The walls were covered with monster thermometers, all hopelessly registering centigrade. I had on a little striped dress with long sleeves, and it felt about ninety already. Janey took off her jacket. She had a matching sleeveless tucked shirt underneath and a blonde crocodile belt.

I got some fruit, some groceries, and some of that ham with sliced olives in it, and a stack of Fantas in two flavors for Derek, while Janey swanned around being gorgeous to shop boys and then catching my eye when they did something silly. We'd got from there to the main market, and I was having a fearful discussion about some big red-and-green tomatoes when this hired car came zooming round from the Calle Antonio Palau, and in it was Derek.

He hadn't noticed us. Janey was quicker than I was. She flung a tomato into the taxi, and it stopped dead with a screeching of brakes. A donkey bolted, and thousands of people quite quickly appeared, as the driver got out. Janey stepped up to him, said six words or so, and gave him a dazzling smile. He stopped boning and began to smile back. So did the crowd, with a few olés thrown in. I paid for the tomato. Derek, roused at last from whatever early-morning trance he'd been in, put his head out of the window and saw me. *"Sarah!"*

His eyes were bloodshot. I must say he looked pretty foul. Then his gaze traveled round to the right. "Miss Lloyd!"

Then Janey smiled, and I got it. The fresh material had not only arrived: it had been sent for.

* * *

He wanted to book in at the Mediterránea, but that was overruled. There was no sense in inviting Johnson's attentions. He must, said Janey, stay at Casa Veñets, with me. He objected quite a lot, actually, but I put most of it down to having to come by night flight: Derek is a very slow starter in the morning. It also turned out that he was seething about being nicked away from his precious experiments, particularly as we both seemed so healthy. I let Janey explain.

It was a line we had thought up that morning, about nasty rumors going around concerning Daddy and his reason for suicide and my anxiety to clear his good name. On the spur of the moment, thinking doubtless of Coco, Janey threw in a bit about Daddy's name being linked with a woman's. It sounded more feasible actually, considering the name he already had among the discerning as a high-grade sponger and drunk. In the middle of it, Janey said casually, "Sarah wondered if Lord Forsey let anything slip to you just before he was found. The time when you came over."

"When?" said Derek. "That was after Father died." When he hasn't shaved, Derek looks awful.

"No: before that," I said. "The other time. Did he say anything to you then?"

"The other time?" said Derek. Fluently.

I got fed up. "Listen, live wire," I said. "You were seen in Ibiza on Friday, the day before Daddy died. What were you doing here? If you saw Daddy, what did he say to you?"

His eyeballs rattled. I swear it, like a computer selecting its programmes. He said, "Oh, that. Now I see what this is all about. Yes, I was in Ibiza.

For one day, that's all. I was back in Holland by lunchtime on Saturday. And Father didn't tell me anything, Sarah, that had any bearing on his suicide, so you can forget that side altogether. As far as the other thing goes, we discussed something which is absolutely personal, and I don't want to talk about it. If I did, I'd have told you about that visit long ago." He looked at me. "The rumor story was cooked up, wasn't it? You were worried in case I'd stayed on and driven the old boy to make away with himself?"

I looked down. He is, after all, a successful engineer. One forgets that. "You didn't like each other," I said.

"No, we didn't. And if you want to know, we had one hell of a row on parting that Friday. But it wasn't enough, if you'll believe me, to drive anyone to cut his own throat." He paused. "What's all this, anyway? Is there a suggestion it wasn't suicide? Or is this just something you've both dreamed up on your own?"

The Maserati swept up the Lloyds' drive and stopped. I could actually hear Janey's brain going round: my own wasn't even running in neutral. Janey said, "Don't be an idiot: of course it was suicide. Only people talk. People want to know why. If one person saw you that time, maybe others did too. Sarah thought for some reason you were trying to keep that visit dark. And you ought to be warned, that's all, not to."

"Well, you're going to be unlucky, aren't you?" said Derek. "Because I don't believe in chatting to strangers about my family affairs. And in my book, you and Sarah are strangers."

People are bitchy to Janey, sometimes, but seldom plain rude. She got out of the car, very elegantly, stretching her long, bare, brown legs. "Then if we're strangers, you can't very well stay here, darling," she said. "Think how people would talk." And slamming the car door, she sauntered in through the wrought-iron porch.

For dramatic exits, you'd go a long way to match it. Unfortunately, one has to be practical. Derek helped me unload the groceries at the back door, not forgetting the ham with the olives in it and the tomatoes. I transferred the Fantas from a paper bag to a holdall and shoved them back in the boot. Then I drove him back to the Hotel Mediterránea, which is the only new show hotel actually inside Ibiza, and saw him booked into a room. I followed him up because my tummy was churning, and I wanted to use his marble-tiled bathroom: there wasn't any hot water, and the soap wouldn't stay on the basin, but everything else worked. When I came out he was sitting on the windowsill of his room, looking down on the morning collection of hippies, and the boy had just put two large whiskies on the table. "Come and sit for a minute. I expect you can do with one," Derek said.

I thought of all those bloody Fantas and stared at him. I had been deceived. "Oh, for God's sake, sit down," Derek said. "I'm not a Boy Scout. But I didn't murder Father either. That's what all that was in aid of, wasn't it?"

I nodded.

"And why you came to Ibiza?"

I nodded again. Neat Whyte & Mackay at nine o'clock in the morning is not my usual form, but I started in on it. Circumstances were exceptional.

"Then you're a silly ass making that girl your confidante," said Derek scathingly. "She'll run your life for you. They have to be boss, that kind, or nothing. You may think you're bosom companions, but I bet you're worth a giggle a minute to her own private circle already."

"Honestly, Derek," I said. Whiskey or no, it was the same old dishwater Derek, all right. "I'm *in* her private circle. We're friends. She was trying to help. For goodness' sake: she saw you in Alt Vila the night before Daddy died. And Coco Fairley says he was up to something shady. We thought it would be just you to go all cubs' honor over the Pater. And you didn't know Daddy like I did. He was an awful old softie inside."

"You drank that far too quickly," said Derek. He frowned.

"I always cry when I'm bullied," I said, and stood up. The floor waved a bit, reminding me all of a sudden of Johnson. "Cessation," I said. It sounded all right, so I sat down.

"What?" said Derek. He fished out a large, immaculate handkerchief and chucked it over, looking both peevish and preoccupied. He said, "Now listen to me. I know you think you're the swingiest chick this side of Chelsea, but you're going to drive back to the house for your luggage, and then you're going to take the next plane with me back to Holland. I'm not having you turn into another drunken, layabout tramp like your father."

That time I shot to my feet, and I didn't care whether I could say cessation or not. "Like hell I will! Talk about Janey bossing my life! She's got a damned sight more horse sense than you have; and what's more, she doesn't sit on her fat bottom handing out bloody naïve advice. In any case, who asked you to stick your bloody nose in?"

"You did," snapped Derek. "At a time when every minute away from my firm happens to matter. But then, I'm not normal. I haven't had a lover a week since I was fourteen. I don't smoke pot. I don't take LSD. I don't consider the rest of the world my inferiors and that it owes me my own brand of superior fun. I don't get so sick of my self-centered life that I'd make monkeys out of decent, hard-working people, for five minutes' fun."

Poor, bloody Derek. I sat down very, very quietly, not feeling angry at all and said nothing for quite a long time, until I realized that I ought to continue the argument. "And who do *you* live for?" I said.

There was a little pause. Then, "I have principles," he said.

I said, "So have I. And one of them is to stick to my family *and* my friends. Janey can laugh at me. She's welcome. I've dined out on a few stories about her. But not ones that matter. By the same token, she could have made quite a good thing about telling how she saw you sneaking about the Alt Vila that night. But instead she chose to help me keep it dark. *You* were the one who flung it back in her face."

"Maybe I should have told her," said Derek. His voice had gone very tight, and you felt he ought to be clearing his throat, but he wasn't. Sometimes he didn't look like Daddy at all. "Maybe I should have told her why I came to see Father and relied on her kind nature to do the right thing. After all, you say you would trust her."

"I didn't say anything of the kind," I said. "In some things I wouldn't trust her an inch." *Men, for instance*. I said, "Oh, for Pete's sake, Derek." He would honestly drive anyone to drink. "What was it you came to see Daddy about? I don't know how the firm managed to spare you."

"They sent me," said Derek. "In a way."

There was a silence. I felt like a piano with the dampers all jammed. "Why?" I said. My whiskey was finished.

"Because," said Derek clearly and nastily, "they had reason to believe that that renowned peer, the fifth Baron Forsey of Pinner, was dabbling in the sale of technical and treasonable secrets, and they had given me to understand that if this were so, I had become an unemployable security risk in this industry and any other competitor on this side of the Iron Curtain, at least."

"That's punk," I said. "For goodness' sake, Derek. When was Daddy ever in Holland?"

"Just before the aural sensator was stolen," he said.

I stared at him. The incongruity of poor, charming Daddy trotting round Europe with a cartload of secret electronic equipment hadn't yet struck me: I was only going by Derek's green face. "So you killed him," I said.

My brother took three strides toward me. He bent down, and clamping his hands on my forearms, raised me out of my chair and held me, barely erect, his face so close to mine that I could see his eyes were all bloodshot. Until then in all our lives, a peck on the cheek was all we had ever exchanged. Now, I could feel the heat from his skin, and smell the whiskey, and see the stubble glittering round his jaws and his chin. He said, "You think that, as a matter of course. People kill other people . . . Why not someone you know? Why not me? I say I have principles, but talk doesn't mean anything, not in your circle. Trust doesn't mean anything. Kinship doesn't mean anything."

My heart was behaving all at once like a body-skin hammer. "It doesn't seem to matter all that much to you," I said. "You need to see a bloody psychiatrist."

He said, "Ha!" and opened his hands so that I lost my balance and sat down again, with a bump, in my chair.

I found I was crying hard, but silently, at least. I got hold of the handkerchief again, my hand shaking, and mopped up till it had stopped, taking deep breaths until the hiccoughs had gone. Then I collected my bag and the carryall with the Fantas and got up. My legs were still shaking. I said to Derek, "I think you're all wrong. I think there's something wrong with you, too. I don't want to hear any more. I'm going back to Janey's."

"Of course," he said. "Curl up in your fantasy world. This is reality, Sarah. You've got to face it some time."

"That's *your* reality," I said. "It's not the same as mine. Mine is Daddy's."

"I know," Derek said. I could feel him standing, watching me as I went out, but he didn't say anything more.

I stopped at Spar on the way home and returned all the Fantas.

I was having breakfast in the kitchen when Gilmore came in juggling three tennis balls, kissed Anne-Marie, and hitched himself onto the edge of the table. He had on a voile shirt and pale hipster pants, and he still looked like Gary Grant. "Your nose is red, She-she," he said.

I said, "I've been drinking."

He caught the balls and began to throw them up one-handed, his eyebrows lifted right up. His eyes were blue, not green like Janey's. I wondered if he wore contact lenses too. He said, "I gather Janey has made a botch of her public relations. Has the worthy engineer gone back to his engines?"

"I don't know," I said. I didn't care, either. I'd given up thinking about Derek. And about Daddy, for that matter.

"Um," said Gilmore. He remained. "Well, now we know you drink. You also cook. You swim. What other talents can you produce?"

I held my coffee cup with both hands and studied it. "I dance. I play tennis and cricket. I skate. I water-ski. I ride. I can type. I think I can wear clothes. And I know how to sew and to nurse and to look after babies."

"Come and look after me," said Gilmore Lloyd, getting off the table. "I want to go riding."

"I have," I said, "your lunch to get ready."

"Anne-Marie got the breakfast and she can perfectly well cook lunch for Janey and Father as well," said Gilmore pleasantly. Anne-Marie, catching my eye, smiled and nodded. "We shan't be in."

It was the kind of day Celeste sometimes hints at, but never for Capricorn. By the time I'd changed, Gil had brought round the Cooper S, dark green and we took off for the stables, where we switched to the horses. Gil had brought saddlebags with him. I knew there'd be cold chicken and a bottle of martinis in one, and a large towel in the other . . . and that they had all been packed long before I got back from Derek. Men like Gil Lloyd don't take a girl out to watch rugby or to teach her to drive. That was all right. We spoke the same language.

The morning was super: blue and clear with a gorgeous fresh heat. And we made our own breeze, cantering over the scrub and between the rows of little green trees, with the fig trees, like ghosts, staked out like maypoles all round their elbows. We passed a bent olive tree with a prop under its knuckle, like "The Thinker," and I asked Gil if all this wasn't someone's land. He said it was. It was his father's. The sun shone harder, and all the cicadas sang, and so did Gilmore and I.

We stopped at a place called San José for a beer and a fizzy stone ginger, and then made our way across unwalled country down to a beach. It was a wild ride, up and down crumbly, overgrown gulches, with a motor road winding in and out in hairpin bends beside us, through a mass of little hot hills, dotted with conifers and bushes and flowers, and all scented by pine trees and thyme.

A flock of little birds barred with bright lemon, like butterflies, got up and fluttered away. A goat, chained and muzzled, looked up as the horses moved past. We rustled at times hock deep in a thicket of flowers: tall, feathery, pink spikes even Gil didn't know and miles of enormous white daisies, their centers all stained deep yellow. There were bushes and bushes of starry things like Christmas roses in lilac and white, and short purple flowers, some with spikes, some with trumpets, and things like vetches, and miniature iris, and oceans of bright yellow stuff that looked like charlock. There were patches of tall sisal cactus and thickets of prickly pear like a crowd of cheering green bats. Gil told me what everything was and the names went straight out of my head because he looked so super, with his French needle-cord jeans, his suntan, and the way he moved with his horse.

We picked our way down to the beach, just about midday. It was simply out of this world: a cut of fine shelving sand underneath a towering cliff of stacked orange sandstone. The cliff had a fuzz of greeny-gray stuff here and there seeded into it and a litter of dead branches and trunks in a queer, electric blue-gray that would fetch a packet at the biennial, I promise you, as Art in the Round. Patching the sand were big fallen boulders and beds of silver-brown flakings of seaweed, so deep it was like walking on cushions. Under the noon sun and the reflected heat of the sandstone, you could see the beach sizzle. It was perfectly empty. We let the horses loose to find shade somewhere under an overhang, and Gil hauled out the towel and spread it for me to lie on, then unpacked the goodies.

It was, actually, the bloody ham with the olives that I'd bought that morning in Spar, with some fruit and some yogurt and a long roll with a packet of butter and some Queso Gruyère ahumado at forty-two pesetas the whack: I'd forgotten who was doing the catering. But at least we didn't have Fantas: we didn't even have martinis. He'd brought a full bottle of Veterano Osborne.

On every first date with a boy, there's a key moment when you know someone's got his finger on the button, and any second now you'll have to choose your line and scamper through all your resources. There's no kick quite like it. Gil poured two stiff drinks, downed his, chucked a corner of the towel over the food and said, "Come on. I'm cooking. Let's cool down first." And leaning down to where I was lying nursing my own empty glass, he slid the zipper neatly from top to bottom of my pink jump suit from Jaeger's.

They all do that. I put my glass down and got up, shaking off the rest of the jump suit. I had my bikini on already beneath. He said, "You little bitch! Where do you think this is, Filey?" And he pounced.

That was O.K., too. I ducked and fled for the sea, with Gil grabbing, but I got into the surf first and kicked a load of it into his face. He still had on his voile shirt and trousers. Then while he was still gasping, I struck out into the water.

He came in, just as he was. He could swim, too, but you can't rape anyone in deep water, or at least if you can you ought to get a certificate. By the time he'd got one strap off my bikini we were both laughing so much we were spouting up brandy, and before very long I made off back to the beach. I got the towel before he did too, and lay face down on it gasping, while he dropped on the sand, his chest going up and down. The voile shirt had a great rip in it. I don't remember doing that, but I must have. I said, "I'm starving."

"Are you, ducky?" said Gil. And sitting up slowly, he pulled his shirt right off and rolled over, trapping my hand. Then he got my other one, before I could kick out, and transferred it till he had them both in one grip. "So am I, ducky," and like a man trained in Spirella, he sprang the clip of my bikini top and followed it up, one-handed in the time-honored way, breathing salt water and brandy. A woman in high-heeled shoes and a man in a suit came onto the beach.

I honestly think he wasn't going to stop. My chin ground into the sand. I could feel his hand turn and get ready, sneakily, to slide in another direction. It wasn't that it was anything but absolutely delirious, but one has to think of one's ground plan. I heaved up my bottom, and as his hand came off, bit him. The yell made the woman look round, but I had the towel round me by then, and Gil was sitting back on his heels, holding his arm and swearing. I stared back, deadpan. His eyes had gone cold, and I hoped suddenly that the couple was going to stay for a while. Then, without saying anything, he got to his feet, found my glass, and filled it slowly and deliberately with brandy. Then he held it hard, against my teeth.

I drank it all, with my hair falling back over my

shoulders, and my eyes half shut, gazing at his. By the end he was smiling. I smiled too. "Hard luck, Gil," I said. "No pills since Sunday: remember?" The smile slowly faded from his face, and I lay back and went straight off to sleep. I like to be organized.

I woke much later, with my tummy rumbling, and lay there getting up the nerve to turn round. But he was still there, asleep also, with the brandy bottle half finished beside him. When he woke, he'd be chocker. I couldn't count on him now at the party, but I should have Austin then. And there would be another day coming. He looked nice, asleep. Spoiled, but nice.

I looked round, and the other couple were just going, still dressed. They were both heavily built. She wore earrings and a black velvet waistcoat suit over a satin striped blouse. I wondered why on earth they had come to the beach. I wondered if I was sorry they had.

I lay for a bit watching the ants, and a thin brown sparrow with large Spanish eyes stood on a rock and inspected me. The rock was gray, with scraps of yellow netting, you'd think, dragged all over it. But it was really a network of hard yellow stone inside the rock, sticking up as the rest wore away. It was funny.

A sort of caterpillar went by, dragging a gray, soft cone of seaweed like a wedding dress. I stirred, put on some sun cream, and decided to occupy myself making the ham into sandwiches. Then I had some yogurt and watched two lizards fighting over the drips in the lid. They were blue-green with thin, black speckled stripes, and they stood with their forelegs braced on one stone and their hind legs and tail miles away, on another stone altogether. I wondered what it felt like. Their black tongues licked the lid, leaving a band of clean silvery foil, and the lid gave little clinks on the stones. Then there would be a dry scrape of feet as they flew at each other and somersaulted apart, streaming up the red rocks into cover. They seemed to like strawberry flavor. I finished my yogurt and woke Gil by laying two cucumber rounds in his eyes.

He was a little cool at first, but he joined in after a bit while I chatted, and by the time we got to the fruit, we had gone through all the people we had in common and found that there was a second cousin of Daddy's who was related to an aunt by marriage of his, that when he was a boy, his father used to take a chalet at St. Moritz near the chalet of some people I knew, and that we had once been to the same bit of the river at the same time for the boat race and hadn't known it. He took all these coincidences fairly easily, but I didn't. I thought it was Fate. I told him what Celeste said about Capricorn and Scorpio, and he said, "Honestly, Sarah. You don't believe all that punk?"

"Yes!" I said indignantly. Men always said this. But they usually managed a grin. "Some are phoney, perhaps. But Celeste is marvelous. She's got me right over and over and over. I promise you. I find it terribly useful."

"As bait?" said Gilmore. Lying on his back, he had lit a cigarette with tobacco in it.

I said, "You've got to talk about *something*." I recognized that this was all my own fault. I was glad that I still had Austin and Clem and Johnson, though.

"What do you want, Sarah?" said Gil. "Marriage at any price to anybody?"

I lay on my elbow and looked at him, but he wasn't looking at me.

"Don't you think I'd make a good wife?"

"For someone who doesn't mind being picked by a pin," Gilmore said.

I picked up a handful of sand and dribbled it down his bare arm. "I think I'd make a good wife. But I wouldn't marry just anyone."

"You'd marry someone rich," said Gilmore. "With a good social position, who didn't mind being bossed around for good by his wife." He opened his eyes. "You should put an advertisement in the papers. Come on: let's pack it in. You've got to get back and cook something sensational for Austin."

The sky was flat milky blue, and the sea to the west was full of running bands of thin sparkle, widening as they came near the shore. We began to pack up.

We got back mid-afternoon, without talking very much more, and Gil disappeared to bounce tennis balls in the garden. But that was an absolutely typical encounter. I mean, something always, sooner or later, comes apart in the middle when a boy takes me out.

I cooked a six-course meal for Austin, using every pan in the kitchen, just to show the bloody

Lloyds what was what. Gil kept out of the kitchen, and he was brief and bored-sardonic when we met. Janey came in once, and sat on the edge of the table while I was stoning olives to stuff in the veal, eating them as fast as I got the stones out. After a bit, as I expected, she said, "What do you think Derek will do? Did he tell you after all what he'd been doing?"

"Yes," I said. It was the half-truth, anyway. I knew why Derek had come back and that he had seen Daddy. What I didn't know was what Daddy had told him and what Derek had done about it. I added, "It was a family thing; nothing to do with why Daddy died. I think it was suicide after all."

Janey stared at me, an olive still in her hand. "You *what?*" Then she looked again at my face and said, "Oh, no you don't. You think Derek killed him."

"I don't," I said. "I just don't want to think about it again, that's all."

"Well, you're going to have to shut Coco's mouth for him tonight then, dear, aren't you?" said Janey. "And what about your precious letter?"

I didn't want to know any more about the letter or about why Janey's father hadn't gone to Barcelona: for all I knew he was the nightclub queen of Majorca. I said, "I think, honestly, if anything had been wrong, the authorities would have found out before now. I was a bit steamed up over it all, and it's not awfully fair, in a way, digging out the old man's lurid past. If you could put up with me to the end of the week, I'll potter off on Monday to Kensington W and forget it."

Three more days would be fair, I felt, to concentrate on my personal life. Austin, for example, had said something about seeing Seville. And Clem was to be at the party tonight. I looked at the clock.

"You can stay as long as you like," said Janey. Afterward, I realized how absently she had spoken. At the time, I just dragged the bowl of olives away from her fingers and started chopping the bacon. I had to wash my hair, yet, and I didn't bother to look when the Maserati tuned up and rolled down the driveway a few minutes later.

She was back before dinner, which was just as well, as I was sliding in and out of the kitchen in housecoat and rollers, nursing the veal, and doing last-minute things, like slicing and bedding the avocados in lettuce. Anne-Marie was off, but Helmuth did the last stages, which let me do my eyes and get into this thing I bought in Hung on You, which was made of kind of white moiré silk with polythene bands in between, which rather showed off my suntan.

Daddy would have hit the absolute roof, and I rather thought Mr. Lloyd might wince a trifle. But it was also jolly smart. If I couldn't frighten Gil, I could shock him. And I could glue Austin, I hoped, to my side, for most of Coco's ominous party. On Clem, I knew, it would make no impression at all. At parties Clem was a model of boyish high spirits: he got sloshed on beer and told a number of rather good, dirty masculine jokes. Flo always said that if Clem ever really fell for a girl, he would fall awfully hard, and I always felt that someday he would meet her: someone jolly, who could live inexpensively off his overdraft. But he made a fabulous bodyguard.

The funny thing was, I had no premonitions at all. And when I looked back in the papers, it said Capricorn was going to have a hell of a time.

They were right.

CHAPTER 6

Mrs. van Costa's house, the Casa Mimosa, hired, Anne-Marie said, from the star of an American TV soap opera, lay in a garden not far from the airport and was landscaped with every soap-opera cliché known to man. Spinning along through the warm night in the Cooper S, the first sight of it, long and white and floodlit among the palm trees, was a bit like finding a cruise liner at night in your bathtub: it was all plate glass and wrought iron and creepers and great wax flowers that dangled into the car as we growled round the drive. There was a fancy lake in the front, surrounded by cacti, small palms, lilies, and white marble seats, and floodlit like an old Korda film. Also, hosts of little strips of tinfoil and plastic hung on threads in the air, slung between all the date palms. On each strip, single words had been written in beautiful script. Walking toward the house, the sequence I saw declared, LOVING IS SUMMER AND HELL IS AN ELECTRIC LIGHT BULB. But as Gilmore pointed out, if you approached the house another way, it read LOVING AN ELECTRIC LIGHT BULB IS HELL. There was a Rolls-Royce Silver Cloud Mark III flying the Soviet flag drawn up before the front door.

Gilmore and I came to a complete halt, and Austin cannoned into us and then listened while we consulted. The concrete poetry party, it was clear, had not yet got off the ground: apart from the Rolls, there were no cars at all to be seen except our own Cooper S and Coco's battered Alfa Romeo, parked rather askew at the side of the drive. The Russian Trade Mission, clearly, were still being entertained to dinner by Mrs. van Costa. Whether Mrs. van Costa also knew of Coco's proposed party and had vetoed it, or whether (as Gil was convinced) she didn't know and Coco was choosing his moment, remained to be seen.

Austin, who had sold a couple of ikons to Mr. Lloyd and felt on home ground, obviously, as soon as he took in the poetry, said, "Now why would Coco Fairley do a thing like that, Gilmore? After all, he's a guest in Mrs. van Costa's house." Americans are the most formal people on earth, maybe after the Swedes.

"It's a happening to celebrate the fact that Coco's being thrown out on his neck," Gilmore said. "I told him not to stop working. The trouble is, as soon as he finds a new billet, he hits the charlie again."

Austin hesitated. I'd expected him to be turned out in white tux, all Washington style, but he was wearing a cream wool-jersey suit by Virgul of Paris, with a strawberry cashmere polo-necked sweater. I saw the label.

He said, "If you want to go in, I guess we might do it without embarrassing Mrs. van Costa too much. I met the Mission when Janey brought them round to the gallery, and they invited me to take a glass of wine with them afterward. That is, if we're not too informally dressed." Gil was wearing a loose silk shirt hand-woven in Siam over beautiful trousers, and I had on my polythene. Austin wasn't looking at me.

"Come on," said Gil.

Mrs. van Costa had brought her own butler. He opened the door in a white jacket, American as a Yellow Cab driver and about as generally welcoming. We asked after Coco and were taken sourly, into a large study lined with stamped Cordoban leather and the finest collection of banned books I've ever seen outside St. Tizzy's, all bound in morocco. Gilmore and I took one each and sat down and got on with it while Austin, who had more inhibitions, prowled round inspecting the bric-a-brac. He came back grining and mentioned that there were more brics than bracs. Then Coco came in, formally dressed, with his long golden sideburns glittering and his face full of early warning signals, and said that Mrs. van Costa had heard we had arrived and would we care to join her in the drawing room. The butler was just behind him. We trooped upstairs, Coco staring at Gilmore. I heard him hiss, dramatically, "What the hell are you playing at? You're too bloody early!" but I didn't hear what Gilmore replied. My polythene crackled.

The TV soap-opera star's drawing room was done in Hollywood Regency, with a fiber-glass Adam chimneypiece and Venetian chandeliers and crimson satin Knole suites. The floor was parquet, with a carpet made of a whole flock of goats sewn together: the air had that strong, randy smell billy goats have. The Russian Trade Mission sat dotted about, drinking vodka.

I had seen them before, of course, at Mr. Lloyd's luncheon. They still looked burly, sweaty and amiable, sitting in their neat cloth suits, grinning at Mrs. van Costa.

Mrs. van Costa was sitting in one of the armchairs with her legs up on a pouffe, her face without makeup, her short, gray hair sculpture-cut by Mr. Kenneth—who else—and wearing a high-necked, navy crepe trouser suit with a long chiffon scarf that showed every elegant bone in her long, angular body. She was smoking a cheroot in a long ebony holder.

It was Mummy.

I think I mentioned she was an actress. There was the polythene peep-dress, of course, and then I had my hair all done up in loops and plaited through with ribbon, with three Littlewoods' Asian hairpieces added in for good measure. My face was the last thing she looked at. Even then, she only swung her feet down from the stool, and getting up said, "What a pretty little girl. I don't think we've met before. Coco, introduce us."

Her neck was stringy and her features were bony, and she hadn't the pink hair any longer, but she still had the huge saucer eyes I remembered, with false eyelashes and then spikes drawn in under the lashes. She wore no other paint. I had the passing thought that Janey would find her common, and then I thought that Janey probably wouldn't. Whatever else she hadn't got, Mummy had always had style. I walked forward, and I could read her expression as if she had spoken. "I'm sorry, honey. But we can't let it be known that poor old Forsey's wife and her boyfriend were living only a stone's throw from where he was killed." I wondered if Coco knew, and then I saw his face and realized why I'd been brought here, and why the whining back there on the stairs hadn't seemed to ring true. And just who the mystery woman was with whom Daddy had had his assignation that Saturday night.

I said something, I suppose, and sat down with my knees trembling while the general chitchat began. The Russian who had sat down beside me was asking me in a smiling way what I thought of Ibiza and how I liked swinging London. I must have answered him, because he kept getting nearer, but my brain was pinking like the old Morris.

Whether Daddy had come to the Lloyds' by sheer chance or whether he had followed Mummy to Ibiza, there was no way of knowing. What did seem certain was that somehow they had come together. And that they had been meeting each other here, in secrecy, or at any rate without it being known they were husband and wife. Except, it was apparent, by Coco.

When had he found out? Recently, I suspected. Or perhaps his jealousy hadn't become sufficient earlier to make it worth his while telling the police. Or maybe he didn't give a hoot either way until Mummy showed signs of finding him tedious, and he thought he'd take his revenge by springing her secret on me.

In any case, that let Derek out. No doubt Coco's silence would have to be bought off by somebody, but for Mummy's sake, not Derek's. And I didn't give a damn about Mummy. The trade attaché moved a bit nearer and Mummy's voice said, "Coco honey, will you do the honors? There's something I just must have your little friend look at. Sarah, will you come here with me?"

Voice from the past. *Sarah, you know that your father and I are just not too good at getting along? Sarah, there are schools in America just as good as St. Tizzy's. Sarah honey, I'm afraid if I had money to buy you a fur coat, I'd have one myself.* I followed her into her bedroom, and she shut the door and said, "Hallo," without moving, with that still, smiling stare that Daddy used to call Bemused Duse. Then she subsided in front of her mirror, without taking her eyes off my face, and said, "How are you, She-she? Are you well? Who's the act for?" Her mouth got wider, and she gave a sort of cluck of amusement. "I don't think I've seen so much of you since you were about five."

I said, "Why van Costa? Have you married again?"

"In a month? Poor, darling Forsey," said Mummy. "It's my incognito, honey. I've had it for ages. Did I give you the most terrible shock?"

I sat on the bed, crackling. "Terrible. Did you know I was around?"

"Of course, darling, but I could hardly step out of character now. I'd even had a cable sent from New York saying I was too ill to go to the poor old thing's funeral . . . I don't know how he died," she added quickly and, turning round, took another small black cheroot from a box on her table and started to fit it into her holder. "I don't know why or how or anything. I'm just sorry it happened that way, and I'm going to remember him the way he was, when we first married."

"It was just coincidence that you were here when he came?" I said. "Or did he come first?"

"How old are you, She-she?" said Mummy. She knows damn well how old I am: she bloody well ought to. She'd got her black cheroot lit. "Twenty, yes. And not married and with no regular boy-friend." She was silent, smoking, and as I didn't contradict her, she took the holder out of her mouth and said gently, "You organize, honey. You mustn't organize. Men just don't like it."

"Women don't like it much, either," I said. Somehow, whatever I did, I ended up being insulting to Mummy. "Did you meet Daddy before he was found dead? Did he come here?"

She got up and roved around smoking. Her bottom was little and angular, like a twenty-five-year-old gym mistress we once had. God is bloody unfair. Then, "Of course," she said softly. "We talked. We were thinking of living together again." She stared at me, smiling. "But that's not why he went off and killed himself, She-she. I don't know why he did that."

I said, "Derek thinks he was a spy."

She dropped her holder. I've never known her make an unpremeditated move in her life but this was, I swear it, although she merely stood, thoughtfully watching it roll, and said, "Don't move, for

God's sake honey, or your nice dress will melt . . . Thank you, darling." She took it from me and sat down, laying the whole thing back on the table. "I didn't know Derek was so romantically minded. Was this at the funeral?"

"No, this morning," I said. I didn't know whether my brother had ever heard of Mrs. van Costa, or if he had, if he knew who she was. But I wasn't going to let on I didn't know. I added, "You remember, he was over here just before Daddy died as well, and saw quite a bit of him."

She stared at me, and a silence developed again: at least a kind of a silence. The house was no longer as quiet as it had been. I wondered how Coco was managing to entertain the Trade Mission in Mummy's absence, and it occurred to me that if it were to lose none of its dewy happiness, the Trade Mission ought to be got out of the villa pretty damn quick. But there were one or two things I had to find out first. Mummy said, "So far as I know, Derek doesn't know that I'm here. I'd rather he didn't know, really. What has he come back for? I thought his test tubes caught cold if he left them."

"I sent for him," I said, and then slid it on the line. "I thought Derek killed Daddy."

The stare was enormous. I think she had had an injection as well. "And did he?" Mummy said. She was sitting quite still.

"I thought Coco knew," I said. "That's why I'm here."

"Coco is a traitor to his art," said Mummy beautifully. "And will have to be dealt with. Come,

She-she." And she got up and walked firmly out of the room.

Coco's was a paper-bag party. They had them in New York in the twenties, and they were just reaching London when I left it that spring. Flo had been to one and her paper bag split: always inefficient. A paper bag is all you wear. On your head.

Not that Coco had mentioned this when inviting Gilmore and Austin and myself to his party. And not, of course, that he had told Mummy, who wasn't expecting a party at all.

I was running after her as she swept out of the bedroom to tell her, but she had opened the drawing-room door before I could catch her, and then she stopped and just stood. I looked over her shoulder. Coco had disappeared. The four red squares were still there, and so were Austin and Gilmore, and I never saw six men so plastered in the whole of my life. If he had been pouring vodka into them with a siphon since the moment Mummy and I left, he could hardly have got a more positive effect. They were singing. I think it was "Auld Lang Syne," but the melodic line was a bit out of the true, and Gil thought he was singing in harmony. Mummy said, "What the hell," very slowly, but they didn't even unwind their arms from each other's necks. She looked round at me.

"Coco's planned a wild party," I said. "For tonight. We were all supposed to be his first guests. We didn't know you didn't know."

"I didn't know," said Mummy. "What kind of party?"

It was then that one of the guests came wandering along the corridor behind us, clearly in search of a loo. It was a girl, in a Heal's carrier bag, and she had pink sequins everywhere. When she saw Mummy she stopped rigid, but Mummy just said gently, "It's third on the left, Madeleine," and went on smoking. The girl disappeared. Then another door opened and Clement Sainsbury came out, his arms full of vodka. He was fully dressed.

"Hallo, Cassells," he said. "Mrs. van Costa? You have a problem."

"This is Clem Sainsbury, Flo Sainsbury's cousin," I said. "He's helping on one of the yachts in Ibiza. He holds the track record for helping."

"I hope I'm helping right now," said Clem. He seemed anxious to accommodate his language to Mrs. van Costa's. "There's a rather extreme sort of . . ."

"We know all about that," said my mother. "And the slug among the delphiniums. Where is he?"

"Running the party, down in the playroom. They all came in the side entrance. They've got your Spanish dancers as well, I'm afraid, Mrs. van Costa."

"Good heavens above," said my mother. "In paper bags?"

"Not yet. But since the Trade Mission were still on the premises, and it seemed very likely that Mr. Fairley would try and involve them . . ."

"You got them plastered," said Mummy. She stared at him, with her eyes very wide, and he blushed down to the neck of his dinner suit. "You have the makings," she said, "of a genius. Put those bottles down. Sarah, ring for Dilling, will you, while I put a disk on the radiogram?"

It was a conga. As soon as the sound came through, on six stereo speakers, my mother laid down her cigarette holder, and snapping her fingers, grabbed a swaying Austin by the hips. I got hold of Gilmore and, shunting, closed him up to Mummy. The Russians, after a little confusion and laughter, tacked on with Clem pushing behind, and clicking and swaying we stamped our way twice round the drawing room to the boom of Latin American hiccoughs, and out the door and down the hall to the shower room. Mummy snaked them right up to the showers and stepped back smartly, pulling me by the arm, and Clem turned the water on full. We closed the door on them quietly.

The butler Dilling was waiting outside in the passage, and Mummy gave him his orders. Then, with Clem on one side and me on the other, she returned and sat down in the drawing room. A moment later, Dilling ushered Coco in.

He was wearing a bathrobe and he was smiling, although his eyes glittered a bit. He said, "I'm rather busy, Geraldine sweetheart, but I got the silliest message from Dilling, so I came for a second."

"It may have ben silly, but I hope it was also quite clear," said my mother. "If there are going to be nude parties in this house, I prefer to throw them myself. Your main possessions are being packed and should be ready for you in the time it will take you to dress. You will then be driven into Ibiza where you may obtain a room in the hotel. Your flight back to New York will be arranged and paid for by me tomorrow, and the rest of your belongings sent after. As you would say perhaps, Coco," she ended with eloquence, "poetry is life, but life is not all poetry."

He was sitting down with his hands in his pockets, and he continued to sit while he called on every form of repulsive imagery in his repertoire to describe the appearance, habits, morals, and cultural pretensions of my mother. Clem started to get up at the beginning, but my mother shook her head and motioned him back. From time to time, Coco spat at him too. "Proud of knowing the daughter of the fifth Baron Forsey of bloody Pinner, aren't you? Now you know what sort of stock she was bred from. An alcoholic goat, alias a penniless sponger, and an old bag who likes sleeping with poets." He waved a hand. "Meet Geraldine Lady Forsey, Mr. Sainsbury."

Clem was quite scarlet, with his jaw set like the ellipse on a turnip. But at this point he got up, said, "I beg your pardon," to my mother, and took Coco Fairley by the neck and the seat of his bathrobe. I suppose he must have refereed worse matches. At any rate, he made light work of lifting Coco clean off his feet, which were kicking madly. Coco screeched, "You'll be sorry. You don't know what I saw the night the old man was killed!" and then his voice died away as Clem carried him out of the door and along to his room. Dilling went with them.

I didn't think it was going to be possible to look at Mummy, but that did it. "Killed!" I repeated, and met her large, open eyes.

After a bit: "Don't rely on it," she said. "He was trying to bargain. I doubt if he knows anything about Forsey's movements." She always called him that, never Eric.

I said, "If he does, won't he make trouble?"

"Not if he wants me to publish his poems," said Mummy. "And on reflection, he will."

"You'll have to find a publisher first," I said cattily. What I had seen of the stuff in the garden hadn't impressed me overmuch.

"No, honey. A cement mixer," said my mother. "That's easy. It's only the postage that's killing." She got up, and I could feel her looking me over. "You came out of that real well, She-she. You're tough. You're nearly as tough as I am. Maybe that's a good thing," said my mother. Then she took my arm. "Come along. Let's put on a towel and join the real sophisticated people downstairs."

I thought she was joking, but she wasn't. We walked downstairs to that playroom with barely a stitch on but a white Turkish towel wrapped Mother Hubbard-like under the arms. With her good legs and flat shoulders Mummy looked incredibly elegant, but my hair was still up in loops anl I felt like a sugar in search of its Daddy. Not, you understand, that I wasn't bursting to get down below.

Coco must have hired a small group from Palma, no doubt at Mummy's expense, and there was a general impression from the noise that a turntable must be going as well. Apart from the music, the shrieking was quite something: enough to tell you that Coco must have imported pretty well all the playmates who have their reasons for lounging around the Mediterranean in the springtime: society, café society, artists, athletes, flower-people, and shady expatriates, to choose a few types from Janey's circle at random. I must say I slowed down a bit as we got near to the playroom door, but Mummy just steamed on like a Monorail in a Harrington square, and I followed, right up to the playroom. Without hesitation, Mummy flung the doors open.

It was like a testing shed for jet engines. The sound came out of a reeling, light-spattered darkness made by dozens of revolving glass lights hung all over the ceiling, which threw heaving, sequin-shaped splashes over the dancers, who were going up and down like ships' pistons. There was a group at one end dressed in boots, white tights, and ponchos, and a lot of sharp shouts and castanet clacking and rolling of r's at the other end from a small party of three Spanish dancers and a guitarist who were deep in a performance. The Spanish women wore high combs and skin-tight décolleté dresses, with loads of frills bouncing along after. It reminded me of the caterpillar on the beach. I noticed that the male Spanish dancer, who also wore frills, was a Chinese.

Everyone else was headless in obscure hoods over which the lights slid in a Hammer-films way. Everyone else was also dressed, as we were, in a natty white towel, fastened under the armpits. No one had seen us come in.

Mother, smiling, was fitting another damned cheroot into her holder. I said, "How the hell did you pull that one off?"

"I didn't pull it off, honey; I put it on," Mummy said. Her saucer eyes stared at me in surprise. "I had Dilling tell them that Coco had infrared cameras hung all over the room *that could see through paper bags*." She paused. "The lucky thing is, there seem to have been enough towels. Now you go right on down there and enjoy yourself. I'll send Austin and Gilmore down to you."

"In towels?" I said. "You're not going to be very popular with the Trade Mission. You must have soaked them all to the skin."

"I think it'll have to be bathrobes," Mummy said. "Why not? They shouldn't have gotten high in a well-bred lady's drawing room, but if she's prepared to overlook it, I don't see why we shouldn't show them quite a good time."

There is a kind of dreadful fascination about Mummy. She has an attitude to life which would drive a phenobarbitone pill up the wall, never mind a civilized drifter like Daddy. But she has Personality too, with a capital P, which is what must have brought them originally together. Then she found that Daddy was nothing *but* personality, and I suppose that was it. Mummy disappeared, the music rose to a kind of frenzied crescendo, and I stepped down into the fray.

I think it was the most energetic dance I've ever been to. And that includes even Highland balls, where you have a houseparty and have to defend your virtue half the night after, as well as dance all the reels. I stepped down into that orgy, and someone got me by the hand and started jogging me up and down, and I got handed from bag to bag for ten, solid minutes until the group finally let up, and we collapsed on the floor. My current bag had a beard which brushed up and down inside the paper all the time he was smooching: with no lips to smooch with, they all made great play with their hands, and it was their hard luck I had all my underwear on. The tennis pro brought me an icy Tom Collins, and I was still breathing hard and parrying his right backhand drive when the lights went up from near-total to mid-total darkness, and a lot of balloons came drifting around.

It was that gruesome game where you have to roll the balloon up and over your neighbor by using your head: one of the Group MC'd it, and there was a fair amount of slipping towels and tearing of bags. They next wanted to do the one where you pass the string down inside the back of your clothing, but after a bit they reckoned the fictitious cameras ruled that out and went back to frugging or whatever.

I was getting so used to recognizing people by their birth marks that I hardly realized Austin had me in his grasp.

His hair was still brushed forward, but it was fluffy with drying, and he had on a rather nice bathrobe in pink. I guessed it was maybe one of Coco's. His eyes had matching pink rims, and he looked very bemused. He said, "I guess I ought to apologize. Over getting plastered back there, I mean. Those guys can sure put back the Smirnoff. Mrs. van Costa's been most considerate . . ." He stopped again and said simply, "I don't get it."

I explained. Coco's vengeful scheme struck him as a great, great pity. Of course, artists were highly strung. They often couldn't be judged by ordinary standards. But Coco's behavior, thought Austin, was unpardonable. But my stars, said Austin, wasn't Mrs. van Costa a sport?

That she was my mother, he had clearly no idea at all. I was agreeing she was dead groovy, considering, and inquiring about the health of Gilmore and the trade mission, when I suddenly saw, dancing together, two paper bags I knew. I stopped dead, treading heavily on Austin's bare feet, for which he apologized like a gentleman. The last time I had seen those two paper bags, one had held my tomatoes and the other my Fantas. One was Janey. And the other was my brother Derek.

I don't know what I was saying to Austin. Whatever it was, his grip kept getting tighter, until finally I had to give my mind to it and ask him questions about his boyhood in Connecticut, and things like that. He told me all about it, and we sat out and had a drink and he told me some more, and still Derek and Janey went on circling, very slowly, with their paper bags blowing in and out with their talking. I realized now where Janey must have gone in that quick drive before dinner. I further realized that whether she told Derek or not, she jolly well knew that it was a paper-bag party, or she wouldn't have brought these two with her. I further wondered if Dilling had brought the towels in before or after they had both arrived. I was never so shocked in my life.

Then I thought, oh my Gawd, Mummy's going to come in. And Derek's going to recognize her. I said, "Darling Austin, I've got to go out for a minute," and as he still clung, I said, "Darling Austin, I've got to go to the *loo,*" and pulled away and ran out.

It was then I realized the party had sort of seeped out of the playroom and was infiltrating elsewhere. All the corners seemed to be full of people celebrating the fact that there were no cameras, and I was scarlet and wishing I had a paper bag on myself when I ran into Clem Sainsbury, in a bathrobe. He put two, kind, brawny arms round me and said, "Hey. Don't look as worried as that. If I can help, tell me. Do you want to go home?"

I said, "Oh, Clem, dear," and kissed him. To be for a second with someone who wasn't on the make was so blissful. Not practical, but blissful all the same. I said, "I'm looking for Mrs. van Costa."

Clem grinned and kissed me back with some enthusiasm, for Clem. "I rather think she's been trapped by the Bolshoi," he said. "They seem to credit her with a passion for congas . . . Isn't Gilmore with you?"

"I've got Austin," I said. "Gilmore and I have sort of developed some cracks in our relationship."

"Why? Did he try something?" said Clem, with some interest.

I sighed. "Everybody *tries* something, idiot. Everyone but Clement Sainsbury, that is."

Clem grinned. "I'm learning," he said. And gave me a proper, long-distance kiss this time, with his hands squeezing my towel and my shoulder hard. I was still standing puffing and gasping and hanging on to my towel when the end of the conga suddenly appeared at the end of the corridor and began to snake toward us, giving tongue as it went.

The head of the Trade Mission led it. He was dressed in red-and-white floral underpants, which I'm damned sure never came out of G.U.M., and a towel draped like a toga over his shoulder and hips. He had an Easter lily over his ear and looked very, very happy. One of the Spanish dancers came next, also extremely high, with her chin tucked in, scowling, and one hand on Nureyev's shoulder while the other held up her frilly skirts and shook them at intervals—no one had tried to get her into a towel. There followed two more Russians in underpants, the Chinese Spanish-dancer, and Mummy. She had both arms round the waist of the Chinese under his bolero, and her hair was standing up in gray spikes, but she had lost none of her sangfroid: in fact her high kicks were better than any of them. There was a large rose pinning up one corner of her towel. "Hi, honey," she said as they passed. The conga whipped round a corner.

"Hey!" I pelted after and caught up on the straight, trotting beside her. "I've got something to tell you."

"Well, hitch on behind," Mummy shouted. "If I let this lot go, the Lord knows where they'll end."

I caught her round the waist and conga'd. The guitarist, who'd been in the Gents, fell in behind and added a little tone to the hullabaloo. Tarara-RAra-ra, Tarara-RAra-ra, Tarara-RAra-RAra-RAra-RAra-ra . . .

I shrieked: "Derek's here!"

"Who's Derek?" said Mummy, hurtling round the next corner so that my feet practically left the carpet. "I do apologize, angel. We suffer from a little clutch judder on takeoff."

"My brother," I wailed into her ear.

"Oh," said Mummy. Tarara-RAra-Ra . . . "O.K. Give me a paper bag, someone."

I feel I have underrated my mother.

Five minutes later, the conga got into the playroom and caught sight of the bar. Ten minutes after that, the Trade Mission was hunkered down on the floor, its hands on its hips, the soles of its feet shooting backward and forward like pistons while everyone roared and hung on to everyone else, counting. After the four separate members collapsed, which they did fairly soon, they instantly got up and launched into backflips and Cossack yells and a kind of chorus of knee slapping and stamping. At the same time, the two Spanish dancers, whose hair was beginning to come down, were stalking to and fro, frowning, with their elbows inside out. Then they flung their arms up and began to writhe a bit, their fingers snaking and snapping while the Chinese stood close by with the guitarist, hissing like rattlesnakes and doing a sort of rhythmic flat clap, hesitating when there was a slight Russo-Spanish collision, which there was from time to time. The girls began kicking up their red satin shoes and roving round, knees bent, in circles, their arms stretched in reverse. Everyone was shouting and jumping. I was dying to know what Janey was saying.

Then the Chinese suddenly hopped into action. He really was dolly, with a long yellow face, loads of black hair and sideburns, and his chins crammed right down into his white frilly shirt. He stood doing nothing, just scowling, and I could have screamed with suspense. Then he began very slowly to do a zapateado, kicking his boots, first on one side, then the other, his fingertips in his bosom and his mouth down round about the second last frill. In his underpants. He was fantastic. It was utterly fabulous. The

126

girls were whirling around with their chests out, their beads all lassoing their Maidenforms, and their surplus frills hooked up like curtains, and from time to time he would break off and stalk round beside one of them, his elbows bent inside out too. The Russians were still doing backflips and not looking very much where they were going, stopping occasionally to cock an elbow and charge up and down sideways, one brawny arm stabbing the ceiling. They gave tongue to intermittent, very loud shouts. Then they got tired of that and made back for the girls.

I never could find anyone who remembered very clearly what occurred after that. The gorgeous Chinese was on one knee by that time, handing a distraught girl in a circle around him, and the guitarist was singing flamenco, very mournfully, in long, minor rises and falls, and short, soulful runs. He had his eyes shut. Possibly the flamenco irritated the Cossacks, or maybe the vodka simply came to the boil. Anyway, one minute the red-and-white underpants were spinning like wheels round the room, arms flipping over and over, like four crazy propellors, and the next, the girls were both on the floor, in a wallow of frillies, and the Chinese, also in a wallow of frillies, was trying to throw the attaché over his shoulder. An earring flew past my ear, and I saw Mummy's mouth open. She ripped the rose off her towel and bowled it straight at the electric portable organ, and Basilio y su Conjunto, cottoning on, struck up the conga. God knows how they knew what to play, for it went out with crinolines; but there was a sort of struggling and heaving and suddenly everyone was attached to everyone else in one long, semi-nude snake and kicking all round the playroom. They went right through the house again too, in and out of the showers, and through the wreck of the drawing room, nicking all the rest of the Smirnoff. Finally, with paper bags and balloons bursting all over the place, they staggered out into the garden. I was stuck somewhere in the middle with Clem and Austin, and almost got the breath squeezed flat out of me. The torque was frantic. It was the hardest-pressed conga I've ever been part of, and if you saw the number of towels left behind on the floor of the playroom, you wouldn't take long to guess why.

Outside, the fountains were still playing and the aluminum flickered under the trees. Pebbles, let into the gravel at intervals, said, TO DREAM IS AN ORGASM. Most of the conga tripped on "orgasm," but none of them was in a state to dig it but Mummy, who turned round and said, "That was rather a nice one of Coco's. The theme is developed in those plastic bullrushes. DREAM NO MORE LIGHTLY."

The bullrushes were on the other side of the fancy lake, under the trees. Basilio y su Conjunto, just behind, changed the tune and the conga gave a convulsive shudder and began twining in and out of small arbors, leaping. Someone had put a towel round a very nude statue and was saying anxiously, "You must go in and get warm." "Coco always did take such trouble," Mummy said wistfully. "The words are all written up the stems. DREAM NO MORE LIGHTLY. EFF AND MAKE POETRY TONIGHT."

"What and make poetry?" I said. The band had

stopped. Clem, his arms crossed in front of me, was nibbling the back of my neck.

My mother turned. "F——" she said impatiently, into the sudden abatement. I said "Oh," and Clem lifted his head and said, "Something's happened."

All at once everyone was running toward the far side of the fountains. I ran, too, with Austin on one side and Clem on the other. I didn't see what happened to Mummy.

The paper bags were all round the bullrushes. Among them, floating like Moses but without benefit of basket, was the fully dressed figure of Coco, with three plastic bullrushes clutched in his dead hand. I had a good look at them. They read, NO . . . MORE . . . POETRY.

CHAPTER 7

AUSTIN AND GIL took me home. I wondered whether I ought to stay with Mummy, but when I looked for her, I found her in the study, telephoning the Consulado de EE UU with Clem standing by her, and Clem told me to push off. I didn't see Derek and Janey. But by then people had started to melt, walking fast round the side of the house with their clothes in bundles under their arms. We saw the gleam of cars, where we had missed them when we first arrived, discreetly tucked under the trees. The party must already have started when Gil, Austin, and I first arrived. Clever Coco. I wondered how many towels Mummy was going to lose, and then if she would lose something more than her towels. Coco had drowned while under the influence of a lethal dose of cocaine, according to a paper bag who claimed to be qualified. But if anyone in that household had good reason to have it in for Coco, it was certainly Mummy. I wondered if I were the only former pupil of St. T's to have cause to suspect my mother and my brother of murder, each within the same twenty-four hours, and lay back thinking while Austin fondled my polythene. Then I made up my mind, and collected his hand idly, and said, "I'm leaving on Monday."

Gil, who was driving, said nothing at all, the rat. Austin brought his damp, white, Virgul arm closer around me and said, "I guess you've had a real fright. Those boys and girls don't mean any harm, you know. Anyone dealing with the creative arts gets out of line a little bit, sometimes. It's the price they pay for their talent."

I shifted my head off his shoulder. I said, "Austin, honestly, it's no news to me. I'm just bored."

"Bored?" said Austin. He gave a perplexed sort of grin. "You sure must be expecting some excitement in London."

"It's the only place I've a return ticket for," I said. "Likewise, goodbye to the real Spanish dancing. I must say, I'm sad about that."

Austin said, "If you had an older relative with you, I'd sure ask her permission to take you with me to Seville."

My better nature staged a brief battle and won. "I don't need an older relative," I said. "People don't get chaperoned any more, you know, Austin. You just get up and go."

"Some people get up and go sooner than others," said Gil, still staring at the roadway in front of him. He drew in, and a Rolls-Royce bearing the

Soviet flag swept ahead. You couldn't see who was inside, or if they had any clothes on.

Austin said, "You mean you would come?"

I said, "I don't see why not. Tomorrow, or whenever you want it. If Mr. Lloyd doesn't mind," I added quickly. Gilmore said, sarcastically, "I'm sure he won't mind in a good charitable cause. Are you going to marry her, Mandleberg?"

I could have killed him. Austin gave an unnerved smile and said, "It's a little early for that?"

"Not for Sarah, it isn't," said Gilmore. "Better make up your mind now. Or you'll see a lot more of Seville than you ever expected to."

"I already," said Austin, "know Seville extremely well. I have a gallery there. And in Gibraltar. And my only purpose in taking Miss Cassells there is to show her a good time and enable her to see a little of that glorious city. I shall make it clear to Mr. Lloyd that my intentions are purely platonic."

I didn't hear what Gilmore said, but I know he jammed on the Cooper's brakes so that I fell off Austin's lap. An old Seat, which had been dogging us, hooting, passed us asthmatically, drew in, and groaned to a stop. The driver's door opened and Johnson got out and came over, followed by Derek and Janey. Derek was white with emotion.

"Hallo," said Johnson. "Their Maserati conked out. I hear it's been quite a party."

Gilmore said, "How did you hear?"

"Clem phoned the Club Nautico," Johnson. "I drove over as fast as I could, but everyone was dressed by the time I got there. All I could find out was that Coco Fairley seems to have drowned himself at a party for eight or ten people, who went through three-hundred quids' worth of booze and used fifty-three dirty bath towels. What happened? Did the Trade Mission liquidate him for the ideological corruption of Portland cement?"

"Don't be an ass," said Janey soothingly, and she wasn't being soothing to Johnson. She sat on the Cooper's window, steadying herself with a hand on Derek's shirt.

"He'd had a row," I said, "with Mrs. van Costa. She told him to get out just before. Why ask? Clem must have told you."

"Clem," said Johnson, "was on the long-distance telephone to New York, London, and Paris, and also, if it matters, to Birmingham, to get a new screw for the heads. Mrs. van Costa was otherwise engaged. Derek says she's your mother."

I'd guessed by now that he knew. She couldn't very well telephone with a paper bag on, and if Derek passed by, he would spot her. I wondered why he couldn't have kept his fat mouth shut and recalled that there was no reason from his point of view why he should. If he despised Daddy, he loathed Mummy as well. Maybe he thought she killed Daddy: although I couldn't see how a woman could have heaved a well-built man like my father up onto a tall horse. He had believed Daddy to be a spy. Maybe he thought Mummy was in the thing with him. Anyway, the shock, on top of whatever Janey had done to him, had done Derek no good. He said to me suddenly, ignoring Janey's fingers pressing his arm, "You didn't think of telling me that. You could accuse me of killing Father with that woman sitting not ten miles away . . ."

Janey said, "Sarah's father committed suicide,

133

and if she accused you of killing anyone, she was getting as bored with you as I am. Also, she had no idea Mrs. van Costa was your mother. Neither had I. My God, would I have taken you there tonight if I had?"

They stared at one another. She had diverted him all right. I shut the book on whether they'd got there ahead of Dilling's towels or not. Johnson said, "Mrs. van Costa sent him packing? Tonight?"

I said, "Dilling and Clem took him off to dress and shove stuff in a suitcase. Someone was going to drive him to a hotel in Ibiza tonight."

"Dilling," said Johnson. "He left him to get the car keys, and when he came back, Coco had gone. Clem had already gone back to the party."

"Yes. I was with him," I said. "So, Coco gives himself a good fix, overdoes it, and wanders into the pond?" I had meant to sound scathing, like Janey, but my voice sort of tailed away. The letter. The fake letter, I thought. Coco might have known I was sometimes called She-she. Coco might have suspected already that Mummy was going to give him the push. Coco might have had the whole nasty idea already written out in concrete poetry in his nasty little overcreamed head . . .

"Picking three bullrushes first?" said Janey.

"If he were drowning," said Gilmore, "he might have come half awake and grabbed whatever he could."

I felt suddenly very depressed. "I believe in Fate," I said. "I bet he was Capricorn."

"Are you Capricorn?" asked Johnson. He was wearing a nameless, open-necked shirt and a botany jersey. He said, "I saw the papers today. It said your day would end drinking a modest white wine in the company of a dark man in glasses. Sarah, I know a place in the Alt Vila where they continue to serve inebriating liquor until three in the morning. Will you join me? And of course, if anyone else . . . ?"

Derek nearly said yes, he was spoiling so much for a showdown. But in the long run, intimidated by the flashing smile, they all turned it down, mumbling. Janey, turning the full lime on Austin, persuaded him to go back to the Lloyds' house for the night, where he could dry out and recover, and then climbing into the Cooper, sat where I had sat on his lap. Derek, hamstrung by Johnson's presence, sat in the back of the old Seat and glared, without a backward glance at the Cooper, while we rattled on into Ibiza and dropped him at his hotel. There had been a notice today in the market: no outside traffic in the town till 7 A.M., Saturday; no public music till Sunday. Johnson ran the car down to the quayside and parked it, and taking me by the hand, walked me up through the Perta de las Tablas into the Dalt Vila.

After the heat and the noise and the beastliness, the old city was quiet and cool. Lamps lit Juno and her headless Roman Senator guarding the walls under which they'd been found, and there were lamps in the roofless courtyard inside and on the houses, blue and yellow, in the square to which it led. We stood there for a moment. Two dark-bereted workmen sat outside the bar, where in the daytime you could see Janey's friends, with their long brown legs, their Labradors, and their casual boyfriends, reading the *Daily Express*. Or alone, in skinny sweaters and bell-bottomed corduroy trousers, sitting with a pack of cigarettes and an English paperback and some yogurt. In the old town were lonely people and dedicated people and people having fun working hard. The hippies were in the other town, outside the portals. Among the people whose island it was, life seemed to go on regardless. They had been there since Carthaginian times. Hairy coats and bare feet and Zapata mustaches weren't likely to have much effect, I supposed, now.

Johnson said, "Death is a sobering institution, isn't it? Even Coco's." He put his hand lightly on mine and said, "Look up, Sarah." I looked up.

High in the sky, caught between the palms and the thick-ridged tiles of the roofs, stood a round, yellow moon, of the kind you always think you're going to stand under one day, with a man. Somewhere, Coco was lying under it too. I wondered if there had been a moon when Daddy died.

"A much-debased image," said Johnson's voice, coolly. "But then, you can't live on nothing but sugar. You can't paint in nothing but pinks. You can't pass your existence indulging in sex. Moons for romance are cheap moons."

He must have known what I was thinking. I said, "It's an expensive moon now. And two weeks ago."

"Yes," said Johnson. He turned the hairpin bend round from the courtyard and began to climb slowly up the hill, taking me with him. He said, "Sarah. Why do you cook for the Lloyds? Did they ask you?"

I didn't look at him, but I remember I stuck my

chin out. "No," I said. "They didn't. They asked me to come for a holiday. I cook because I want to, that's all."

I could feel him looking at me; and I knew he was smiling. I wouldn't look round. His nice voice said, "You may have the moon, Sarah. Your only real handicap is youth."

He didn't speak again and neither did I.

Johnson knew the *Dalt Vila*. We didn't stay on the main road but went climbing through the steep, broken lanes, flattening once as a Simca loomed from the darkness reversing toward us, its engine cut off. There was, somewhere, a smell of incense among the other small, teasing smells in the air. I followed Johnson, without speaking, until he stopped and opened a door in a wall, and I walked through and found myself in a garden, small, dim, and latticed with vines, in which tables had been set under the palms, with low candles flaring.

"Come in," said Johnson. "There's no music tonight, but they'll serve us some food and some wine. You don't need to talk."

A young man came for the order, quietly, and then went away, leaving us nearly alone. One other table was occupied, by an old man half sleeping over his copita. Behind us, someone touched a guitar softly now and then, and sang under his breath absently, forgetting the embargo: only moved by the still night and the flowers and the dimness. Far off, you could see the steady lights lining the Santa Eulalia road and the bright lights at the end of the yacht club. The apéritifs came.

"There's *Dolly*," said Johnson. He was a restful man, in some ways. Or maybe all men were restful,

137

and I'd never allowed myself time to observe it. I felt the way I did the last night at school, when I had to leave, and I didn't know what to do. That was when Flo's mother turned up and took me home for the weekend.

I found I needed to blow my nose.

Johnson said, "Clem should be back on board later on; Spry will wait up for him. I'm afraid it will be pretty rough going for your mother, now it's known she was in Ibiza while your father was here."

"Does it have to be known?" I said. I shoved my hankie away. "Janey and Gilmore won't tell, and I don't suppose Austin will if we ask him. Derek . . ." I faded it out. I wanted, like an ache, to tell Johnson everything. And I couldn't. Bloody, bloody Derek. I couldn't.

"Derek hasn't told anyone so far," said Johnson. "According to Clem, who will keep his mouth shut also. Do you still think Derek murdered his father?"

My tummy turned over. "I don't know," I said. "But if he did, he probably murdered Coco Fairley as well. Coco was busy shrieking that he had seen something the night Daddy died, when Mummy had him turned out."

"You couldn't guess what he'd seen?"

"No. But from what he hinted earlier, he knew that Daddy had visited Mummy that Saturday night. He might have seen him leave or even followed him to watch where he went."

"Who heard Coco say that, Sarah?" said Johnson.

I thought. "Clem and Mummy. Dilling, perhaps:

he wasn't far away. Not Austin and Gilmore: they were in the shower with the Russians."

"And Janey and Derek?" said Johnson.

"I don't know. I saw them on the dance floor later, but I don't know when they got there. If you want to imagine Derek listening outside the door, I suppose he could have been, at that. No one could identify anyone else. They were all wearing those bags."

There was a little pause, while we pushed down our drinks. Johnson had got me Anis del Mono. I liked it. Then Johnson said thoughtfully, "You realize. If your father was murdered, then Coco was certainly murdered, although I doubt if anyone will ever prove that he didn't take that shot and fall into the pond by himself. And with the exception of Gilmore, who you say was certainly under the shower, every single suspect from the death of your father was equally a possible suspect tonight."

"Except for Mr. Lloyd," I said. "This time at least he was at home."

"How do you know?" said Johnson gently. And of course, I didn't. For with Janey and Gilmore away, there was no reason at all why their father should not have left the house and successfully gate-crashed that party. Why not, in a paper bag?

I finished my aniseed stuff in one positive gulp. "I give up," I said. "I'm going to Seville with Austin."

For a moment, Johnson's glasses were still. "Alone?" he said.

"Of course, alone. For goodness' sake," I said, my voice rising in spite of myself. "Austin and

Gilmore and Clem are the only three boys I know who couldn't have murdered my father."

"It's a sweeping claim," Johnson said, "but I know what you mean. Unless they're hunting in couples."

"Oh, my Gawd," I said wearily, and he laughed and poured me more wine and began to talk about other things.

Later, when we'd had ice-cold gazpacho, and paella with all the right things in it—squid and octopuses and chicken and lobster tails and paprika and sherry and peas and onion and pimento and pork, all done with saffron rice and shimmering in the quiet air—he took me out of the garden, between walls and through archways, up steps and along passages, climbing further and further until we came out at the highest point in the town, the little piazza of the Cathedral.

In spite of the time, the doors of the Cathedral were open. It was very small, with its high, square clock tower looking out over the flat sea and land far below, and the light from inside fell across the beaten pebbles and dirt of the little square, and the short old walls of the *curia* and the museum adjoining. A black lane led, Johnson said, to the castle now used as a barracks, and a big double green door to the episcopal palace. The wall was peeling, but the palm branches laced in the wrought-iron balconies were still fresh from Sunday.

The smell of Easter lilies and carnations came through the church door. "I can't go in," I said. "Can I?"

"I don't see why not," Johnson said gravely.

There was a scarf tucked in the neck of his tatty jersey: he hooked it undone and held it out.

It was silk, and Hermès, at nine guineas a whack. He was so ordinary, one forgot. I folded it over my hair and my shoulders and slipped in, keeping well to the wall. I didn't expect Ibiza to see eye to eye with polythene.

It was only a little church, dim and Gothic, and filled with the smell of incense, wax, and massed Easter flowers. The altars were all draped in purple and the holy figures concealed. People were kneeling instead before a shrine decked like a bridal with carnations and lilies and roses, with candles and silk. No one looked up. We stood for a moment, looking at the dazzle of light, and then my eye caught something else in an alcove. "Look," I said.

It was a hand litter, propped on two benches, bearing the Virgin, weeping, candelabra unlit at her feet. Her robes, of heavy velvet worked in gold thread were quite real, and the handkerchief she held in her hand was banded with gorgeous lace. There was a jeweled dagger stuck in her robe. "Are they going to carry that in the procession tomorrow?" I said.

"That and three or four others. Plus a cartload of flowers, a number of great whacking batteries and sundry cloaks, veils and robes with solid gold adjuncts. Or silver at least. Quite a load to carry down all these perpendicular lanes."

"I didn't know they wore clothes," I said. "I mean, real ones. The stones in the dagger aren't real, too, are they? What if somebody nicked them?"

"Up there, in full view of the worshipping throng?" Johnson said. "It's not very likely. In any case, there'll be someone here all through the night. The very best jewels will come out tomorrow, when the figures are finally dressed. People donate the stuff. Conscience money, maybe you'd say. In Seville, women lend jewelry, too. Sometimes the Madonnas wear hundreds of thousands of pounds' worth of diamonds. But that's Seville, not Ibiza. Ibiza's only got the Saint Hubert."

"Wait a minute," I said. "The Saint Hubert collar?"

"It's on all the postcards," Johnson said. "In fact, I thought we might see it here. It was left to the Church by a banker called Hubert, on condition it was worn by an effigy of his name saint alone. Wait a minute. Let's try in there."

"There" was through a couple of doorways and into a long, marble-flagged room at the back, with tattered notices directing traffic to the Cathedral museum. It was a robing room, clearly, with stacks of ancient old cupboards and a chest of drawers in black oak, labeled like an apothecary's with the names of the owners: Canon Gimenez, Canon Tamas, Canon Anton. Heavy, gold-embroidered vestments belonging to the top dog, I supposed, lay out on a table, beside a broken electric candle and a saucer containing a slice of dry bread and a lemon. Johnson went across to look at a dim painting done on cracked wood, which hung on the plain, whitewashed wall. I began to look at some postcards.

They were presumably for sale on less-exalted occasions. One was of the float with the Madonna we'd just seen inside. The other was of the Saint Hubert. "Strewth," I said. "Madame Tussaud's."

In fact, Hubert, robed and bearded and mitred, looked rather a patsy, with one hand uplifted in classical blessing and the other parked on the head of a stag. The litter was huge, with lots of ormolu, candles, and frills and a sort of tree at each corner.

"Saint Hubert," said Johnson. "You'll see him tomorrow. Or are you going to Seville with Austin?"

"We haven't settled it yet," I said. I was thinking of something else. I said, "I've seen that collar somewhere before, do you know that?"

"No, I don't," said Johnson obligingly. "Where?"

The incense was making my head ache. I stood still and tried to think back. Then I remembered. "In the exhibition," I said. "In Austin Mandleberg's exhibition. Or no, it wasn't. It was in the basement downstairs. I sneaked off to look at the workshop, and I didn't take more than a glance, because someone turned up. Jorge, the old boy who works there. But I'm sure the necklace lying on one of the benches was exactly the same shape as that. Rubies?"

"Rubies," said Johnson with interest.

"That's it. They were red. I thought they were there for mending or cleaning."

"No. The Saint Hubert rubies," said Johnson thoughtfully, "are cleaned, they say, in Barcelona."

"Oh. Then I must have been wrong," I said.

"Not necessarily," said Johnson. "Describe the room and the old man you saw in it."

I did, and also Gregorio, the director. "He lives in the basement, I think. The rest of the staff seem to come in daily. Why do you want to know all this?" I asked. It was rather exciting. "D'you think someone's pinched them?"

"Maybe. Or maybe even just made a copy. But it would be nice to know which. Do you think Mandleberg knows?"

"I'm sure he doesn't," I said. "Anyway, he's been away for months and months: Janey checked when we were sleuthing. He really was in Paris when he said he was."

"Then the staff of the Mandleberg gallery may be indulging in a fiddle without him," said Johnson. "I wonder if Señor Gregorio believes in the power of prayer?"

"Why?" I said.

"Because I'd like to pay him a visit, and I'd like it even more if he were safely in church," Johnson said. "But I'll take you home first."

I had nothing to lose, except a trip to Seville and Gibraltar. "I'll come with you, if you'll paint my picture on *Dolly*," I said.

The black brows shot up. "Are you sure? I'm not wholesome at all."

"I don't want to *eat* you," I said. "Just to get painted."

He took my arm. "We may end up like your mother, phoning the Consul de S. M. Britanica, from jail."

"She phoned the Consulado del Estados Unidos," I said. "I'll come. Will you paint me?"

We walked back through the church and out into the square. The moon was still there, and the leaves of the three little trees stirred in front of the lanterns, throwing flickering shade over the old, gray carved stone and worn steps and the tops of the trees in the small, dusty garden underneath. From the barracks unseen behind us, a faint beat of undistinguished pop music made itself heard, from some invisible transistor.

The view was fantastic. At our feet, the blocks of white houses stepped down into darkness. You could see the dim lights of the market and the few neon signs in the low town: a bank, a cinema, the red Philips shields. There was floodlighting near the harbor, and far out, the big aviation petrol installation blazed with blue flares. But elsewhere there was little. The new road to Talamanca, bridging the harbor, with its lights pooling the dust and the water. On the right, the dark spit of land dividing the bays, and the flashing beam of the lighthouse. On the left, the line of lights round the marina, ending in emerald green.

The country beyond was all dark with, here and there, the finest sprinkle of lights. Johnson said, "I drive a harder bargain than you do. I'll paint you if you promise not to go to Seville or Gibraltar. Or anywhere else where Clem can't keep an eye on you."

"But Austin—"

The bifocals flashed in the lamplight. "Austin Mandleberg," said Johnson pointedly, "I make no doubt belongs to Rotary, is head of the Lodge and chairman of the local hospital fund, loves his old mother, and is kind to little children and animals. Other people are not quite so pure-minded. I still want you under surveillance."

I was struck. "Was that why you drove all the way from *Dolly* to Casa Mimosa when Clem phoned you?"

"Yes, it was," said Johnson. He was smiling, but his voice was perfectly level. "I wanted Clem with your mother. For if Coco was murdered, it was because of something he knew, which he might have passed on to your mother."

"But he didn't," I said. "He was threatening us about it when Dilling took him away."

"So I am told," Johnson said. "I'm also told that several people now know that Mrs. van Costa is Lady Forsey, your mother. Suppose then that your father was murdered also because of something inconvenient that he knew. Who is to know whether," said Johnson, "your father told Lady Forsey the night that he died? And whether she in turn has told you?"

"She hasn't," I said.

"We're talking about appearances, not what actually happened. Why did Derek come back?" said Johnson suddenly.

I smiled. "To see Janey," I said.

Johnson took my arm again and walked me slowly down the steep slope. "You're a rotten-bad liar. I happened to be in the Télégrafos y Correos office the day you sent off your cable. What made you think Derek might have killed off his father? Surely he had made a life of his own by now in Holland? It isn't likely, you know."

"You know," I said, "too bloody much."

He stopped. "Sarah. I don't want another murder. Yours or anyone else's. You don't want scandal. I don't want to be mixed up in an international incident. If it can solved quietly, let's do it. But I can't work in the dark."

The lane was pebbly and steep, and you could almost touch the high, continuous buildings on each side with your two outspread hands. Even in the

146

dark you could see they were fine houses, with crested stonework and heavy bossed doors and, lower, with deep sills filled with cactus and cages and flowers, and sometimes a high, rattan-roofed sunroom, with roses and creepers in round Moorish pots, spilling over in the glow from a lantern. Wire skeined the canyon below us, black against the near blue-black sky. The sound of a drumbeat, suddenly, just out of sight—Tuck. Tr-r-uck. Tr-ruck, tuck tuck, and Johnson abruptly broke off.

We had turned off the main passage by then and were plunging down something much more dicey: a broken lane bordered with dank, peeling houses, where the light hardly reached, except to pick out a sunken, barred window, a swaying curtain of reeds, a double door rotting in all its planks. Above us, the houses on each side suddenly joined forces, two stories high, and we entered a tunnel, utterly lightless—Johnson's dry, warm hand gripping mine hard. Then the blackness became dimness, and we turned right and passed down between steps and walls and big buildings, the cobbles firmer and broad to the foot until we reached a wide flight of steps to the left, tumbling down against a high wall to what seemed a small square. Johnson took one step down, and I said "Look."

They were passing through the small square far below: so silently that but for the drum I shouldn't have seen them. They were roped together, in two long, thin lines: tall faceless men in long-sleeved black gowns sashed in purple, a crucifix glinting on each. Over each head was a long, slender cone sheathed in light purple which fell to the shoulders. Each nose was merely a cut triangle of cloth; each eyehole a circle of flesh. Drums glinted, with gold fringe and purple, and short bugles shone in the hand. But while we watched them, they were silent, picking their way up the difficult path, the tall spires swaying against the shadowed white walls, the shod feet and bare alike making no sound.

They passed. "The penitents," Johnson said. "They will have carried their image round the low town and are now delivering it back. Does penitence frighten you? No, I'm sure. As I've said before, you're too young." He was leading me down the wide steps.

"I'm frightened," I said. I hoped he'd forgotten.

He hadn't. He stopped and said quietly, "So. Did Derek come to Ibiza before? Before your father died?"

I gave up. I needed help, and he was helping, more than anyone. I said, "Yes. Janey saw him. He came to see Daddy, and he had a quarrel with him on the Friday. That's all he told me."

"He didn't tell you what the quarrel was about? Not your mother: he didn't know evidently that she was here."

"No."

"What then? Not you: you go your own sweet way, or so the evidence tells me. Not money: he's one of the technical salariat and doing very well, thank you. Some other aspect of his job? Was your father queering his pitch? Making a display of himself with people Derek thought mattered?"

He was quick. "It was because of his job," I said, my eyes on the square. "He had found out his employers regarded Daddy as a bad security risk. They thought he was an enemy agent."

"What?" said Johnson. "Oh Christ, my dear girl," and he started laughing under his breath, so hard he had to take his bifocals off, and I looked at his eyes. I don't know what color they were because the surprise was somehow so great. His eyes were tired. He said, "And what did your father say?" He had put the glasses back on.

"Derek didn't tell me," I said. "We sort of quarreled ourselves, and I walked out. I haven't seen him since till tonight."

"But Janey has," Johnson said. "Maybe Janey has had better luck. I should ask her, if I were you. If we're not both in prison."

Austin Mandleberg's workshop was not all that hard to break into. It couldn't have been: Johnson did it so easily. We didn't go into the garden. We walked along the dirt lane running behind Gallery 7 and found a row of windows, covered with fine, blue-painted netting, which must belong to Austin's own rooms. Below them was another window, with no nets but a balcony, not too far up from the ground. Johnson's theory was that this would lead us to a room off the inside first landing. When I remembered the slope of the ground, I realized he was probably right.

I got up without any help on the balcony and crouched there, behind the pots of red-flowering cactus, while Johnson messed about with, he said, a hairpin. There was a click, and then he messed about a bit more with a knife. No one came along the lane but a dog. It looked up at us and then trotted on. Then Johnson said, "How nice," with a rather satisfied sound in his voice.

"What?" I said.

"The burglar alarm," Johnson said. "A good make. But not very well fitted. One of the hazards of living abroad. Are we clear?"

"No one's coming," I said. I was still frightened: the smallest bit frightened. Of Johnson. Then he opened the window, and in a moment, we were both inside Austin's house.

It was dark and stuffy, once the window was shut, and smelt of glue and fresh paint and carbonized metal and food. The room we were in appeared to be some kind of office. Producing a little torch from his pocket, Johnson swept it over the few elegant furnishings: a filing cabinet; a typist's table and chair; a larger desk with a tape recorder and a telephone on its green leather surface.

The door was open, leading onto a lightless landing, devoid of all sound. Johnson closed it and, drawing both blinds on the windows, proceeded to kneel at the desk. I said, "Hey!"

The first drawer was open, and Johnson, very quietly, was ruffling at speed through the papers. I said, "Hey!" again. He shut the drawer and opened another. "Don't worry," he said. His voice was so low I could barely make the words out. He sounded mildly amused. "If I come across any love letters, I'll tell you. I want to see the receipts for the production and sale of his jewelry. This is Gregorio's desk."

"Oh," I said. He went through all the drawers in turn, looking at everything but taking nothing out. He didn't speak again, and neither did I, until he had finished and relocked the lot. I said, "That wasn't Gregorio's desk."

He grinned: a flash in the dark. "I know, dearie," he said. "But if he likes you enough to ask you to go to Seville, I feel we ought to view his credentials."

"And?" I said crossly.

"Clean as a whistle," said Johnson. "Now take me to this lair in the basement." And opening the door, we pussyfooted out onto the landing and then down the white marble stairs to the hall. Then we turned left, away from Austin Mandleberg's ground-floor antique room, and opened the little green door.

I found the creaking stairs and went down making very little noise, and I noticed Johnson did the same. At the bottom, all the lights were switched off except one: at the end where Gregorio had his apartment. It was a very dim bulb, encased in a lantern framework hanging with dirt: American efficiency obviously hadn't penetrated belowstairs to the native quarters. To my horror, signing me to stay out of sight, Johnson felt his way first away from the workshop and toward where the dim light was hanging, listening at doors as he went.

He saw the cat the moment I did, lying in the shadows by the far wall, curled inside its tail, fast asleep. He stopped, but the beast had sensed him: it raised its head, the end of its tail twitching, and then got up and let loose a meow like a train whistle. Then it stared at Johnson, stared at the last door of the corridor—the door farthest away from the stairs—and stalking toward it, meowed over again.

There was a line of light under that door. I saw Johnson wait for a moment. Then, very softly, he leaned forward, and with one gloved hand, he turned the knob of the door. He did it slowly, and in absolute silence, while the cat watched him, its ears pricked, its tail switching. Then, when the latch was just disengaged, he pushed the door gently open.

The cat stalked in, giving a view of a small, heavily furnished room with a fire smoldering behind a wrought-iron guard. It was quite empty.

Johnson smiled, and heaving the door slightly ajar, came back to me. "Come on," he said, and made for the other door, the workroom door right beside us.

Seen in the light of the torch, the workshop looked like any room used by craftsmen. The broken floor tiles were littered with curls of metal and shavings, and the heavy benches were piled with raw materials and work in various stages of process, together with all the appliances—the vises, the lathes, the soldering and welding equipment—needed for the trade of repair and reproduction of jewelry.

"Three men, perhaps," said Johnson. "Under Jorge, the old fellow you saw." If you looked closely, you could see the empty packets of cigarettes, the greasy sandwich paper which hadn't fallen into the square box of rubbish; the stained jackets hanging on rough hooks by the wall. On the opposite wall was a safe.

It was the only receptacle with a lock in the room. I remember Johnson stood before it for a long time, just looking, until I got impatient and said, "Gregorio will be coming back. What is it?"

"It hasn't got an alarm," Johnson said.

"Poor thing," I said. "What does it matter? We couldn't open it."

Johnson walked forward briskly. "With the aid," he said, "of a stick of well-cooked spaghetti, any child over the age of six months could open that safe. Observe." And indeed, he had hardly touched it when it did actually swing open. Inside was a packet of gold leaf and some worn bank notes, packed beside a tray of rather dishy, reproduction antique rings. The total value of the whole thing was probably about twenty quid.

"So?" I said.

"So there's a safe somewhere else," Johnson said. "Not upstairs. If they're doing anything shady, they don't want to be carrying stuff about through the hall. I know."

I followed him along that hellish corridor again, bleating. He paid no attention but, reaching the door at the end, listened for a moment again, then gave it a push and went in.

The cat, which had settled comfortably this time in front of the fire, looked up, recognized him, and bristled with superior hate. Johnson went on in, and I followed.

It was a room devoted to the total dominion of cloth. You could tell a Spaniard, or so Daddy said, because he liked his cutlet frills done up with tassels. All the furniture was square, heavy and dark; the religious paintings were hellish; and the lampshade had bobbles and went up and down. "It would fetch a fortune in Lord and Taylor's," said

Johnson. "Where do you suppose he keeps his money?"

"There," I said, lifting the Prodigal Son.

"It seems a bit obvious," said Johnson.

"It's a safe," I said. "In the wall. Under the picture. Not everyone has seen as many old movies on telly as you have."

He said, with slightly more interest, "This one has an alarm," and started in to disconnect it. I made no comment. The time one might expect Señor Gregorio to remain at his devotions was running out fast. I wanted out.

The safe door creaked open, and Johnson's black head disappeared inside. After a moment, he withdrew it. "About two hundred pounds in pesetas and nine thousand used dollar bills, a bundle of personal papers, some rather good silver plate, some old-fashioned family jewelry, and two tins of cat food," Johnson said.

"Let's put the cat in beside it," I said. I hated that cat. "No rubies?"

"No," said Johnson absently. He was still staring at the safe.

"Come on, then," I said. The cat moved, stretched, and arching its back, leaped from the hearth rug to a dusty, plush armchair and lay down again, watching us. Coinciding with the soft pad of its landing, I thought I could hear, somewhere in the house, a double click which could have been a key in a lock. I pulled Johnson's arm.

He shut the safe door with a blessed alacrity. "Back to the workroom," he said. The cat bristled.

I said, "Someone's coming!"

"Well, if it's Gregorio, he'll come in here, won't

154

he?" said Johnson reasonably. "Back to the workshop. I've got an idea."

I could feel all the little octopuses lying dead at the bottom of my paella. I said, "Why can't we get out?"

"Because there are two people on the floor above," said Johnson. He had, I admit, a logical brain. He also had nothing wrong with his hearing. As we hared along the dark corridor in the direction of the other room at the end, I could make out the quiet footsteps too, coming along the hall above from the direction of the front door. They walked up to the head of the stairs and went, so far as I could judge, to the study. "Hell," said Johnson, placidly.

"Why?" We were in the workroom again, with the door shut.

"They'll feel the draught from the window." He was moving, very fast, back to the safe, and in two seconds, he had it open again. He said, "Stand behind the door, Sarah, will you? If they come in, try and slip upstairs and out through the front door." All the time he was speaking, the beam of his little torch was probing inside the safe. I saw the small circle of light dim as he put his hand in and heard him say something, quietly under his breath as I felt my way, in the dark, to the door.

I had hardly got there when it opened, slamming into my arm. Light from the main switch sprang, dazzling, into the room. I had a picture of Johnson turning, his arm dropping from the still-open safe, the other hand in his pocket. There was a terrific report, like a lorry backfiring, and a sort of popping sound immediately after. Johnson crashed to the ground, and behind my door, someone yelped sharply. There strode into the room a tall, heavily built man followed by another clutching his rib cage and groaning. The wounded man was Austin Mandleberg. The other was Anthony Lloyd, Janey's father, and he had a smoking gun in his hand.

CHAPTER 8

LETTING GO THE DOOR, I ran round it to Austin, and held him up. He looked fearfully surprised, in a dazed kind of way, and then let me ease him down onto a stool. I can't bear to see people hurt. It's the retriever instinct, Daddy used to say. Then I remembered I wasn't supposed to, and looked round at Mr. Lloyd and at Johnson.

Johnson wasn't hurt: he had just taken cover in time. There was a hole in his jacket pocket, and a gun with a long thing on its muzzle was still in his hand. Mr. Lloyd said, "Good God." Then he said, "Put your gun down."

"Oh, dear," said Johnson. He put down his gun. "Have I hurt you, Mr. Mandleberg? But really, you shouldn't let your friends fire on people unseen. Mr. Lloyd might have killed me."

Austin Mandleberg's voice had got very high.

"He was doing me a favor," he said. "Anyone is perfectly justified in defending his home against thieves."

"I've lost my pipe," said Johnson, hunting. "Oh, there it is." He picked it up and, fishing out tobacco, started to load it.

Moving very quietly for a man of such bulk, Mr. Lloyd walked forward and confronted Johnson. His revolver made a small movement. "We'll have your attention, please," said Janey's father. "What are you doing here? And Sarah?"

Johnson sighed. "Playing at detectives," he said. "An obvious error. But we were not, I promise you, attempting to steal anything. Rather, to save Mr. Mandleberg some trouble."

"Detectives?" said Austin. He sat up, jerking the rolled-up handkerchief out of my hand. Blood was spreading over the side of his cream jersey suit. It would never dry-clean. "There was gold leaf and money in that safe. How did you get it open? I don't know what pretext you've thought up to take Sarah with you, but you are a thief, sir. The fact that you carry a gun is quite proof enough."

The bifocals looked surprised. "Mr. Lloyd carries a gun."

Anthony Lloyd said, "I'm a businessman living in a foreign country. I don't pretend to be a painter on holiday. Are you a painter? Or is your name perhaps not Johnson at all?"

Johnson looked down at his pipe. A torn sheet of tracing paper lay on the workbench beside him. Leaning over, he knocked the pipe bowl into it, hard, and then laying it aside, ground his thumb into the brown charcoal mess and straightening, considered Mr. Lloyd for a moment, his head on one side, his glasses repeating: two large men; two steady revolvers. Then he ran his thumb softly over the tracing paper in a half circle, another; a line, a line, a dot, a squiggle; a mass of soft ruffled shadow.

Anthony Lloyd's shadowy face lay on the workbench before us. "They call me Rembrandt Bloggs in the underworld," Johnson said.

"Why, then?" said Austin. His ribs had started bleeding again.

Johnson told them. Not the detail, but the substance: how I had caught sight of some jewelry I had later realized was identical with the Saint Hubert rubies; how it occurred to us something odd was going on in Mr. Mandleberg's absence; how, after a visit to the wine garden (Johnson's voice was apologetic), we thought we would see if we were mistaken or not.

"You didn't think to get in touch with Mr. Mandleberg, who could have investigated the thing properly? It was, after all, his business, not yours?" Mr. Lloyd said. "Or was this a drunken fantasy, with no substance at all? I am quite prepared to believe that Sarah saw something, but that she could have seen that particular collar is highly unlikely. I don't suppose the thought would even have occurred to her if you hadn't put it into her head."

I opened my mouth, and the glasses flashed in my direction. "I fear I did lead She-she astray," said Johnson contritely. "But we were passing the house, and I wanted to show off my safe-cracking technique. It's very handy, you know. I once painted a stockbroker who'd come up via Wormwood Scrubs, and he paid me in kind. You do it." And Johnson swung the door shut and took out his hairpin. After a moment's hesitation, Mr. Lloyd laid down his gun and craned forward.

They opened and shut the door twice, Johnson's voice instructing Mr. Lloyd, while I got Austin a glass of water and found the first-aid box for him. It was full of Beecham's pills. The bullet had gone, he said, right through his side; and he was looking quite frightful. He wouldn't let me send for a doctor.

It was all very well, not wanting trouble; but I felt that Johnson had rather asked for any trouble he'd got. Austin didn't even listen to what I was saying. When there was a break in the burglary class, he called, "Mr. Lloyd!"

Johnson came over, even quicker than Janey's father. "Our wounded! I do apologize. There you sit suffering, while we amuse ourselves with safeblowing. I'm afraid I returned Mr. Lloyd's shot quite instinctively. I had no intention in the world of inconveniencing you."

I was furious. I said, "He's got a hole right through his ribs, and he's bleeding."

"A doctor," said Johnson. "Mr. Lloyd, where can we get a doctor?"

"I'll ring one," said Lloyd. He looked at Johnson. "If I do, you know it'll mean trouble."

Austin said weakly, "I want Mr. Lloyd to do something first." I never knew anyone so hopeless as men for sheer waffling. I let him go, wet pad and all, and went off to find a telephone. I don't know how Johnson got to the door ahead of me but he did, and tucked my hand in a friendly way under his arm. I tugged.

Austin went on speaking. "If what Sarah here says is correct, then there's something far wrong. I'd like to know first what it is. Mr. Lloyd, would you look in that safe?"

"There's nothing there," said Johnson helpfully. My muscles cracked, under his arm.

"There's nothing there," said Mr. Lloyd, a moment later. "No rubies, that is."

"Right," said Austin. "Then if I may trouble you, sir, there is another safe in Señor Gregorio's room." He described where it was and repeated the number. I looked at Johnson, but Johnson was sucking his empty pipe, his glasses raised to the ceiling. A moment later, Lloyd called from the other room. "Nothing here, either."

He reappeared in the doorway just as Johnson said, "Are these all the safes you have, Mr. Mandleberg?"

"Yes," said Austin. He swayed. "Could I have . . . ?" Mr. Lloyd jumped forward, but Johnson had already taken a hip flask from one of his pockets and was holding it out.

"Try that," he said. "I have news for you. You have one more safe than you thought."

It seemed to be brandy, which has not much, medically, to recommend it, but Austin didn't complain. He handed the flask back, his eyes bleary, and said, draggily, "What?"

"Didn't you notice?" said Johnson. "It's very cleverly hidden: you should come here and look. There's a safe inside the safe."

He let go my hand, and I helped Austin to his

feet. Mr. Lloyd was already there, swinging open the old safe door as far as it would go, while Johnson shone his small torch inside. There was nothing to see, except for the money and the leaf gold at first. Then Johnson put in his muscular fingers and pressed something hard. The grain of the wood moved, like a ship being launched, from one side to the other, revealing a small recessed dial. Austin's eyes were like blue plastic marbles. Mr. Lloyd's voice had lost a lot of its measurable warmth. "I should like to see you open that," said Janey's father.

"You open it," said Johnson cheerfully. "If you look, I'm sure you'll find the combination in Señor Gregorio's safe."

He did, too, and opened it. We all craned round while he felt about and brought out the only thing that was lying inside. I don't think any of us were surprised by then to see a replica of the Saint Hubert rubies.

"Gregorio," said Austin, and fell back against the edge of the workbench. "Or Jorge." Mr. Lloyd stood, looking at the elaborate collar. He said, still studying it, "It isn't an offense to copy fine jewelry."

"No," said Johnson. "But it is a little disturbing when the copy is so painstakingly hidden. Gregorio couldn't make this himself?"

"No! No," said Austin. "Jorge, my goldsmith— he must have made it under Gregorio's instructions. The three others are juniors and recently added to the staff. I would not expect them to know anything . . . May I see?"

Mr. Lloyd handed over the necklace. He said,

"I suppose there's no doubt it is a replica? No, I see that it is . . ."

And indeed, even to me, the clumsy metalwork and the sharpish red of the stones were quite clearly false. I do know the look of a ruby, in the same way that I know sable and ermine and mink. One always knows where one is going, even if one doesn't quite know how to get there.

Johnson said, "You had no idea this safe was here?" and Austin shook his head, dropping the stones on the bench. I said, "If you could stop talking for two minutes, he needs to get into bed and have that thing bandaged."

They ignored me. "So you were right," said Mr. Lloyd to Johnson. And to Austin he said, "Well, it's up to you, Mr. Mandleberg. Do you want the police told?"

Austin shook his head. "There's nothing worse than a scandal in my kind of business. I'd be happy, Mr. Lloyd, if you'd take that collar and throw it away, or break it up and dispose of it in some way, so that we know it won't be misused. I'll look after Jorge and Señor Gregorio myself, and I promise this won't happen again. My God, I couldn't afford to let it happen. Honesty is the strongest card we have in our trade . . . Mr. Johnson, I can't say I'm happy that you felt you couldn't bring your problems to me, and I sure wish your aim had been better, but I won't say I'm sorry now that it's turned out the way it has. Mr. Lloyd, I have to thank you for tackling what you thought was an intruder on my behalf . . ."

"What made you come back?" I said.

"You didn't expect us, did you?" said Mr. Lloyd.

He didn't sound very pleased. "Gilmore drove the Cooper through Ibiza just as I was getting into my own car in the Bartolome de Rosello. He stopped when I waved to him, and Mr. Mandleberg offered to get out and take me back here for the two ikons he promised me, while Gilmore drove Janey on home." He paused, and then said to Austin, "I think you had better do what we originally planned and come back to the Casa Veñets with me. If you insist on having no treatment, my daughter is fairly knowledgeable about nursing and could make you comfortable, at least. If any complications develop, naturally we shall have to call in qualified aid." He slipped the necklace into his pocket and shut the double safe door.

I did three months more of that first-aid course than Janey. Janey left after four weeks. I opened my mouth and then shut it again at the expression on Mr. Lloyd's face. We all crawled upstairs, switching off lights and locking doors as we went.

Mr. Lloyd had a not quite new Buick, parked in the Plaza España, just down the road, by courtesy of his friends in the police, or Austin's status as resident. We lifted Austin into the back, and Johnson stood waiting to walk down to where the Seat was standing. Mr. Lloyd stopped at his side. "What you did was, to say the least, both foolish and criminal," he said. "You or the girl might quite easily have been shot as a result. I cannot say that I am sorry about anything that has happened, except that it should have been Austin and not yourself who eventually suffered."

Johnson stroked some sawdust off Mr. Lloyd's jacket. "Never trust an artist," he said. "It's a corrupting profession. I shall take up something healthy, like tennis, instead."

He waved cheerfully, as I got in, but Mr. Lloyd didn't wave back. In fact, as he got into the driver's seat, I could see by the dim light from the lamppost that he had gone rather red. I also saw, sticking out of his pocket, a corner of tracing paper. At least he hadn't had the nerve to get Johnson to sign it.

Helmuth put Austin to bed, and Janey and I fought a ladylike battle over the nursing which Janey won quite unfairly by dint of her father coming in and sending me sharply to bed. I kissed Austin good night, and he opened his eyes and said weakly, "I guess this puts paid to that trip to Seville, meantime at least. You're a crazy girl, Sarah."

"I'm not so crazy," I said, sweetly, for the benefit of Janey. "Johnson's going to paint my portrait."

For the first time, the annoyance in Mr. Lloyd's face gave way to a kind of unwilling respect. He put his hands on my shoulders. "Sarah Cassells, I hope you know what you're doing."

"I always know what I'm doing," I said, and squeezed Austin's hand, and let myself be steered out of the room.

Capricorns had had a big day, all right.

Anne-Marie did the shopping next morning: I wasn't up to it. Over a late breakfast which nobody ate, I affirmed my decision to go home on Monday; nobody rushed to persuade me to stay either, except Janey, and she was in two minds because of Austin. Austin, it seemed, had had a reasonable night, and no doctor had been called. Gilmore, perhaps because of the after-effects of the vodka, spoke to practically nobody and went to knock some tennis balls moodily against a wall. Mr. Lloyd, who had taken one or two telephone calls, informed us that the Russians had left for Madrid and that it appeared that Coco Fairley had died through drowning following a severe overdose of drugs. He told us after Gilmore had gone. He also took occasion to take from his pocket, before witnesses, the fake rubies, and smash them with a coal hammer on the terrace, breaking one or two of the paving stones in the process. So that was that.

I got in once, to see Austin, but Janey stayed there with her manicured hand on his brow the whole time, and I felt a bit spare. I had brought him another pillow, a jug of fruit drink with ice cubes that I had concocted myself, and some paperbacks I'd had on the plane, but he was practically sleeping and didn't pay much attention. I got both him and Janey to promise they wouldn't mention who Mummy was. Austin gave me a queer look before he closed his eyes, and I suddenly realized that this had made me a bit eccentric, to say the least of it, in his eyes. But if he could tolerate any scab who could write poetry or paint letters on boxes, I couldn't see why he couldn't be broadminded about Mummy and me.

I could see Janey taking his temperature with her thumb, and hoped he wouldn't go into a high fever while I was out of the house. Then I prepared an elaborate luncheon, beginning with iced melon balls and going all the way down to petit fours with the coffee, and lit out to the Hotel Mediterránea to see my brother Derek.

He wasn't there, so I scouted off (in the Maserati) to find him. I hadn't expected Janey to be very forthcoming about the exchanges between Derek and herself last night, and she wasn't. No one said anything about spying, and I thought it very unlikely Derek had unburdened himself to that extent. He had told her that he had come back briefly, for a personal talk with his father, and that was all, she said, that he had mentioned. Then when he caught sight of Mummy last night, he went off like a rocket, because, Janey assumed, Daddy had said nothing about the primary purpose of the Ibiza exercise being to allow the stagey bitch and the old drunken cadger to get together again. Although she didn't put it quite like that at the time.

With all that had happened, the spying story seemed to me to become less and less likely. It was much more possible that somehow, Daddy had stumbled on the funny business with the rubies, and someone had made sure he wouldn't give them away. In which case, Derek was surely quite innocent, and might even, in his ignorance, know something involving Jorge and Gregorio. The nuisance was that I couldn't imagine Gregorio manhandling another man onto the back of that horse. And for Jorge, it would have been quite impossible.

Coco could have, of course. I played with the idea that Coco might have been in league with Jorge and Gregorio and might have killed Daddy because he found out about the collar, summoning me out of sheer ill-will in order to confront me with

Mummy and confuse the issue still more by making her presence public.

If that were so, it was quite on the cards that Jorge or Gregorio had something to do with his death. On an impulse, I passed Derek's hotel, and parking the car in the Avenida General Franco, walked up through the Dalt Vila to Austin Mandleberg's gallery.

An old, sallow-faced woman in black was whitewashing the walls with a long-handled brush dipped in a bucket. When she saw I meant to say more than good morning, she set the brush down, wiping her hands on her apron, and gave me a long story. It was in the local thick accent, and I couldn't make out a word. After a bit, I said, "Momentito," and embarked on my own tale: Señor Mandleberg had been taken ill—not seriously, Señora—and was safely in the Casa Veñets with Señor Lloyd, where he was being nursed back to health. Any urgent messages to go to Señor Lloyd. This was the address; this the telephone number; could I see Señor Gregorio?

Only then, making a great effort to speak clearly with all ten fingers, did she manage to convey a few, shattering facts. Señor Gregorio was not at home last night. His bed had not been slept in, and no clothes were missing. Also, although the three young men had arrived, Jorge was missing also, and the chica of the house where he boarded said he also had been out all last night. Meanwhile, who was to open the gallery? Receive the visitors? Conduct the shop?

I told her to close everything and tell the three

men to go home: Señor Austin would come later and make his arrangements. It was possible, I said, that he knew all about Jorge and Señor Gregorio; we hadn't wished to disturb him this morning to ask him. I left her standing, her gnarled hands clasped and her deep-set eyes smiling gratefully under the gray, scraped-back hair. She was probably aged about thirty.

I got to the big silver teléfonos kiosk on the Vara de Rey and rang Janey. After a bit, Mr. Lloyd came to the phone. I told him again what had happened and waited. I wasn't going to inform the police and get everyone excited if there was nothing to get excited about. On the other hand, there had been two deaths already, and if there were going to be any more, I didn't want them on my conscience. After a bit Janey's father said hang on and he'd try and see Austin.

I hung on, feeding the phone rows of pesetas, until finally he came back and said better do nothing. "Gregorio might have come back," I said. "He might have found the rubies gone and guessed he'd been found out and got off the island?"

"It had occurred to me," said Janey's father, who had, I was discovering, several irritating habits of a tycoon. "And since there are only two ways of leaving the island, you may leave that side of the inquiry to me. If they have gone, it is perhaps the best thing that could happen."

"Poor Austin," I said. "No director."

"If the man was a criminal, I hardly think Austin will be any worse off," Mr. Lloyd said. "I am obliged to you for calling, Sarah. I trust we shall soon see the end of the matter."

I don't know how tycoons get to be tycoons. I came out of the phone box, shoveling pesetas thoughtfully into my handbag, and found my way blocked by Mummy.

"Hello, darling," she said. "I saw you in the phone box; you could hold a dance in it, couldn't you? Do you know where Derek is?"

She wore a pale blue tunic with trousers and a silver chain, and her urchin cut was brushed down and her eyelashes cropped. At the curb was a Humber Imperial. It must have been at least thirty years old. I guessed the soap-opera star had either locked up the sports car or she had crashed it, and this was the best the island hire service could afford in the style she demanded. No Seats for Mummy. I said, "At his hotel, I should think. Have you been there?"

She shook her head. "He isn't. And he hasn't left for the airport. He ordered a packed lunch and went off after breakfast; he said to queue for a bus. What are you doing?"

"Looking for Derek," I said. "We may as well join forces. Would you rather be cool in the Maserati?"

"It is rather dashing," said Mummy, looking it over with approval. "I don't know if Dilling can drive a Maserati. But Clem, I'm sure, does."

"Clem?" I said.

"My bodyguard," explained Mummy. "When Mr. Johnson phoned, he insisted. Never less than two able-bodied males, in full-time attendance. If someone had just said that to me," said Mummy, "around thirty years earlier."

I looked through the front picture window of the

Imperial and waved. Clem's face, shiny with sweat, grinned modestly back. Mummy made beckoning gestures. "Come and join us," she said; and we all piled into the Maserati. I put my dark glasses on again and gave Dilling the wheel.

It was a nice tour. We did the bus queues first, and then went out at random on the San Antonio road, clutching a badly printed timetable which Mummy insisted on reading, changing from her dark glasses to her long-distance glasses to her reading glasses with extreme rapidity and with a non-stop flow of comment.

It turned out, to my surprise, to be quite a sensible choice. There were about eight different services out of Ibiza, but they nearly all left before breakfast, or not until lunch. There was one for Santa Eulalia at 9:30 A.M., but I'd passed it myself, by the grace of God, and Derek wasn't on it. But the buses for San Antonio left every hour. I looked, with a certain respect, at my mother. Considering she had been up all the night with doctors and police and undertakers, she looked remarkably fresh. Coco's nearest relative, she said, was a sugar planter in Trinidad who was a member of the Plymouth Brethren, and how nice to think of all that money going to a good cause.

"What money?" I said.

"The money from his posthumous works, dear," said Mummy. "You know how values rocket on death. And he was a good poet."

"You'd better watch no one pinches the bull-rushes," said Clem, and chortled but briefly, out of respect for the dead. Mummy took him up and we went right on talking. It turned out she thought the Plymouth Brethren was the name of a hot trumpet combo on Radio Luxembourg. Dilling put her right. In the middle, we saw a bus in the distance, and chased it, but it turned out to be full of Spaniards staring at Mummy. Derek wasn't in San Antonio either. We crawled up and down streets and then sat under the trees on the seafront, and I had a fizzy stone ginger, without seeing a whisker. Then we piled in the Maserati and set off back, on the round trip through San José.

"We shan't find him," I said. The general support and hilarity were making me incautious. "He'll be with Jorge and Gregorio."

"Who?" said Mummy.

There was no harm in telling that story. Mummy was in no position to spread slanderous rumors, and Clem was on Johnson's side anyway. I related the tale of the rubies.

"Why?" said Mummy, at the end. "Did he hope to sell them as real?"

"He couldn't do that: they were too well known. And they were bad copies anyway," I said. "No, our guess was that they were meant to replace the real ones somehow, while the genuine collar was stolen and sold."

"I thought they kept them in the bank," Clem remarked. "Or is there a vault in the church or something?"

"I think they're kept in the bank. Somewhere safe anyway," I said, "eleven months of the year. The only time they come out—"

"Is in the holy processions. Of course," said Mummy, delighted. "The night procession of penitents. They must have planned to take the real ones—"

"Today," I said. I'd heard Johnson work it all out. "Tonight is the great procession, and they go back to be locked up right after. Just think of it. Someone was going to have Asprey luggage this summer. And now he's got to run for his life."

"Suppose Gregorio turns up and says he knows nothing about it?" said Clem. "You haven't much proof. It might have been Mandleberg."

"Well, hardly," I said. "He wasn't even there. And tell me how he could have a false safe not only made but put in, without Jorge or Gregorio knowing? He wouldn't even have known he had been burgled, if Mr. Lloyd hadn't rushed down with a gun."

"What about Tony Lloyd then?" said Mummy. "Maybe he was directing this man Gregorio in Mr. Mandleberg's absence. That would explain why the two men haven't turned up. Maybe he spent the morning quietly getting them out of the country."

I must say the thought had been in my mind too. I said, "The only thing is, he hardly needs the money, you'd think. He runs half the foreign commerce in southern Spain already. And I don't suppose even these rubies, broken down from their mounts, would give more than, what, twelve thousand, eighteen thousand pounds?"

"It isn't much," Mummy agreed. "But it mounts up, honey, you know. Maybe that's just how he got to run half the trade on the coast. It sure helps grease the wheels."

I said, "The thing is, do you think Daddy found out? Do you think that's why he was killed, not the

173

other thing? And do you think Derek might know it?"

She took off her glasses. Inside the rings of horse-hair I could see that her eyes after all were blood-shot and a good deal less than fresh after her violent night. "My darling girl, I don't know," said Mummy. "For all I can detect behind the nut cut-lets, Derek might be preparing to pinch the rubies himself."

"That," said Clement firmly, "is nonsense, Lady Forsey. Apart from anything else, how could Derek possibly organize a thing like that from a large firm in Holland? He's probably never even heard of the rubies."

But he had. Janey had phoned him last night. Although we didn't know that, of course, when we spotted Derek at the cross-roads to the airport, with one foot on a bicycle. Mr. Lloyd's Buick was standing beside him.

Clem saw them first and got Dilling to draw in behind them; while I explained to Mummy who Mr. Lloyd was.

"I know, honey. You told me," she said. "The gentleman with a gun who tried to blow apart your Mr. Johnson. If you would bring him, I'd like to meet your Mr. Johnson someday."

"His fees are a thousand guineas and over," I said coldly. Mummy is pathological about being painted. She has been done in forms tachist, sur-realist and cubist, in paint, wax, mud and gravel. Someone even sculpted her once in Scotch cheddar, and she kept it until the microbes had chinchilla earmuffs and the housekeeper fainted.

She tapped me on the neck with her reading

glasses as we got out. "Don't be old-fashioned: no one uses money nowadays," she said. "You arrange payment in kind."

"That's all right," I said rather nastily. "You've got lots of kind."

"And you keep yours for special occasions. Let's see," said Mummy, "who gets painted first? Dear Derek. Whoever would have thought of a push-bike?"

I put on my dark glasses. Derek would have thought of a push-bike. If he didn't want to be followed. We piled out and walked over to join them.

Derek stood quite still and glared, but Mr. Lloyd waved when he saw me. He was evidently alone in the Buick. I introduced Mrs. van Costa and Clem, and he gave a quick look at the pale blue trouser suit and the chains and kissed Mummy's hand. He said to her, "I don't know how much you know . . . ?"

"I know it all, pretty well, I guess," said Mummy. "Sarah here has been telling me. But what brings you out here?"

Derek said, "We think we've found what happened to Jorge and Gregorio."

The subsystem logic flip-flops were working. Since Janey phoned, he'd been on the track of Jorge and Gregorio all night. Gregorio had gone to church and then had visited the house of some friends, which he had left about three in the morning, since when no one had seen him at all. At Jorge's lodgings, Derek had discovered that a man had called for Jorge in the early hours of the morning with an urgent message from Mr. Mandleberg. Jorge had dressed and gone out, and had been seen no more.

"It wasn't Austin," I said. "He was flat out and besides, there was someone with him until at least three o'clock."

Clem said, "There is a third person in the ruby thing, then. Do you think, Derek, this is why your father was killed?"

"I'm sure of it," Derek said plainly.

Mr. Lloyd said, "It's the first I've heard of this theory, but I'll tell you my end. The airport clerks tell me neither Jorge nor Gregorio has flown out. The *Compostela* left Ibiza for Barcelona at four o'clock yesterday, so they weren't on that. The steamer people know them both well and say likewise that they haven't sailed on anything else: they haven't bought tickets, and they couldn't have slipped on board unseen. Now the airport and the docks are alerted; they won't get out either way. And I imagine, now they know the game's up, it's very important to them and to the unknown third man that they do get out. And there are only two ways they could do it. One is by private boat, and I've checked that no one put out after 2 A.M. this morning in a boat likely to make landfall anywhere else. In fact, only one large boat did leave the island very early this morning, with a crew list we can't check."

"The foreign ship. The steamer from sa canal, the anchorage for the salt mines," said Derek. "I thought of it too."

They had just met, I gathered, and formed an anti-Johnson alliance, and good luck to them. We parked Derek's bicycle. Clem and I got back into the Maserati and Mummy and Derek and Mr.

Lloyd into the Buick, and we set off down the road to the airport. Just past San Jorge, we took the left turn for the salt flats.

It was the watery sort of plain we had seen from the airport, Austin and I: a shallow lake marked into squares and stretching for miles. You could see the control tower sticking up, and every now and then a big passenger plane would come droning in. Then we turned our backs on the airport, and the road dived in between a set of low, scrubby hills and turning to the right, became a sort of causeway across the flat water. On the same side, not very close, was the long sort of table of salt that we'd seen that first day, with railway tracks running from it, and beside us was a road sign showing a dear little steamy black train.

"Train?" I said.

Clem had his arm round my shoulders and it was sort of wandering: I hoped Dilling hadn't noticed. I must say, Clem had improved, but it might just have been the hot climate. I wondered when he was coming back to London. He said, "They used to run the salt in trucks to the anchorage along here, but they use lorries now. I think the rails are under repair. How much do you really like Gilmore Lloyd?"

"He's fun," I said. "We had a ride the other day. And a swim. I wish I could look at the salt. What does it taste like?"

"Salt," said Clem. Beyond the railway lines on our left, the water stretched into the distance, broken by patches of trees and small buildings. On the right, the ground rose abruptly in a long, low escarpment, covered with small, cushiony pine trees,

177

and juniper, and masses of purple and yellow and white Spanish flowers. It was baking hot, and the smell of the pines and the thyme and the flowers came off the hill like an ounce bottle of Floris and stirred me up too. Clem said, "Wait. There's some salt. Dilling, could you draw in just there?"

"Never mind the salt," I said, getting out. I could see it, where it had dropped from the lorry, in a drift of dirty-white chips at the roadside. "What's the heavenly smell?"

"Lavender," said Clem. "Come and see."

I looked along the road. The Buick's dust was just visible at the end. "To hell," said Clem quickly. "They'll wait."

I saw the lavender, I suppose, out of the corner of my eye. The stalks looked about six feet tall, with a spike like a delphinium at the end, all open and reeking of perfume, and stuck full of bees. It grew in big, pillowy mounds all over the hillside, and I was going over them like Mary Rand, at the rate Clem was hauling me up that damned hill. We struck a level space, where a new road was half under construction, and then plunged into the fir trees beyond. Then Clem grabbed me and got going.

He got going so fast that my zip was half down before I grabbed hold of his wrist. He let go at once and, instead, got me in a half nelson and proceeded to kiss.

There are kisses and kisses. That one had about thirteen stone behind it and a lot of big silver cups. It gradually became apparent what Clem had been training for. It never crossed my mind in a long and varied experience that one could ever be kissed actually unconscious, but we nearly made it right then. I remember making a hollow, booming noise, inside my head, since I'd been deprived of all the usual agencies for communication, and Clem lowered me onto the grass and drew off, looking as if he were going to cry. "Cassells," he said. "Now I've done it. You'll hate me."

"No," I said, panting. My zip had lost the top three inches of teeth. "I'm just surprised. Clem, I thought you didn't like girls?"

"I thought so too," he said. He looked even more worried. "I haven't any income to speak of. I don't know what I'll do. You won't want me, anyway."

He sat there on a stone, big and brawny and simple, and rubbed his face with one trembling hand. It left a red smear.

I went, quite unexpectedly, off my rocker. I took his hand in both of mine, and said, "What makes you think that?"

"Oh, Cassells," he said, in a kind of whisper, and sort of tumbled across to me, taking little short breaths, on his knees. Then he put his head on the undone zip, and I held him, my heart going like a roadmaking machine. I wasn't even thinking of his worn-out jeans and his overdraft, but I knew I should have to. I think that apart from knowing very well what was going to happen next, I was chiefly thinking: Flo's mother would be my aunt as well. Then we heard Dilling's voice, calling.

Something always happens when I'm out with a boy. By the time Dilling reached us, I'd wiped the smear off Clem's face and he'd lent me a safety pin. I even had grabbed a big bunch of lavender. We

179

got back down into the car and set off and didn't say anything at all.

The road came to an end at the anchorage, and by the time we got there, the Buick was already standing empty. It was quite a big settlement, dumped in the midst of the hills and the sea, with a long, marble-tiled office and its own generating plant on the landward side, together with a number of decent white houses with gardens and washing and children running around. On the other side, on a low cliff overlooking the shore, were the working installations: rollers for crushing the salt, warehouses for equipment and so on, and a deep well like a bullring, half full of salt, with long yellow wheeled chutes, standing ready for loading. Next to it was the jetty, reached by iron stairs from our level. A notice barring it said: SALINERA ESPAÑOLAS, ZONA DE TRABAJO PROHIBIDO EL PASO. I took a handful of salt, which looked like white coffee sugar but tasted, as Clem had predicted, of salt, and wandered along past the buildings. Up on the wall was a rusty green bell and two colored lamps: below them, two labels said MENOS SAL by the red lamp and MAS SAL by the green. I giggled and then stopped. Reaction, Sarah. Then I turned and walked past the thumping powerhouse and under the trees to the houses. Among them was a bar.

It was cool inside. Mr. Lloyd and Mummy were drinking cointreau which, at 125 pesetas a bottle, I noticed everyone was putting down like milk shakes. Derek had a bottle of cold pasteurized drinking chocolate. Clem, who still hadn't spoken a word, let them fill the glass right up with brandy.

I had fizzy stone ginger. It was a day I felt I might need to be quick off the mark.

Mummy's eyes, of course, went straight to the safety pin, but Mr. Lloyd saw nothing wrong. They'd been to the office. A Swedish boat had left at first light with a cargo of salt, but no one knew whether she had taken two extra passengers or not. A car had arrived at some point through the night, and people had been heard to get out. The car had then driven off. There was an inlet next to the jetty with any number of small rowboats in the water or on the slipway. No one knew if there was one missing or not, but there were some footprints on the grit there this morning which had definitely not been made by salt workers' boots.

It was pretty conclusive.

"Where does the Swedish ship make her first landfall?" asked Clem. He had, clearly, pulled himself together. "Couldn't we call at the Salinera head office in town and find out?"

"If they're on board, they may well have landed already," said Mr. Lloyd thoughtfully. "Of course, we could always ask the company to contact the captain. Let's do that. Let's get back to Ibiza."

It then appeared Mummy was dying of hunger. She lifted her hedge-clipping lashes to Mr. Lloyd, and he agreed it was maybe too hot. There was between them already, a certain air of *rapport*. Clearly all the stuff about Coco had already been covered, on Mummy's terms, in the car. Mr. Lloyd was not only softened up: he was melted. Mummy is nothing, if not expert.

Everyone began to move back to the cars. I hoped he wouldn't ask her to lunch, or I'd have to cut some more melon balls, but he did, without even glancing at me.

Derek came to luncheon as well, and he got melon squares, because I was damned if I was going to sweat all day in the kitchen for him.

I didn't sit with them: there were too damned many, and although Mummy never stopped looking at Mr. Lloyd, I knew perfectly well she was enjoying herself. At least I got Austin to myself. Between courses I ran in and out with some white wine and an egg soufflé in brandy; he was looking tons better, with his ribs done up in crepe, and talking of getting up later. I discouraged it. I needed time to think about Clem. I had already told Austin about Jorge and Gregorio, and he said good riddance. On the whole, I think he was glad not to take it up further. Then, after I'd shoved the petits fours on the plates, Clem came into the kitchen and said, "For God's sake get out there and relax," and hurried me into the dining room while he helped Helmuth with coffee. It was Anne-Marie's afternoon off.

There was an empty chair next to Gilmore. It wasn't fair to Clem, but I couldn't resist it. Gil had been swimming: his hair was still damp and curling a bit at the edges, and he had a new coat of suntan. I was a little alarmed by his smile. He said, "When are you fitting in Johnson?"

I knew perfectly well what he meant. "This afternoon, maybe," I answered. "He's painting my portrait."

"Before Monday?" said Gil. "Or are you taking up residence on *Dolly?*"

I'd forgotten I was going home on Monday.

"He'll need a cook," Gilmore suggested. "Someone to sew on his buttons. He could even teach you to sail. And there's Clem, for variety. Two in the hand, She-she. After all, you can't count Austin now."

I raised my eyebrows. Steam always makes my hair come down like a broken umbrella, and my nose had peeled, but you have to have dignity. "Austin is a sweet boy," I said. "So is Clem. I don't know why you should be so stroppy about them. You've got Louie and Petra."

The names I had had, in confidence, from Janey. But there comes a moment in everyone's life when they've got to use every weapon they have.

"That's true," said Gilmore. "And they're very sweet girls. I'm water-skiing with Louie after lunch. What a pity you're going to see Johnson."

I could have screamed.

I went down to *Dolly* after the siesta, leaving Janey talking to Austin in two lounging chairs by the pool. I couldn't get her away. Mr. Lloyd and Mummy had disappeared, I suspected to look at Mr. Lloyd's paintings and/or listen to his new classical records, and Clem, bodyguarding, was lying full length in the lounge, a thing I suppose he finds hard to do, if not impossible, on *Dolly*. Gil had gone off in the Cooper, with his towel, surf pants, and skis, and also with Derek, who was going back to Ibiza. I took the Maserati, without asking.

There was no one on *Dolly*. I have never in the whole of my life had such a stroke of good luck. What was more, I knew where Louie's beach was: her uncle had a house party in a villa near Portinaitx. I turned the Maserati and set off north, singing—Janey's water skis snug in the boot.

Last summer, I spent two whole months cooking for a family with an estate on the banks of a very cold loch in Scotland. It rained. Except for me, everyone came down with flu, and no one wanted to eat. There is absolutely nothing like a very cold loch in Scotland for teaching you to stay upright on water skis. I stopped at the edge of an orange grove and brushed out my hair, remade my eyes and put on my dark glasses, which is not at all the waste of effort it may seem, and starting the car, did a bomb round the bend and screeched to a smoking dead halt on the road above Louie's beach. Then I played all the chimes on the horn.

Gilmore got to the car first, with two others whose vaccinations I recognized. I said, "He wasn't in."

"But you've brought your water skis," said Gilmore Lloyd.

"Why should she waste her time water-skiing?" said the shorter of the two others. I gave him a polite smile. With me, it is either the wrong kind or the right kind trying to make their established girl friend jealous. This was the wrong kind.

Gilmore said, "It's Louie's party really, but come down and have a drink anyway."

A nice girl would have said, "No, thank you," and punted off on her scooter. People always call me a nice girl, and truly, I can never see why a nice girl isn't supposed to want to get married. I want to get married, terribly. It's the only thing I do want. I mean, I want a great many things, and there's no other way to get them. I said, "Thank you: I'd love to," and Gil squired me just long enough to get me introduced to Louie and one or two well-mannered men, and then took off on his skis. I waited until he came back, having shown off until he was exhausted, and asked, very sweetly, if I could possibly try.

I hadn't got a Pucci swimsuit or a Tobago suntan or a rich father . . . or a father. But I had long yellow hair, natural, and a bloody good figure, natural, and a Jantzen swimsuit that a cousin had grown out of, and a strong sense of discipline. I did my nut on those skis, and if there wasn't a soul looking except Gilmore, it was worth it.

On the next trip he came with me, zooming backward and forward. I was meant to be scared. I felt scared all right, but I was too busy to show it. He shouted, "You say you can cook?"

"And dance," I shouted back. When he whizzed back again, I said, "Does Louie ski?"

He swooped away, the spray flying. When he came back, he said, "Not till June. She had a crash at Zermatt in her whirly-bird."

"Hard luck," I said, and capsized. You can't win all the time. But you can try.

We had a sort of snack on the beach of French loaves and whole stems of lettuce, with anchovies and tomato and chicken and salami and red peppers and olives and rounds of small hard-boiled eggs.

It was a marvelous party. The crowd were nearly all English: I'd met some with Janey. There was also a party of Spaniards who roared up a bit later in a Mercedes and a lot of gray-green Lambrettas. I'd seen one or two of the girls in Ibiza. They wore cloaks, long brown boots and little white kilts with bright, high-necked silk jerseys, and wore their hair tied severely back in pearl rings. They were wearing a lot less, I noticed now: in fact their suntans seemed to be all over. The new way to wear dark glasses, I noted, was not goggle-like on the forehead any more but with one leg hooked into your bosom. Louie's specs were like catherine wheels. There was also a boy who stood around, hands on hips, with two-inch sideboards, a gold locket, and a beach towel hung straight down from one shoulder. He stood just like that for ten minutes, and you could hear all the Englishmen hissing with hate. Then a couple of cruising yachts put in with some boys from Minorea.

They all knew Mr. Lloyd. One of the really good-looking boys, who was already engaged to a Portuguese heiress, lay down beside me for some courtesy snogging over the doughnuts and said, "Janey's a nice girl, but her old man keeps her wrapped in cotton wool, doesn't he?"

"Janey?" I said. Anyone less needing to be wrapped in anything but maybe asbestos I have never met in the whole of my life.

"Well . . ." said the nice boy, offering me a pack of sugar almonds like curling stones. He had had four gins and half a bottle of Sauterne, but you really would hardly notice it. He said, "I dunno why he doesn't tell Janey. Janey's broad-minded. Would Janey mind?"

"Mind about what?" I said, stroking his biceps. He had a beautiful tan. "Go on. Gil isn't listening." I wasn't sure if he was out of earshot, but I didn't care.

The nice boy rolled over and began to experiment, in the same mannerly way, with my bikini.

"Oh, you know. The love nest in Palma," he said. "Why not bring the woman back home and be done with it? I can't see why Janey should mind."

Palma. Where Janey's father had actually gone on the night of my father's death, although claiming to be in Barcelona . . .

A shadow fell over us both, and Gilmore Lloyd, bending down, cuffed the nice boy in a cursory way off my back. "It's hooked on the other side," he said calmly. "And despite what She-she may fancy, her trustees, I'm sure, would prefer it to stay hooked." Then he jerked me to my feet with a snap that nearly knocked the fillings out of all my back molars and returned with me to Louie. "We'd better be going. Johnson's expecting you, isn't he, She-she? And Father's making up a party to watch the high jinks tonight."

I wrenched open my teeth, and said to Louie, "It was super of you to let me gate-crash, and it's nearly my last day: so sad. Could we have a meal maybe back in London? Gil can give me your number."

Louie, who was a heavenly brunette, linked her arm in mine and Gil's and made all the right noises, much more sweetly than mine, right back up to the road. She was going to San Francisco after Easter. I remembered an aunt of mine who used to stay in San Francisco and gave her the address. She left us by the cars.

"Goodbye," said Gilmore.

There were a lot of things I had been going to say, but at the look in his eye, I didn't say one. "Goodbye," I said. "Thank you for having me."

It might, I thought, sting him into a little action

tonight. After all, I'm not really a prude. It's simply my code of ethics needed a little revamping to meet changed conditions. Such as having four steadies and going back to London with none.

Driving back through the corniche road south, I had time to think of a great many things, alone in the car. Until Gilmore mentioned it, I had forgotten that tonight was the big Easter procession in Ibiza, the Procession of Silence, when the floats would be carried down from the Cathedral by the faithful and all round the town.

Today was Good Friday. Someone had said Coco's party would offend the natives. It hadn't, because Mummy's house happened to be secluded and her staff were discreet. The beach party I'd just been to was innocent enough, too, compared with some barbecues we'd all attended back home. We could all look after ourselves: we'd been brought up to it. But there was a shocking difference, one could see, between that and the people one passed in the Maserati, dressed in their best black lace and silk shawls, going with worn faces and knotted hands to and from Mass.

The odd thing was, I felt at home somehow with both. I mean, one has to meet the right sort of people, and no one can say it isn't fun playing footsy in snorkels or whatever. But I could enjoy chaffing the children that morning in the Salinas buildings, and the teasing I got in the market. Come to that, there was more life in the fishwives than in Louie's lot, never mind poor Coco and his sad paper bags. But that was their life, and this was mine. I'd seen the English girls in stained anoraks and torn jute-soled shoes, bargaining in guttural

Spanish in the market. The market women didn't like *them*. You couldn't go native. You just went into a limbo between their nationality and your own.

I noticed Janey was different. At home, Janey treats every shopgirl like dirt, and she did the same here. The funny thing was, they didn't seem to resent it.

Driving along, I ran my mind over the others. Austin condescended to his inferiors. Very politely, but a complacent self-centeredness was certainly there. Mr. Lloyd was plain and brisk and rather impatient. Maybe his staff didn't love him, in any of his lucrative businesses, but they'd respect him, I thought. Gilmore was exactly like Janey. The only two who treated everybody the same, high and low, were Johnson and his mate Clement Sainsbury. And Mummy, I suppose. But she could hold forth by the hour about Bartok to a hopped-up Chinese waiter in Soho and come away firmly in the belief that she'd had a useful and intelligent chat.

I suddenly wanted to see Johnson. I passed the turning to the Casa Veñets and ran right on into Ibiza, where I parked the car on the right, opposite the boatyard. Then I crossed to the Club Nautico and walked quickly inside the gates and along the quayside to where *Dolly* was berthed.

They were winching up a sardine boat. The big, powerful horse plodded steadily round the dirt circle, in his straw hat and worn leather harness, the round woven pads like reedy bifocals, fixed over each eye, as the chains inched slowly up. I didn't look at it much: you had to watch out for the hose pipes and the bollards. Johnson said it took twelve

189

hours to fill *Dolly*'s water tanks for a bath, and looking at the bore of the pipe, I could believe it. I ran up the gangplank and stood on deck, calling his name.

There was a movement inside the cockpit, and my mother climbed out, wafting the odor of cheroot smoke before her. "Hello, honey," she said. "Johnson's clean out of ice. Be a darling and run along to the store. You know where it is?"

I did, as a matter of fact. It was just along the main road. But I kept on coming and said, "Mummy, I just don't care who you've got in the cabin. I just want to see Johnson."

"He isn't here," Mummy said. "I don't know where he is. The skipper isn't here either."

"Then who do you want the ice for?" I asked. I was getting fed up, calling on Johnson.

"Oh, that's for Clem. You know," said my mother, "he's lying on the floor right in there, and I think that he's dead."

CHAPTER 9

THERE WAS A SMELL of paint in the saloon, of good
food and alcohol. The table hadn't been let down
after lunch, although Spry had cleared it. Under it,
folded upon the floor, was the solid person of my
suitor, Clem, still wearing the blue levis and crumpled shirt he'd had on up the lavender hill. His hair
was too short to be ruffled, but his fresh skin was
very pale, and he didn't move when I got down
fast beside him.

"I never could take pulses" said Mummy, looking
over my shoulder. "Either he's alive and I'm dead,
or the other way round."

"I think you're both alive," I said, letting his
wrist go. The banging inside my chest settled down
to a steady jog trot. "He's been hit on the head."
The deck was sticky with blood. "Look, if you
take that arm . . ."

We heaved him onto one foam-padded side bench. I'd forgotten how strong Mummy was, in spite of the stick-insect physique. I found a cloth, wrung it out in the galley, and began to wash the blood out of Clem's hair. "How did it happen?"

"Search me," said Mummy. "Use my hankie. That cloth's got paint on it. We dropped by to see Johnson, and I walked to the front to get a good view of the town while Clem went down below to find someone. Then when he didn't come back I came down myself, and there he was. Wham."

"Alone?" I said.

"Alone," said Mummy. "It seemed mad to me, too. I went up on deck to look for anyone running, but there wasn't a soul. Then Pepe came along— you know, the man who looks after the quay—and I sent him along to the Club Nautico to fetch Dilling: you know how he goes in there to gossip. I'd just come down here again when you arrived."

"You came here in the car?" I said. "With Dilling?" You could see the neat, white face of the yacht club from where *Dolly* was tied.

Mummy took the holder out of her mouth and said, "If that mechanized mating call of yours is in the car park, you must have noticed the Humber."

"I didn't. The Humber isn't out there." There was a lump like a tennis ball and a cut that looked awfully deep to me under Clem's hair. He showed no sign at all of wakening.

Mummy sighed. "Dilling's on hash again. Sweetie . . ."

"Listen," I said.

"Drums?" said Mummy. "Those drums give me the creeps."

"No, listen. Someone is coming." You could hear the footsteps now quite clearly, on the uneven dirt of the quayside, getting nearer.

"Johnson?" I said. But I knew that it wasn't.

Mummy got up, rather gracefully, and took down the aerosol fire extinguisher. Sitting, she appeared surprised at my stare. "A woman's got to think of her future." We heard the footsteps slow down, and then become light and hollow as they traversed the gangplank. They arrived on deck and crossed it, heavily.

"Hullo?" said the capped head of Spry, appearing upside down at the top of the gangway. "I beg your pardon, Mrs. van Costa. I thought there was no one aboard."

"By no means. It's like the Schweitzer settlement down here," Mummy said. "Someone's attacked Mr. Sainsbury."

I wanted to stay. Clem still hadn't wakened, and he looked awful. But Mummy was adamant. "There's nothing you can do that Mr. Spry can't do better. He knows where to get a doctor, and he knows all the yacht-club men who can help him if need be. Impulse buying is no good in your situation, She-she," said my mother gently. "Less than twenty-five thousand a year is not truly advisable."

My cheeks were still burning as I marched back through the harbor beside her. "I suppose if Coco had had twenty-five thousand a year, you'd have suggested him for a husband."

"Goodness gracious me, no," said my mother. "You'd have killed his art in a week, and anyway, he was perfectly impotent. I guess you'll set out to have six children and call a halt about three."

"I happen," I said, "to think children are important."

"I know," said my mother. "That's why I said three. Forsey always thought you'd be fecund. You don't mind, do you, giving me a lift home?"

I stopped dead. "Honestly. I think you're the most selfish . . ."

"But you weren't doing Clem any good," said my mother patiently. "And I've got to get home somehow."

I glared at her, and then got into the Maserati, letting her get in on her side by herself. As I revved up, she said absently, "You know, She-she: I never did have that soul talk with Derek. Where did he go?"

"To the salt company office, I think," I said. "At least Gil dropped him by the quay in Ibiza. You were too busy to notice."

"Tony Lloyd? He's rather a pet," said my mother. "Slow down, darling. If we see Derek, I'd like just a word with him."

"He's got a love nest in Palma that's the talk of the countryside," I said spitefully. "With six children in it, for all that I know."

"*Derek* has?" said Mummy. It was the first time I'd ever seen her reduced to a bleat.

"Mr. Lloyd has." I swerved, to miss beheading a hen. "But I bet he's got more than twenty-five thou a year."

"He'll need it," said Mummy. "You remember the Vesey-Jacoby court case?"

"The people you sued for defamation of character?" It had been going on while I was at Mother Trudi's.

"Yup. I won it," said Mummy.

I missed another hen by a fraction. "You *won* it?"

"Two hundred and forty thousand dollars," said Mummy. "Am I beautiful in your eyes?"

I put on the brakes hard, and a horn blared behind me, so I put her into gear again and drove on. "When I wrote in October, you said—"

"I was damned if I was going to give you forty quid to impress an LSE student at his half sister's wedding. Check. Have you ever seen that boy since?"

"No."

"Do you want to see him again?"

"Yes!" I said. "Clem's sick, Gilmore's furious with me, Austin's in Janey's clutches, and Johnson's disappeared. I suppose you'd *like* me to go to parties in tatters?"

"You will learn," said my mother, "that lack of clothing never hampered anyone's style. Whether it attracts the right type is another matter. There's Derek."

I drove on right past.

"There," said my mother distinctly, "is Derek. Please stop."

I said nothing. To hell with the Forseys by marriage. We were in the middle of Ibiza. Mummy leaned over and took the ignition key out.

She was out of the car calling him before the engine had petered quite out. The car behind me didn't like it a bit. All I could do was look sweet and helpless, and finally everyone pulled out and passed. I couldn't even draw onto the side as she'd taken the ignition key with her. I could hear the

New England cadences and the voice of Cambridge approaching and sat, staring stonily ahead, while the car door opened, and they both squashed into the front. "He's coming too," Mummy said cheerfully, and put the key back in the slot. I started the car without speaking.

Derek didn't speak either. He smelt hot, and his expression, when I got out of town and managed a look, was exceedingly grim. Mummy said, "He's been tracking down Rodgers and Hammerstein."

"Who?"

"Jorge and Gregorio," said Mummy. She made it sound like a crack circus team. "He went back to the salt flats and went down to the anchorage."

"Why?" I said.

"Because," said Derek, "no one answering to their description boarded the Swedish vessel this morning, and nothing but salt has disembarked since she sailed. The trail was a phoney."

"They didn't take a car last night to the anchorage?"

"No," said Derek.

"They didn't sail from the island?"

"No," Derek repeated.

"Then they're still here?" I said. "But where could they be?"

"That," said Derek, "is what I'm going to find out."

Mummy sighed. "Darling boy," she said. "All those brain cells, groomed by all those trustees. Sometimes you make me feel perfectly stupid. Are you really bent on tracking down those two tedious Spaniards?"

"Yes," said Derek.

She put a long blue arm round his shoulders and tweaked the little curl over his ears, in the way that he hated. "Well, you're in the right place, honey," she said. "For they're both at my house."

I hit the hen that time. By the time I had scraped together my pesetas and got back to the car, you could hear Derek's voice in Minorca. Mummy was sitting enthroned in her grin, like morning glory in a company window box. I told you she was an actress.

She stayed that way all the way to her house, and sweeping round that drive in daylight, past the lake and the bullrushes, I got pretty quiet myself. Derek drew a deep breath, and as we came to a halt in front of that familiar portico, he said, "You understand, Mother. No matter what our relationship, if there is something criminal going on, I intend to report it."

Mummy got out uncreased and regarded him with those spiked saucer eyes. "You didn't report it when you knew Forsey was spying," she said.

Was spying. Derek's color got less, and I knew he'd noticed it, too. He said, "My father was of poor character, his will power weakened by drink . . ."

"So you felt protective," said Mummy. "I'll say She-she and you are a pair. Why I didn't have the sense years ago to take to a wheel chair, I'll never know. Come on in. The butler's just putting the knockout drops into the cocoa."

The mad thing was that Dilling was there. He opened the door with a bow, and if he was on hash, I didn't see any sign of it. Derek said, out of the side of his mouth, "Sarah. Does anyone know that you're here?"

I shook my head. Clem was flat out on *Dolly*. Janey, I supposed, was still with Austin and Mr. Lloyd as well, in her own house. Gilmore would have left Louie's party and be on the way home by now. Johnson had vanished. In about an hour, perhaps, someone would wonder why I wasn't there to make dinner before they all went on their boring jaunt to the processions. Then when I didn't turn up, Anne-Marie would take over or Janey would open a tin. We followed Mummy, who took us into the room where the Russians had been and poured us three brandies and soda, with ice.

I didn't care, I drank it. And so, after a moment, did Derek. Mummy, standing over us in her silver chains and blue suit, smiled sentimentally. "Dear children," she said. "If only Mother had had me taught knitting."

"What?" said Derek, anxiously, hunting data in everything.

"A crochet hook," said my mother, "isn't long enough. Ah. There you are."

Dilling had opened the door and ushered in Johnson.

His glasses looked just the same, and I suppose the pattern above and below was unaltered: he had his pipe in his hand. He said, mildly, to my mother, "You make people feel insecure. Anyway, you're in the middle of the wrong play. I said leave Sarah and Derek out of this."

"I couldn't," said Mummy quickly. "Dilling drove the Humber away. And Derek has found out about Rodgers and Hammerstein. That they didn't leave Las Sadinas, that is. I know Derek. He's hell unless he gets facts."

I said, "I don't know, of course, if it matters, but someone has tried to kill Clem. He's lying on the bench in *Dolly*'s saloon with his head cut half-open, and Spry looking after him. I think it's time we knew what's going on."

"Time, for one thing," said Johnson. He walked slowly forward, took another brandy from Mummy, and sitting down with it, proceeded to light his foul pipe. Without looking at anyone, he said, "It depends. I don't see why I should be expected to explain anything unless you turn out your pockets as well. You haven't told either Sarah or Janey, but I think you'll have to tell me, Derek. What did your father say, that night you came back to Ibiza and accused him of being a spy?"

"I didn't kill him," said Derek. "As I presume you know, if you're mixed up in the whole thing yourself. I had the opportunity to kill him and to kill Coco, but I didn't. I just wanted to find out who did."

"I don't think you did either, Derek," Mummy said comfortingly. "But you haven't answered Johnson's question. What did Forsey say when you accused him?"

My brother looked straight at me. "He said, if I left my job, he'd pay me five thousand a year and expenses."

"He *what?*" I said.

"I gather Forsey didn't take an interest in the LSE student's half sister either," said Mummy.

Five thousand a year. I felt betrayed. Utterly, utterly betrayed . . . I'd taken him a three-pound box of Bendick's bittermints last time I'd gone to stay with him, "Did *he* win a law suit as well?"

"He was earning money, I guess," said Mummy. "Undercover. What happened, Derek?"

"What do you think happened?" said Derek bitterly. "It was a bribe: as good as an admission. I knew as well as you do that he'd never had that amount of spare cash in his life, at any rate when *we* were all living with him. And when you think of it, of course, his was the perfect life for picking up secrets. He was on chatting terms with all the intelligent business world and all the peers in public positions—not in the boardroom or during the working day, but on the beach or at the drinks party where the yashmaks got dropped . . . I said if he didn't give it up, I'd report him."

"And?" said Johnson.

"He took my hand and patted it and said, 'My dear boy,' and grinned. That Roland Young grin. You know, She-she."

I knew. "Oh, hurry up," I said. "Did he clip you one?"

"He said he didn't really see me going back to Holland and denouncing him, which was true. And that he couldn't see me either going back and saying he was innocent, which was equally true. So, he said, the only possible course was the one he'd outlined. Living off his technological spin-offs was, I think, how he put it."

"Then when you spurned him?" Johnson said.

"He asked me to go back to Holland and say nothing and do nothing for four weeks. After that, he promised my job would be safe, and I needn't worry any more. I was to tell my firm that I wanted four weeks to complete my investigations."

"So?" Johnson's voice was quite gentle.

"So when I heard he had cut his throat, I knew—I thought I knew—that this was. what he had meant. And that in a sense I had killed him."

"What made you change your mind?" Johnson asked.

"The blood. There wasn't any," said Derek. "I saw him, you know. And the winch. And I spoke to old Pepe. The Guardia Civil were so hopeless, and no one seemed to understand, and of course the last thing I wanted to do was to stir up all the dirt about Father. But I knew he hadn't cut his own throat: he'd been taken there after it was done. The question was, was it done by his own wish? Or had someone murdered him?"

Johnson said, "Why should it matter?" but I didn't need to ask, nor I suppose did my mother.

Derek said, "You see, if he'd been murdered, in a way it was all right."

"Well: you can relax now," said Johnson, and put the pipe in his mouth. "He was murdered."

There was a little silence. No stanza of poor Coco's poetry could have been more concrete or more chilling than that.

I didn't want any more brandy and soda. "Who killed him?" I said.

"He was killed," said Johnson, "over some rubies. Derek's instinct was right. It seemed too much of a coincidence that there should be some nonsense going on over rubies and that a man should be killed at the same time. My guess would be that your father got to know, somehow, about the proposed theft of the rubies and that he was killed to keep him quiet."

"By Jorge and Gregorio," said Derek. Color had come back into his face.

"No. By someone else," Johnson said. "Someone who also killed Coco, because Coco watched your father when he came here by night to visit Mrs. van Costa and because on that one vital night Coco must have seen where he went. I don't suppose Coco had any motive other than jealousy, coupled with malice, when he sensed that he would soon be asked to go. He must have followed Lord Forsey hoping to uncover some dirt or some trouble. And he certainly found it."

"Who, then?" said Derek. My mother hadn't uttered a word.

"We don't know yet," said Johnson. "But we shall. We have a very good opportunity, later tonight. Jorge and Gregorio are not the most cooperative of prisoners, and the old man is half dead with fright. Since I couldn't use force, Lady Forsey, I took the liberty of bugging your cellar. I don't know who killed your husband: I suspect they don't know either. But I did find out one thing. There were two copies made of the Saint Hubert rubies."

Mummy was first off the mark. "Huh? There's another replica? Aside from the one that was smashed?"

"Check," said Johnson. "The first one, the one we saw, didn't pass muster. It was pretty clumsy, as Sarah will remember. A second copy was made."

"We didn't find it?" I said.

"No. They took no chances with that one," said Johnson. "It was already removed from the workshop by person or persons unknown. All ready to be swapped for the original on the one night in the

202

year when the original is within reach of the public, passing through the old city by drumbeat, at night."

I put my hands over my mouth, and Derek half got up. "Tonight?" he said. "During the Procession of Silence tonight? The people who killed my father are going to steal those rubies tonight?"

Johnson took his pipe over to a table, laid it down, and had a swig of his brandy. "I looked up Capricorn, She-she," he said. "It says pension matters are overdue for serious consideration and that you will sparkle tonight."

"Never mind my pension," I said. "Let's get the police."

"Now—" said my mother and Derek simultaneously.

"Now nothing," I said. "The heroines I've seen come to a sticky end because, while the murderer's still running around, no one calls in the police. You've evidence of two murders and a forthcoming robbery. For crying out loud, dial nueve, nueve, nueve. Policia, Guardia Civil, and Bomberos."

"Someone has, dearie," said Johnson. "That's why I'm here." "Meet," said my mother, "the Man from the Prudential."

"You meet him," I said. "I'm going home. I don't want to go the same way as Clement and Austin and Daddy and Coco."

"You go on home, honey," said Mummy.

I stayed.

I suppose I would have thought more about Johnson's work if he hadn't had glasses. I mean, what special agent on films ever had glasses? Bifocals, anyway. I did wonder in passing why he carried a gun and found safecracking so easy, but he simply said he'd been on special-branch work in the war, and once done, never forgotten. And that when you'd spent a few years on the waterfront, you learned the best way to take care of yourself and your boat. If an internationally famous portrait painter told you that, you believed him. Despite anything Derek upbraided me with afterward, I am definitely not naïve.

It was Derek who went on and on when Johnson was trying to swear us to silence. I knew what Derek was thinking. He thought Janey should know. And he resented Johnson anyway for a perfectly obvious reason. If a British agent had been called in to look into Daddy's murder, then Daddy must have been what Derek's firm thought him. A murder in a foreign country is dealt with by the police. Not by people like Johnson.

He gave his word, in the end, because Mummy browbeat him into it. Johnson let her. Johnson was a man of unusual talents. Then he took us, very slowly and clearly, several times over his plan for that night.

Spry phoned, before it was over, to tell Johnson that Clem had now wakened but wasn't up to much: he suspected concussion. They couldn't lay hands on a doctor. We heard Johnson hesitate. He said to Spry, "I want you to take over guard duty at Mrs. van Costa's within the next hour. Could you leave Clem? Or isn't it safe?" Johnson's face, as he laid down the receiver, bore perceptible signs of concern. "He's going. He thinks Clem will sleep," he said. "It's rotten luck, but we really can't do anything else, with Austin laid up as well. She-she: where is Mr. Lloyd planning to stand? At the Monument? In the Vera de Rey?" All the processions in Ibiza arrived at the boulevard and took a turn round the Monument.

"He said something about the Monument," I said. "Janey and Gil and I should be with him. He was joining friends there."

"But the four of you, and possibly Derek, will be the only guests for dinner tonight?"

"I hope so," I said. "I've only ordered enough food for four." I paused and said, "Johnson, why should someone cosh Clem?"

Johnson's black eyebrows rose, but his voice remained perfectly calm. "Are you sure it was Clem whom they wanted to cosh?"

The ash broke from Mummy's cheroot as she sat suddenly upright. "Me? It was an attempt to hurt me?"

"I should think so," said Johnson. "It's perfectly easy to hide in the fo'c's'le and escape up through the hatch later, when the fuss has died down. You've got short hair. In the half-light he might easily have mistaken his victim."

"Clem is a dear boy," said my mother, wide-eyed. "But I must say I am not flattered. What is more, I don't get it. If Coco had imparted to me any of his vital secrets, surely by now I've had time to pass them all on?"

"Maybe . . ." said Johnson.

"I know something I don't know I know?" said my mother.

Johnson nodded his head.

"I don't know anything I don't know I know,"

said my mother in a positive voice. "Or if I do, I'll sue my psychiatrist."

"You do that," said Derek coldly. "Then if someone does wipe you out, Sarah and I will share in the proceeds."

It was one thing I had never thought of: that Derek and I were heirs to everything both Daddy and Mummy had possessed. Since we thought neither of them had a bean of their own, I for one had never given it more than a sigh in the passing. But now . . .

Johnson finished briefing us just after that, and I got up with Derek to climb into the Maserati and drive back to the Lloyds'. Just as I was getting in, Johnson called me back to tell me something he'd forgotten. Derek looked at me as I climbed into the driver's seat for the second time. "What was all that?"

"He forgot to ask what time we usually finished dinner."

I put her into gear and drove off. The concrete curb and the cactus at the edge of the drive shone intense green and white in the headlamps; and then we were on the gray, pockmarked road, with its broken, yellow dirt at the edges. The pale stems of a fir wood swam toward us, the gray-green clouds closing over our heads, Dazzling red-and-white triangles and circles appeared far off, like eyes, and flew past us—50, 30—and warnings: children, skidding, CEDA EL PASO. Red-and-white netting, bright at a corner. A cyclist—a double red lamp clipped to each side of his calf. A swaying grouping of lights, that turned out to be a lorry, with extra sidelights on the top of its load. A bus, with triple

lights also. Ibiza—the yacht club—the broken inn
opposite the Talamanca road with its sign: BAR—
STOP.

The last of the road lights glittered on something
on the mat under my feet. I changed down as we
rounded the corner, and holding her in low gear
between the long, dark avenue of bare trees, bent
and fished the thing up. It was one of Coco's bits of
tin bunting, from the Casa Mimosa. It said only:
DEATH.

CHAPTER 10

IN THE END, I made them all curried chicken except Derek, who got eggs Mornay and lumped it.

There had been no trouble over getting Derek added to the party, although there was a slight air of inquiry over how we had spend part of the day: a good few hours had passed since leaving Gil. I said I'd been having a sitting with Johnson and then I'd come across Derek by chance in Ibiza.

"Helmuth told us," said Mr. Lloyd, pouring himself a San Miguel pilsner cristal. It was a rather hot curry. "Wasn't Mrs. van Costa there too? You apparently blocked the whole roadway."

"That's right. I gave her a lift. Dilling had gone on a trip with the Humber and left Mrs. van Costa stranded," I said. He could interpret the leading phrase there any way that he liked. Johnson had said, "Don't mention Clem's head, and don't tell them I've been with your mother." He hadn't needed to tell us to keep quiet about Rodgers and Hammerstein. I had a moment's unease when Austin asked Derek if he'd found out anything that mattered at the office of the Salinera Española, S.A., but Derek just said no, they didn't keep any records. Thereafter there wasn't much to be heard but the opening of beer cans.

I got dressed, ages behind everyone else, to the sound of the record player, and came down in my black crochet dress and black anorak to find Janey and Austin, with his bandage undone, dancing to "Itchycoo Park." He broke off after a bit and gave me a whirl. Janey said, "You're in hot-cross bun country all right. Why the black, She-she? You're not Roman, are you?"

I wasn't anything, except obeying instructions to wear something dark.

Then Mr. Lloyd came in wearing a fur-collared car coat, and Gilmore dressed in a sweater, with a great scarlet wool cloak for Janey. I didn't look at it. I was so busy not looking at it that I hardly said good-bye to Austin, who was curling up with a good book in the grotto. We all piled into the Buick, waited patiently for Derek who was in a sports jacket with a raincoat over his arm ("A *raincoat?*" said Janey), and then Mr. Lloyd let in the clutch, and we snarled up into the gear changes which would land us in Ibiza. The moon had got up, and the telegraph poles and the trees were black now against the light sky. Where the planting was sparse, you could see the hazy blue of low hills on the left, till they flattened, just before the bend round the harbor. Then the lights of Ibiza leaped out before us: blue-gray, with the Cathedral floodlit a deep golden yellow. We crawled in, behind the crowds and the buses, and parked.

The holy images for the procession were dressed in the Cathedral in the afternoon, Johnson had said. Nobody had seen it being done, because *Dolly* had spent her time sailing back from the Salinas anchorage with Jorge and Gregorio and guarding them until it was safe to drive them to Mummy's villa. It wasn't until late afternoon that Johnson had learned that there was another set of false rubies: that the scene was set for the theft of the real ones after all.

But, said Johnson, he also understood that the dressing was done by the senior officials of the Church, plus a handful of devoted Ibizencans. This, in his opinion, made it impossible for anyone to depend on being able to substitute the false rubies for the real at this stage.

From then on, they were guarded by never less than six people, most of them priests. By afternoon, all the images had been fixed on their litters, and candelabra, real or electric, and flowers, real or waxen, set round about.

Johnson, he had said, would be with the Saint Hubert. How he proposed to manage that I couldn't tell. The order of the procession was always the same: it started at the highest point of the old town, the images assembling from all their various churches, and then wound its way down the lanes, accompanied by its files of churchmen and penitents, plus contingents of armed forces and local officials, spaced out with sad music and drums. It sounded wild. In the big cities, Johnson had told me, the statues alone could weigh up to five tons, and needed thirty stevedores underneath to carry them. I wondered if Johnson proposed to get underneath the Saint Hubert before it left the Cathedral or if the union would veto it.

I had only three firm instructions from Johnson. To stick to the Lloyd party. If I could, to keep them together. And not, under any circumstances, to go off by myself. He had added a comment. If a theft had been planned, it was likeliest to happen in the low town, where the thief could get away easily. If Mr. Lloyd stayed in the low town it would, said Johnson, be nice.

Mr. Lloyd thought it would be nice, too, until he saw the Vara de Rey, which was pandemonium from end to end and three high in the middle with people standing on people round the Monument. I saw quite a few of the types who sit with their woolly socks on the chairs every morning outside the Mediterránea, including the German girl in the lime-and-gold sari and the five million bangles, the girl with the ticking nightshirt and boots, and the boy with the skinny sweater and necklace, who went about with the barefoot fat woman with pink and orange and green paisley painted all over her face. It was mild, and the lamplight shone under the palm trees. I got pinched black-and-blue while we struggled, fruitlessly, to find Mr. Lloyd's friends. After a bit he got fed up and said, "Let's get out of the scrum. We should be in the Alt Vila. Much more dramatic."

"Well, you won't get there now," Janey said. "Look at the crowds." She was mad anyway because Derek wasn't looking at her and the others hadn't turned up. I expect she wanted to play them off against one another.

Mr. Lloyd said, "The procession won't have started. We can get there if we try. Hang on to each other."

I hung on, with my arms stretched like chewing gum, until Gilmore complained, and I actually had his lizard belt with the bull clip off twice. The curbs were packed with beak-nosed Spanish women with lots of eye-black and jewelry, and old types with long, gathered, black sleeves, black silk headsquares, and cut-velvet shawls with silk fringes under their pigtails. Children seethed. We crossed five streets and got to the market, where the stalls were dismantled and the square jam-packed with crowds. The balconies of all the town houses round the walls were also crowded with people and draped with red and yellow, the national colors.

There Mr. Lloyd had an earnest discussion with a man in a uniform, and next thing, we were scurrying up the ramp to the Portal into Dalt Vila. We went under the long arch of the Portal and into this roofless place I've mentioned before: a kind of paved, high-walled room which connects the arch into the old town with the arch into the new. There, Mr. Lloyd hustled us behind one of the pillars and we stood, looking around us and waiting.

It was a super place, I must say. We faced a blank wall about thirty feet high, in the right corner of which was cut the portal onto the ramp. Through the arch, you could see the whole market lying below: the lights and the people. We stood with our backs to another blank wall and inside a long, pillared portico, which held up a strip of tiled roof jutting over our heads. On our right, our wall was joined to the wall of the portal by another arcade:

a double arch with a room built above, with no windows but a green double door giving onto a rusty, railed balcony. The roof of the high room was tiled, and behind it, the end wall rose up another six feet or so, covered with creepers, with a path at the top. There were plants growing out of all the cracks in the stones, and a sort of yellow flower in the tiles over our heads: I had seen it, turning up the hairpin bend in the Maserati with Janey. On our left, the fourth wall was a short one, and the whole lower part nearly formed the entry and the pools of lamplight on the white walls and the moon shining on the cobbles, like an incline of paperweights, round which the procession would come.

I was staring at it, mesmerized, when an officer came up and asked us to move. Mr. Lloyd talked to him severely in a low voice, but it didn't do any good. We shifted out of the guard place and through the arch into Dalt Vila itself.

It was all right. We stood looking at the outside of the arch, among the crowd in the square, squashed up to one another, giggling, and making witty remarks, until Mr. Lloyd suddenly said, "Hush." Then we heard it, high up in the darkness. The flat tuck of the drums.

I felt Derek shiver. My curry was also starting to do salaams. I wondered what Johnson was doing: what could one man do? I wished I'd been able to stay nursing Clem. I wondered if Spry knew what to do for concussion. Clem would make a decent husband. A nice one. One who didn't throw paper-bag parties. My stars. He couldn't even afford paper bags.

The people round about us were Spanish. The

woman next to me turned out to be one of the helps in the fish market, and she kept smiling and talking in short, clanging outbursts of patois. Instead of the jersey and skirt and the square-fronted apron, she wore a black crepe dress and a black lace mantilla. She still smelt of fish. I asked when the float of Saint Hubert appeared in the procession, and she said nearly last. I don't think she approved of him. I suppose he was a bit secular to have all those rubies. The drums were getting louder, I thought. I looked at Janey's father.

He looked preoccupied. If he were going to snatch twenty thousand pounds' worth of rubies, I suppose he would look preoccupied. I supposed anyway he had seen it before: they had had the villa in Ibiza a long time, before his wife died. You forgot Janey was half-Spanish. I wondered why she wasn't a Catholic, and then thought that perhaps the mother wasn't. He would have no religious scruples, anyway, about pinching jewels from the Church. And I didn't suppose he cared a damn about deer. But would he have killed my father and brought me out to Ibiza? Then I remembered what Johnson had said. If he thought Daddy had written to me, then he might.

Gilmore said, "That's the music," and if you strained, you could just hear it, far up the hill. Not creepy stuff in the least, wails and rollings of drums, but stern, tinny tootles, four beats to the bar, above the conversational roar of the crowd. Above our heads a caged finch, wakened by the noise, suddenly started to twitter, and some others answered him. Gilmore said, "Don't be alarmed if some of the stations look a bit tottery. The canopy poles are fitted with fairly loose sockets so that the whole shooting match sways if they want it. It whips up the excitement."

"Do they never tip one right over?" I said.

Gilmore shrugged with his eyebrows. "It's been known," he was kind enough to explain. "In places like Seville, they go in for sensationalism a bit more than Ibiza. You might get a hitch here if the bearers stop for a swig in a side street. Now and then there's a little contretemps, too, if the candles get too near the costumes. But that's about the extent of it."

Derek said suddenly, "I wish we could see the start of the thing. I think I'll try and work up a bit, and then come down alongside it. Would you mind?"

I didn't know who he was asking, but I said I wouldn't mind, and Mr. Lloyd said he wouldn't, although he didn't think he had a hope, and Janey didn't say anything. In fact, I minded more than somewhat because I had to choose whether to go with him or stay with the Lloyds.

I was a coward. I stayed. If Derek was going to do something awful, it was now clear to me that I wasn't going to stop it. But at least I wouldn't know anything about it.

He went, and we stood with the crowd and looked at the steep incline before us, edged with tall, balconied houses, down which the procession would come. It would come down into the square, and folding back on itself, would march through the arch into the empty guardroom before us, and turn left, through the Portal and down the ramp to the town. After that, the long threading of streets to the Vara de Rey, the circumnavigation of the Monument, and back and up through the Dalt Vila again. The thought made my legs ache: I looked at those glassy rounds of scratched stone and thought of Johnson.

"Here it comes," Mr. Lloyd said. And we looked up and saw the top of the slope crowded, in silence, with tall, faceless, peaked masks and torches, and smelt the incense, in silence, rolling down on our heads. Then a masked, barefooted man advanced alone down the path, his purple robe brushing the cobbles, a banner in purple and gold held high in his hands, and a double file of purple robed figures came silently after, linked hand to hand by a thin, swinging black cord. On their heads were the tall cones of purple I had seen with Johnson before, and purple hung over their features. In one hand, each carried a torch like a lily sheaf, and a priest in white walked between them, moving from side to side, encouraging.

They came down the long path in silence, and padding round, turned their backs on us all and marched steadily through the arch, past the gallery, and left through the other arch leading to the low town. At the entrance they slowed for a moment, and you could hear, from the changed quality of sound outside and below the high walls, that the crowds out there had seen them. Then they resumed their slow, swinging pace and continued, and we turned to the high slope again and watched to see the file of penitents end and what was to follow.

Although only half my mind was thinking about the procession, I remembered it afterward with fantastic clarity. Of course, the setting was fabulous, and whatever anyone says, I am hung up on creepy processions. I remember the heave in the curry when behind all the wagging, thin peaks a red glow appeared, which turned out to be a little float, carried on four penitents' shoulders, with a figure of Christ knee-deep in candles and greenery, with whopping Victorian lamp brackets at every corner. The penitents were coming down a bit warily, clacking along with kind of walking sticks to fix under the litter when the weight got too much. They came down the hill without stopping and turned through the arch, the guard space, and the other arch and disappeared, going steadily out of sight. Janey said, "Ooo look. White ones," and the crowd behind us swayed and pushed us forward, so that we had to redress our line.

The white penitents wore layers of coarse snowy-white cloth, white peaks and masks, with big red crosses sewn over their bosoms. They had red crosses, too, on the plastic lanterns which they carried on long, thick, white poles. Behind them was another blaze of flowers and light: a float with the Madonna and Son, filled with red carnations and arum lilies, with pink plastic foam thoughtfully bound on the poles to save the shoulders of the sailor boys carrying it, their navy caps slung round their backs. They were the first naked faces we'd seen since it started. I noticed Janey craning a bit.

She had a good look, too, at the escort of soldiers who came next, with gold-banded hats off, but then we were back to the hoods and gowns: all white with pale blue masks; all white with blue hoods; all white with black hoods and buttons, like a gingerbread man, all down the front. A stout man in uniform and gloves came stepping down, like a *haute école* act without the horse, and then a ringing noise broke the silence

217

and, turning a corner, rattled backward and forward among the high houses as the municipal band appeared on the slope and descended, blowing and beating. They had their music stuck out in front, and the flute had a little torch pinned to its chest. There was a clarinet, as well, and drums. The racket squeezed through the arch and ricocheted back and forth under the gallery before being swallowed, abruptly, by the jaws of the Portal. A body of upright men with long coats and epaulettes breasted the lane: they all caught Mr. Lloyd's eye and smiled. "Hullo?" said Janey.

"Public relations," said Mr. Lloyd. "Pay no attention."

They wheeled round before us. The room between the two archways was filled with bobbing caps and a few retarded white peaks. Things were still pouring down the slope. Church dignitaries in velvet and thick gold embroidery, edging downward with care. Two wooden crosses borne at intervals by robed figures, their black-soled bare feet padding securely down over the stones. The figure we had seen in the Cathedral of the sorrowing Virgin, in a halo of silver, with her lace hankie still in her hand. Some women, veiled in black lace, carrying fancy black missals. A large block of civilians, in their good suits, medals catching the light. A Cavalry with the figure in a purple velvet sort of apron, a thick silver belt round the waist.

The silver flashed under each lamp as it came down the hill, and I stopped watching Gil and started to nibble my nails. Any minute now. More robed figures. A regimental band of cornets and drums, deafeningly letting off down the slope, the brass dressed in scarlet with fringes. The echo of the drums, banging backward and forward inside the arch, was like a heavy cavalry charge. Janey put her hands over her ears, but I was enjoying the mixture. You could hear, far off in the low town, the bugles and drums and flutes which had already passed us, playing something different. It was a bit like the *1812* being played by Boy Scouts in two different drill halls. Then the band got through and down to the ramp, and I had time to look up the slope and see the Saint Hubert.

Hubert is not one of my very favorite names, and what the fishwife had told me hadn't changed my mind much either. After beating it up as a courtier, he was startled into repentance when hunting on Good Friday, say the books, by the sudden appearance of a stag bearing between his horns a radiant crucifix. He renounced all worldly pleasures and ended up as a bishop, in afterlife giving much help to those bitten by mad dogs and taken over by devils.

Anyway, there, obviously, seesawing at the top of the slope, was the form of Saint Hubert, in a bishop's mitre, robed and bearded, with one hand uplifted, as in his photograph, and the other resting on the head of a stag. The heads in front of it moved, marching downward, and you could see that instead of a canopy, the float had a tree fixed at each corner, with flowers and leaves realistically made out of wax. Round the trees, lay the carved statues of various hunting dogs, one with a hare in its mouth, and the rest of the space was filled in with flowers and half a million candles with their flames all bending one way, like a happy crowd at a tennis match. Then it got a little nearer, and you could see something else: the candlelight flashing crimson on a sort of necklace slung round his shoulders. The Saint Hubert rubies. He still had them, then. So somewhere near, Johnson must still be lurking, but I couldn't see him. Nor could I see Derek.

I looked round. A contingent of soldiers was goose-stepping past us: little, sallow men with mustaches, with rifles reversed held by white gloves, the ranked helmets shining like fishing floats. Both Mr. Lloyd and Gilmore were staring at them, their eyes slightly glazed. Janey wasn't looking at all. I followed her gaze with my eyes and found a wrought-iron balcony with a carpet flung over it and a family party sitting behind on tall, straight-backed chairs. At the end of the balcony, a perfectly super type with one of those long, brown Spanish faces and sideburns was carefully picking geraniums out of one of the window boxes and throwing them to selected females in the crowd, most of whom were Janey.

I suppose, up to then, the retreating noise of the bands had drowned the sound of the barking. At any rate, it was only then that I noticed, and everyone else beside me, that the float of Saint Hubert was behaving in a peculiar manner. For instance, it was traveling sideways. It then moved backward, and sideways again, and then with sudden and extreme rapidity, disappeared up a side lane. There was a heightening of noise, and the procession halted behind it, while the crowds all inclined upward, pushing. It was the nearest one could get, in performance, to actually rushing to see what had happened.

For a moment, everyone shouted and shoved and asked questions, while nothing else happened. Outside the walls, there must have been a block on the ramp, for the band and the float and the penitents between the two arches had stopped, too, and those who could were craning round to watch the happening behind, while the lot stuck through the arch in the guardroom kept calling up questions. The soldiers stood at ease and swayed without moving their boots, their eyes wandering vaguely. Then, as suddenly as it had gone, the Saint Hubert float shot like a roller skate out of its side street, turned round twice in mid road, and began to charge down the slope. At the same moment, creaking, the procession before us got moving again, and draining out through both arches, disgorged itself into the town, leaving the cobbles in front of us perfectly clear.

Alone and jolting, its velvet skirts flouncing, its candles vibrating, and Saint Hubert posting above, the paso of the poor hunting bishop came rollicking past, accompanied by every dog in Ibiza.

They were happy dogs. High and low, white, black, brindle and tan, with or without ears and tails, covered with dust, scabs, and layers of incense, leaping and driving and fighting and snapping and barking—about two dozen dogs ran round and after that float, under it, and scrabbling half up its sides. And every time a boot lashed out from under the valance and caught a dog in the ribs with a squeal, another three dogs ran in, teeth bared, and another voice joined the shouting and swearing which we could now hear, emerging with passion from under the litter. It joggled, dancing. Impelled by a series of snaps, it took a short run to the left, and another back to the right, stopped, and then suddenly set off, like a clockwork mouse, dead downhill. It passed us, going like steam, with everyone within reach on the cobbles giving gratuitous help to kick the peripheral dogs out of the way: the rest were quite beyond stopping. For a moment, it looked as if it were going to crash into the crowd. Then, lurching, Saint Hubert swerved, instead, sharp right and shot through the arch into the galleried guardroom.

The roofless space between the two arches was now quite clear of people. There was, in fact, nothing in it but wind. As the float slowed and turned, snarling, to move with its dogs out through the Portal de las Tablas, the flames of the candles suddenly bent flaring over, and the bishop's robes burst into fire.

I think Mr. Lloyd was there first. I never saw anyone move so fast, although Gil was not far behind, and Janey and I flailed our way through the arch after, the lines of penitents pounding beside us, their torches streaming, their hood points fighting like pelicans. I saw Mr. Lloyd force his way through the dogs and jump onto the float, at the same moment as I saw Derek scramble up on the far side, with a bunch of Penitent Brothers ahead of him. You could see the palinquin tremble as the extra weight piled on top. It tilted; the dogs squealed, the men underneath shouted, and just as one of the hooded figures flung a cloth over the blazing Saint Hubert, hugging and smothering him, the litter came cracking down on its legs, throwing everyone on it off balance.

For a moment, there was a smoking heap of

limbs, flowers, candles, shattered china, and dogs. Fighting my way through, with the crowd pushing me forward, I saw no faces I knew. Then beside the statue, a hooded figure stood upright, still clutching the end of the cloth which had put the fire out. It let go the cloth and turned, clearly about to get down, when from the end of the float rose another figure, also hooded, purple robed and gloved. It advanced on the first, picking its way over the struggling bodies and ignoring the guttering candles, and drawing back its gloved fist, socked the first man clean on the jaw.

Whoever he was, the assaulted Brother must have had a neck like a bullock. He shook his head once, staggered, tore himself free, and turning, jumped. Not for the ground, where rows of upturned faces, aghast as I was, waited for him. But upward, to the rusty rails of the small balcony which hung over the galleried wall. For a moment he hung there, in a swirl of stained robes. Then, swinging himself up and over, he disappeared through the green, double-leaved, broken door and reappeared two seconds later, on the shattered tile roof. I think he glanced down at us, once. Then turning, he began, hand over hand, to climb up the creepered wall to the bulwarks.

It was so unexpected that we all stood and gaped, while the dogs pushed and swarmed and barked and the heap of men on the float scrambled upright again, groggily, in the mess of bent trees, chipped dogs, and real dogs hysterically barking. Alone in their midst, the painted hand of Saint Hubert stretched out scatheless in the benign gesture of blessing. The lower half of his robe was a peeling

223

mess of layered and blackened embroidery, but the mitered head was untouched. Round his neck, knocked awry and evidently not quite refastened, was the ruby collar, with Mr. Lloyd peering at it. Gilmore knelt at his side.

Pressing with Janey at the side of the float, we could hear her father speaking quite clearly. He said, "That's not the true collar! Follow that man in the robes!"

He was pointing up to the room with the balcony, with the wall rising behind it. The man who had received the crunch on the jaw, his agility unimpaired, had just disappeared over the top; but now a second figure came into view through the roof. The hooded man who had hit him was hard behind his victim and climbing like crazy. Our mouths open, Janey and I watched her father and brother likewise make a leap for the rails and, with a good deal of grunting, begin to swing up them. "Are you game?" I said to Janey.

"There's Derek," she said suddenly. "Look. Right at the top. Come *on,* She-she!" and we both jumped for the wall.

One or two of the more agile penitents were intrigued enough to come with us, but not enough understood English or were near enough to hear what Mr. Lloyd had said. The rubies were still hanging there, most publicly present, and you would have to know a good bit about rubies and have your face practically in them to tell they weren't quite real. In any case, other things were rather rapidly happening.

The bearers, having let the float down with a crash when half the populace of Ibiza appeared to

224

have jumped on their backs, had finished rubbing their bites and their sores and were crawling out, bellowing from under the valance to lodge appropriate complaints.

No one knew, afterward, who had had all the legs of the float fitted out with new Shepherds' castors. All we saw at the time was that as soon as the bearers had left it, the litter stood trembling slightly, a mess of reeking wax, smashed flowers, and dogs scrapping, biting, barking, and making the most of the trees. Then, very slowly, as a Cunard liner moves down the slipway, it began to move inch by inch down the steep slope of the guardroom, steel rumbling, ruination rising in clouds like the rust from its chains. Then, traveling like a torpedo, it shot through the Portal de las Tablas and veering right, dogs going crazy, went sheer through the window of the marketplace butcher's shop.

Saint Hubert, patron of hunting, rested, they said, outside the door, one hand rocking benignly, as every hound in Ibiza tumbled smack into paradise.

Janey and I both missed that bit. We'd got to the top of the wall, through a door and down a slope to the Avenida General Franco, and were thrusting uphill against the rush of people, penitents, priests, and drummers pouring down to get an eye view of the disaster. Here and there, in the patchy dark, you could see the dark spire of a hood far ahead, forcing uphill the wrong way as we were. Occasionally, still ahead, I could catch the gleam of Mr. Lloyd's gray head and Gil's sandy one following.

We climbed another wall, and as the noise from

the crowd thinned and the tail of the procession dropped down below us, we continued running—threading through the dark, uneven lanes, going up steps, stumbling into half-made trenches and through builders' rubble—our footfalls strangely flat and distinct against the faint rumble of crowds and music and drums far below.

We were easily the last in the race. Sometimes, turning a corner, we would glimpse a dark figure skidding fast round the next: once I distinctly saw Derek, face uncovered, running at the end of a lane. We followed, pelting along until we came to one street where we saw and heard no one, where the road end was empty and there were no side paths up which anyone could have possibly gone.

"We've missed them," I said.

"No, we haven't. Not all those people. They've stopped running," said Janey, and raised her voice. "Gilmore! Daddy!"

No one answered. I kept turning round, like the float. I didn't want to be coshed on the back of my neck and find myself in the Lebanon market: *for sale, white slave with pills who can cook.* "Where *are* we?" I said. And almost immediately answered myself. "Wait. I know where this is."

Janey got it in the same instant. "So do I. I know where the rest are, as well. I've never been here before in the dark."

"I have," I said. "But that time we got in through the back."

We were standing a few doors along from Austin Mandleberg's Gallery 7, where the replica rubies had been produced.

CHAPTER 11

WE ACTUALLY PAUSED for a moment outside poor
Austin's door before going in. To the street, the
house was dark and perfectly silent. Austin, of
course, was in the Lloyds' house still convalescing
and by now, no doubt, thankfully slumbering. As far
as the Lloyds were aware, the men who made the
fake necklace, Jorge and Gregorio, were out of the
country; to my knowledge they were not, but at
least they were in Johnson's keeping.

In this house, therefore, must be the man who
had stolen the rubies tonight: the hooded figure who
had exchanged blows in the smoking mess of the
float and then bolted; the man who had murdered
my father, as well. Someone touched me on the
back, and I made a sound like tearing paper: a large,
well-kept hand was pressed over my mouth. "Shut
up. It's all right," said Gilmore Lloyd. "We're all

here more or less, inside the door, and we think the chap we want is bottled up in the gallery."

"You might have come out sooner," said Janey furiously. She didn't seem to be frightened.

"We hoped you'd go away," said Gilmore simply, and shoved us in through the door.

Inside, it was not perfectly dark. The lights to the big showroom were off and also the lights in the basement, where Gregorio's rooms and the ill-fated workshop were. But in the office, the room at the top of the stairs where Johnson and I had illegally entered, a dim light seemed to be burning, and there were more lights round the corner, from the other door on the landing, which led to the exhibition of Art in the Round.

Around us on the tiled marble floor, doing nothing, was a fair-sized group of people, most of them hooded and masked, although here and there I saw a perspiring bare face, and one or two that I knew: Mr. Lloyd's, Gilmore's—and suddenly— Derek's. In the midst of the Ku Klux Klan, I suddenly felt calm and perfectly confident. Of course, they were all waiting to make sure all the exits were guarded. I smiled at Mr. Lloyd, who looked absolutely clean through me, just as a low whistle sounded from the door of the office. With some reluctance, the gathering shuffled its feet and then moved, slowly at first and then with gathering momentum, toward the bottom of the stairs.

I suppose the first two or three had set foot on them when a door opened straight across the small landing and printed a square on the wall. In the middle of the square, Janey and I now observed, was the shadow of a tall man, standing upright and still in the center of the gallery doorway, with a gun in his hand.

"These are private premises," said Austin Mandleberg's voice sharply. "If any one of you moves a step further without my permission, I shall certainly shoot."

Austin!!! Presumably he'd gone off his rocker. I started to move to the corner, but Janey was even quicker. She sang out, "Austin!" and dodging round to the foot of the stairs, was three steps up before anyone managed to stop her. She said, "Don't be an ass, it's us. Father and Gil and She-she are here. We've just brought some friends."

"Oh," said Austin. He lowered the gun and said stiffly, "I'm sorry, Miss Lloyd. But since no one knocked or rang before entering . . . People get excited as you know, at these times, and the police are busy. Premises are sometimes entered and rifled." He looked green. His ribs were probably giving him hell.

"I see," said Mr. Lloyd dryly, "you were protecting your property?"

"Naturally," said Austin. For a moment, he stood on the landing, just glaring at us; then he wiped his free hand on his stunning cord trousers and stepped back, stuffing the gun in a pocket. "I beg your pardon, sir. I'm not maybe right at my best. Come in. Please. Thank heavens you called out to me, Janey. You see, I just got to thinking of this after you left, and the more I thought, the more I got worried. With Gregorio absent . . . So—I hope you'll forgive me—I took out the Maserati and ran here just to make sure everything was all right."

"You must have had a hell of a job," Gilmore

said. "Getting the car through these crowds." He finished climbing the stairs and walked into Gallery 7. We all followed. "So this is your traveling show?" His gaze took in the quilts, the Perspex, the colored circles, and the printed sections of wood and traveled slowly upward to where "Cumulus Cloud with Tartan Traveling Case" was rocking gently, spurred by one hood point succeeding another.

"That's it," said Austin. He walked across to the large oak dresser which occupied most of one wall, and took out some sherry and glasses. He glanced back at the doorway, where most of the hooded figures, embarrassed, were standing on one another's shiny black boots. "Do come in, all of you." He was too well-mannered to ask a direct question; but the query in his voice was quite something. Since his own clothes were spoiled, Gilmore had lent him a high-necked twill shirt and a blazer, a little tight over the shoulders. He added, "You must let me make up at least for my unfriendly welcome. Was the procession a hit?"

"Mr. Mandleberg," said Mr. Lloyd. Janey crossed the room and, tucking her hand into Austin's arm, said, "Let me hand those out for you. Oh, Daddy, never mind those boring old rubies. Have a drink."

Austin turned. "What rubies? There hasn't been trouble?" He shouldn't have been out of bed, really. He was a sort of pale biscuit color, and his hair looked unkempt, like a rattan chair in a cat's home. Janey got her hand away, at last, to take some glasses across to the hoods.

"They've been stolen," said Mr. Lloyd. He paid no attention to Janey. "Another collar, a copy from God knows where this time, has been put on the statue. There was a fight on the float, and we all followed a man here. You didn't see him?"

"*Here?*" said Austin. He put down the sherry bottle. "What did he look like?"

"He was dressed in a hood," said Mr. Lloyd, staring at Austin. "You didn't see or hear anyone?"

"No!" said Austin blankly. He took a grip of himself. "Hell, you can search if you like. In fact, I think that you'd better. If anyone's hidden in this house, I'd sure like to know it. Do you think he's still got the rubies?"

"I think it's likely," said Janey's father. "We'll look for those too. If you've no objection?"

"None at all, sir," said Austin. He grinned a pale grin. "Maybe you'd like to search me as well." And before anyone could stop him, he pulled off his blazer and slung it across to Janey's father, and then proceeded to turn out every pocket until the linings were showing. He had beautiful Swiss handkerchiefs, a croc wallet and handfuls of pesetas, and bennies, plus a key ring with a very authentic-looking scarab attached. There was nowhere else he could have carried anything so large as that collar. Mr. Lloyd got a bit red and said, "There was no need for that, Mandleberg, but it was very decent of you to do it. Gil, come on."

Half the room emptied. One or two people began crawling around the gallery itself, and Austin, after some hesitation, packed the stuff back into his pockets and got into his blazer. Janey said, "Well? We're waiting for the rest of those sherries," and he smiled at her and began pouring again. A voice behind me said "She-she," gently.

I hate those hoods, and if I hadn't known it was

Johnson, I wouldn't have let myself be drawn gently backward and halfway down the stairs. "It's going rather well, don't you think?" he said. I could see the bifocals, flashing behind the slits in his hood. "Where's your brother?"

"I don't know," I said. "Janey said she saw him at the top of the wall. After the rubies were whipped. How did the dogs . . . ?"

"Aniseed," said Johnson simply. "Brilliant, don't you think? Will you do something for me?"

"I don't think so," I said.

"Nothing to do with Derek," he said. "Would you go down and watch for your mother? She ought to be here about now."

"Wearing a hood?" I said acidly. I didn't know what on earth Mummy had to do with all this. I thought of something else too. "Were you the man who punched the other chap on the flat? The chap we're looking for now?"

"No," said Johnson. "That's the other piece in the puzzle. The man who got punched ran in here. The man who punched him must have dodged into a doorway when he saw half the town about to catch up with him, and let us go by. My guess is, he's here now, too."

I said it in the end; but don't think it was because Janey and he were drinking out of the same glass. "Austin's got a pink patch on his chin."

"I know," Johnson said. "Look. Here's Lady Forsey."

She didn't have a hood, but she had a bloody mantilla, with a comb and a rose stuck through her urchin gray hair, and a red dress covered with white spotted flounces, slit right up to the knee. She

232

had gorgeous legs; she still has. "Hi, darling," she said. "Where's the action?"

I said, "Oh for *heaven's* sake. You didn't stand watching an Easter procession all dressed up like that?"

"I had the best seat in town," Mummy said. "The chief of the Guardia Civil is an old friend of mine. The dress was a present."

"You wear it on *Sunday*," I said. "I promise you. The poor old chief must have been sitting in agonies."

"I hope so, darling," said Mummy, admiring her kneecap through the top of the slip. "I've got a police pass for the rest of the holiday, and I've donated the van Costa Trophy for the best turned out Guardia Civil with more than eight children. I smell sherry."

"In here," said Johnson. "Sarah, take her in, will you? I'm sure she'd like Mandleberg to show her the exhibition."

"What, *now?*" I said. "In that getup?"

"Every color blends in a garden," said Mummy, and striding forward, cocked a hip in the doorway. I edged past the elbows and said, "Austin: you remember Mrs. van Costa?"

"Of course," Austin said. With the ease that all those years and years and years in college always give to Americans, he advanced without blinking once, kissed Mummy's hand, and, in a voice in which there was only the faintest trace of despair, said, "You're most welcome, ma'am. Would you do me the honor of taking a small glass of sherry?"

Mummy smiled silently into his eyes, bridging the generation gap like a harpoon from a whaleboat.

Her technique hasn't changed one little bit; in a way I suppose that it's ageless. "If its manzanilla," she said, her eyes still wide open. "I hate gluey sherries."

It wasn't manzanilla, of course; hardly anyone stocks it, but he wasn't thrown in the least. He found and poured her a fino and handed it over, doing a great line on vineyards. To my surprise, Mummy listened entranced, and sipping the fino, said, "Delightful," into his eyes. He tore himself away to give a drink to Gilmore and Mr. Lloyd, who had just come back, and one or two hoods who had also wandered in. Mr. Lloyd gave the thumbs-down sign to Janey. No man and no rubies. Austin said, "I don't know if you all know Mrs. van Costa? Why don't we all sit down? I'm sure you gentlemen would be much more comfortable without that cloth on your heads."

"But they mustn't!" said Mummy. "Don't you know it's forbidden to unmask before the floats are all back in church? Mr. Mandleberg, I just wanted to tell you how much I appreciate the splendid work you are doing in placing the creations of these talented boys and girls before the public they deserve. Marshall Cheeseman has long been a close and dear friend of mine, and I have watched his work mature from a minor art to the bagged landscape with chickens, which I see you have hanging there now. I have the honor also of knowing Mackenzie Hall-Bassen since he set up his workshop in New Orleans, and I have seen his art flower into those marvelous shapes: so strong, so virile, so refreshingly clear of the mainstream of current art thought. Mr. Mandleberg, you are performing a service to aesthetic man."

Austin's eyes lit up. They really did. He put down his sherry, and advancing, said, "Mrs. van Costa, I have some things here which even you may not have seen before. There is an example here of what I might call a condition of dynamic equilibrium, a sensory experiment with light waves with induced emotional and intellectual response, which has the organically disturbing function of the greatest discoveries. When you see these items, you know yourself, Mrs. van Costa."

"Indeed," said Mummy, hitching up her frills and threading her way after him through the banks of exhibits. Her flat bottom waggled. "As the great Paul Klee once said, 'Art does not render the visible, but renders visible.' What is your opinion of the Blaue Reiter school, Mr. Mandleberg?"

She was in her element. It was the stuff that drove Daddy to drink. At my elbow, Johnson's voice said, "Let's follow." Mr. Lloyd had sat down, and Gilmore was picking, moodily, at a canvas covered with nails. The sucking noise of sherry being imbibed reached us from a number of hoods. I walked, with Johnson beside me, down the gallery after Mummy, and Janey came with me. "It's Johnson," I said; but she didn't answer. She was looking at one of the man-sized circular boards painted in those stomach-turning concentric bands of bright color. Beneath it, you could see Derek's shoes, still all stained with seawater from the Salinas harbor. I kicked her, and she said, belatedly, "Oh? In the hood?" Luckily, Johnson didn't seem to be paying any attention, and we all stopped within earshot of Mummy engaged in putting pressure on the dollar.

They were standing in front of the board with

the rows of round wooden slices, and Austin was telling her the significance of the words stenciled on each. She seemed to understand him. I think she probably did understand him, which is a comfort in a way. I mean, it's nice to know someone does. He had just moved on to something else and was saying ". . . abandoning figurative painting for a lighter and gayer construction, of piping and mesh . . ." when Mummy said, "Mr. Mandleberg?"

He turned back, still pointing onward. "Mr. Mandleberg," said Mummy, "the condition of this exhibit seems to have altered a good bit since I last saw it in Boston. Are your people keeping this gallery humidified suitably?"

"Er, no," said Austin. He didn't come back. "So close to the sea, Mrs. van Costa, there's no need for that. Certainly, as it travels about from country to country, one cannot always ensure that packing and transport conditions are all that one would make them oneself. Certainly, I always personally inspect the galleries that they go to, and many of them, as you know, are my own. But I regard the risk of a slight deterioration as being part of the price one must pay for bringing this unique and brave exhibition before the philistine world. You wouldn't have me stop it on that account, Mrs. van Costa?"

"Why no," said Mummy. "But I tthink your wooden framework would repay watching." She put her finger along one of the printed wood slices. "Look, there's a split right along there."

I don't know if she pressed it or if she dug her fingernail in. At any rate, there was a small creak. Then, slowly, in front of our eyes, the wooden boss swung smoothly open, revealing, nesting inside, a massive piece of brand new machinery, with the name SCHUYTSTRAAT—AMSTERDAM printed on it. "Now that," said Mummy, "is a Happening, if you like."

I think for the moment he thought she'd done it by accident. I think perhaps he even thought he might get away with it, if the woman was stupid enough. He just didn't know Mummy. While Austin was saying, ". . . not unlike Mitchell's work: petal shapes cut out from boilers and tank ends . . ." she just kept on pressing. Three other sections of the exhibit swung open to show other pieces of plant, and by that time Austin had stopped speaking and was at the end of the room, with the gun back in his hand.

Johnson shoved back his hood. "Don't be silly," he said mildly. His glasses had got steamed up a little. "When you threw your blazer over, we took the bullets out of your gun . . . We seem to have the aural sensator, so you might as well tell me. Where are the rubies?"

Austin took a deep breath and let the gun drop. He said, "I guess . . . When I saw the machinery, I knew you'd blame me. You'll just have to believe me. I didn't know these things were there . . . How in hell could I know? I've been abroad."

"You were in Holland," said Johnson. "Just after the machinery was stolen. So was Lord Forsey, as it happened: that's why Schuytstraat got hold of the wrong end of the stick. We know you didn't steal them, any more than you were meant to touch those rubies today. Someone else does all that for you, and you simply act as a vehicle to anyone who will pay you enough for your trouble. One, the item

237

is stolen. Two, it's delivered at once to your gallery. And three, it leaves the country in due coure, concealed inside one of your special exhibits." He rapped his knuckles, smiling, against a hoarding studded with glued rope and metal. "You could carry anything inside these, couldn't you? Hashish inside the quilts, chemicals in the bagged landscapes, microfilm or documents anywhere."

Austin went liver color. "All right. That's it," he said, and began to walk forward. "I don't know who you think you are, Mr. Johnson, but it's obvious you don't know anything of me or my work. Have you any idea what it costs to insure and pack and ship these exhibits from country to country? If I were in need of money, Mr. Johnson, as you imply, I should hardly be able to finance an undertaking such as this. As it is . . ." He stood face to face with Johnson—a big, clean, indignant man reflected in the bifocal glasses—while Johnson stood unmoving, like a Welsh soprano, the pointed cap clutched under his arm.

"As it is," said Austin, "my work is philanthropic, Mr. Johnson. For the benefit of the whole of mankind. Mrs. van Costa, whoever she may be, was right about that. And I cannot permit pure, dumb, low-grade sensationalism to interfere with it or me."

"Was that," said the grating voice of Janey's father, "why you attempted to pass this piece of stolen machinery off just now as a fine work of art?"

"Never mind, Mr. Lloyd," said Johnson mildly. He hadn't moved. "Spry spent the afternoon rigging a camera. Whatever Mr. Mandleberg did when he ran in here this evening will be most fully recorded."

"Oh, really," said Austin. "I'm not a schoolboy,

you know. And I really doubt whether many portrait painters carry a night camera along with their brushes and a technician to rig it. In any case, where could it . . ." He stopped.

"That's right," said Johnson. He turned and strolled backward, then pausing, reached up an arm to the "Cumulus Cloud with Tartan Travel Case" and pulled back a zipper. Held within by an efficient structure of cord, the shining lens of a camera glittered down on us all. Johnson rezipped it and turned just as Austin, cornered at last, began to run for the door.

There were quite a lot of people in the room by that time, but he also had a great deal of cover. Austin wheeled and, overturning a heavy, self-colored canvas, dashed for the protection of a bank of lit double-skin boxes, containing large and significant patterns assembled in washers.

Gilmore was there. Austin attempted to turn, lashed out at Gil and got a kick which shot him through the double-skin window: the washers poured out like fruit-machine tokens, and Austin, twisting, made off this time and began doubling in and out of the lines of exhibits in the general direction of the door. He had nearly got to the end when a group of hooded men, jumping in at a tangent, neatly cut off his exit.

He was saved by one of the quilts. Ripped from its moorings, it burst on the struggling men, feathers shooting from every overstuffed symbol. Blinded, hood struggled with hood. Other hoardings rocked and came hammering down, to further the blizzards of feathers. There was a sort of heap of men on the floor. I saw Mr. Lloyd sprinting to join it, and then Gilmore. The hump of men zigzagged up, struggling, and overhead, a "Bagged Landscape" burst. The other works, rocked wildly by buffeting cowl peaks, hardly held out much longer. With a sigh, one by one, punctured as if by bayonet charge, the great bladders died, pouring upon the locked figures a long, sad, steady stream of cold, colored water. A spray of small plastic ships settled, like locusts, and one of the figures, detaching itself, suddenly rolled to its feet, shedding dolls' eyes like aniseed balls, and made for the door.

It was Austin. Janey shrieked. I belted along one narrow passage of oscillating disks of shrill color, aware, out of the side of my eye, that one of them seemed to be moving. As I ran, I saw it detach itself: a thick eight-foot circle of spiraling yellow and pink, rumbling into deliberate movement. It was making straight for the door. I saw Austin look back once, his eyes white as single-spot dice, before he crashed through the doorway and jumped four at a time down the stairs.

I couldn't have reached him in time, but the disk did. It thundered through to the landing and, taking off on the top step, sailed down through the air sideways taking my eyeballs, revolving, along with it. Austin had got to the bottom step when it hit him, and he didn't even give a cry: just a grunt, as it dropped like a lid. He didn't get up.

Derek, who had propelled it, stood beside me dusting his hands, with an expression of microelectronic satisfaction under his dripping wet hair. "As Paul Klee didn't say," Derek said, "art does not render the visible, but renders invisible. Let's go and pick him up, shall we?"

It took three men to lift off the disk and get Austin back to the room. He groaned as we got him into a chair, and groaned again, a bit more, when he opened his eyes and saw the shambles of his Art in the Round. Johnson tied his hands to the arms of his chair and patted Derek on the back. "Well done. I don't suppose you know where he's hidden the rubies?"

"I'm a stranger here myself," said Derek, who still looked as if he had had four gins in a row. It was the first joke I'd ever heard him make, which explains its unremarkable nature.

"Look here," said Gilmore. We left Austin in the charge of a masked man who turned out to be Spry and walked through the shop to where Gil was kneeling, in front of a block of wood covered with steel wire and cotton reels, labeled "Maternity." From the area of the right hip he twisted a screw and drew out a small drawer concealed in the thickness of wood. Beside me, Austin shook his head and sat up. Everybody craned over.

"What a pity," said Johnson. "It's empty."

The shout from Austin distracted us from the movement we should have been looking for. Everyone looked round at Mandleberg, who was sitting forward tugging like a mad thing at his hands, shouting amazing Bronx epithets. I saw Mr. Lloyd and Gilmore look at one another.

I don't suppose anyone really expected the first hiding place they found to be the home of the rubies. The whole collection was presumably honeycombed with secret pockets, large, small, and middling. It was perhaps coincidence or perhaps the fact that, in haste, Austin hadn't quite rammed home the drawer which caused Gil to spot it. So it seemed to me then. In any case, there was Austin on the verge of a stroke, the veins bulging on his fair, well-scrubbed brow as he howled in a formless outburst of rage and mortification. Johnson came over and slapped him on the face, very neatly, with the flat of his hand. "Did you put the collar in there?"

Austin sobbed and, panting, got some words out. "Yes! They were there seconds ago! The effing bastard! The double-crossing . . ."

They were the last words he spoke. He was still honking when a spark of flame lit the far end of the room, and there was a sharp pop, a clang, and the zinging noise of a ricocheting bullet. Austin fell back in his chair. One of the steel chimpanzees developed a navel. And the final bagged landscaped, shot true in the belly, began to shed slowly out of its lining a drip of Bueche-Girod watches.

Austin was dead. I was looking at him, stupidly —the nice man who had held my hand on the plane to Ibiza—when the impact of a robed body knocked me back on my heels. A hooded figure, the gun still smoking in its hand, flung itself on me, twisted my arm hard up my anoraked back, and shoving me sideways began to carry me with it through the door and off down the stairs.

I saw everyone in the gallery stop moving, suddenly, and realized that if they hadn't, I was going to be shot. I realized if I struggled, I was going to be shot anyway. The man holding me was powerful enough to drag me as far as the door before he had time to say *"Walk!"* and to make sure that I did walk by shoving the gun hard into my skin. I stumbled down the staircase beside him and discovered

I was squealing, anyway, at the top of my voice. Above, I could hear Johnson's voice shouting something, an order, in Spanish.

Ahead was the doorway, with an armed policeman in it. He must have heard what Johnson shouted. On seeing me, he dropped his gun and stepped back. Hauling me with him, the Penitent Brother dodged out into the street. Without conscious effort I was still shrilling like an alarm clock; my assailant stopped, for a second, in the dark, echoing street and clouted me once on the ear with his gun. "Be quiet." I cut out, and with a jerk that nearly took my ball and sockets apart, he started to run.

A roomful of grown, bloody men, and a fat lot of protection they'd been.

Behind, I could hear people pelting down Austin's tiled hall. Above, here and there, dim faces attracted by the brief screeching looked down, with interest, from the lit balconies. And in the street, one or two knots of people turned around.

The tricky thing was the gun. I could have yelled, or tripped the brute up, if it hadn't been for the gun. I'm as strong as most men, though this one was big: bigger than a Spaniard, I'd say, and he'd spoken in English. The words, whispered, told me nothing at all. There was no smell of curry.

That, at least, had a negative value. It wasn't Gil or his father, hastily got up in robes. It wasn't Spry, because I'd seen him a moment before. It wasn't Derek, because I know the feel of Derek, and anyway, he'd been the one who caught Austin. And it wasn't poor Austin. It was someone whom Austin knew . . . an ally, a partner, who had robbed

Austin, in turn, of the rubies Austin had stolen. And who had killed Austin to prevent his name being known.

We were running fast, dodging people, while I was thinking. My Penitent Brother had problems as well. He had to gain enough ground to get out of those clothes without being recognized. Until then, he'd need me as a hostage. Afterward, he wouldn't want me at all. Living, that is.

I was gasping. The gun was now in my side, and it tightened when I made to look round. I couldn't tell if the others were following. My heart was drumming: it seemed to me that bugles rang in my ears, that the music had come back, louder, with the hum of crowds watching. I suppose I realized at the same moment as my captor that it wasn't a dream. It was eleven-thirty, and the Easter Procession of Silence was on its way back from the Monument, about to enter the Portal, and retrace its weary steps up to the top square again. In a moment, the road we were on was going to be crowded with people.

There were steps on our left, wide cobbled steps with trim marble edges plunging clean down into the dark below Austin's handsome paved Calle de San Guillermo. The hooded man beside me shifted his grip on my arm and, swinging me round hard against him, drove me before him down the black stairs. I thought I heard, as we went, the sound of running footsteps behind. So long as pursuit stayed quite close, I didn't see how this man could kill me. The moment he shook it off, he most certainly would.

We went down those stairs like two roller coasters, slewed right round the blank wall of a house, and debouched into a narrow, dirt lane full of uneven white houses with broken steps and poles of washing like ghosts over our heads. A low wall on the left showed, as we flew, a glimpse of tiled roofs, lights of the harbor, and distant hills black against the dark sky. It looked peaceful and free. Turning, I missed my footing and stumbled and for a second was dragged off balance down the black, stony track.

The lane was a cul-de-sac. The hand on my arm spun me round, and we reached the steps again and resumed the headlong rush downward, twisting again and again between narrow, high walls until we reached another flat, stony space in the darkness, lined with dim, peeling houses, their blinds rolled up over rusty railings, the windows all empty except, here and there, for a flickering light and the sound of a child's thin voice, wailing. A wireless spoke, and a cat, surprised, made a high sound. I thought of the dead rat in the ditch, the night I met Austin, and shivered. The man with me slowed down and stopped. Then, pulling me, he melted into a deep, broken doorway.

It was very dark. A lantern fixed to one of the houses threw a limited light, like dust, on the ground, and a lizard, moving into its circle, rustled off into the rubble. The bugles, starting up somewhere not too far away, were like a sudden scratch on the nerve endings. I felt the man beside me jump too: we were both breathing hard, trying to subdue it, but not hard enough to drown the light patter of steps coming down the stairs we had left and continuing past us. They receded into the blackness below, and the sound vanished with them.

We waited, and I thought, "This is it. Goodbye, Sarah." A shot through the heart—the crochet wasn't going to offer much resistance. And then my Penitent Brother, whoever he was, would merely peel off his Penitent clothes, walk up and mix with the crowds, in his usual identity. I felt the hand on my arm beginning to relax and his other hand, his gun hand, lift and alter its grip. A voice, calling, said "Cassells? Sarah!" from below; from the foot of the steps. Not near enough to come back and spot us. But too near for murder.

The man beside me said something under his breath, and the hand on my arm tightened, and the gun muzzle moved back again to my side. Then he said "Run!" in the same eerie, hoarse whisper and set off, pulling me, up to main street again.

Just now, I had been lucky. This time, his luck was in. In a burst of torchlight and music, the procession had reached the end of the calle but only just. The drumbeat echoed: Tuck, Tr-r-uck, tru-uck, truck, tuck; and the sound pattered, like shuttlecocks, back and forth along the double row of fine houses. We didn't wait for the crowd. My hooded friend ran before it, deeper down the dark street, and found the steps he must have been seeking, I realized, the first time. As the main road curled steeply up to the left, a stepped, cobbled lane led downward, past big houses set at different levels, with double doors and light shining bright through their fanlights.

Perhaps I hesitated as we passed. Certainly the gun hurt my ribs, grating against my side as we went, and the hand on my arm was hot and soaking with sweat. The steps were wide, sweeping down between white walls covered with roses. Their scent came plain as the bugles in the quiet night air, and through a wrought-iron gate you could see a garden, the lacework of a trellis, a glimmer of water, and the sparks of two cigarettes being smoked at ease, under the palms. At the bottom was another narrow dirt lane, with a row of low white houses facing us to left and to right, flowers on their deep sills. A lantern, glowing dimly, showed an orange bead curtain, still swaying, and on the left, a bastion of the old wall, on which stood a Gothic gallery, with arched windows and massed flowers in pots. We swept past it and into an unpaved square with a concrete pump in the middle. Two men, talking in low voices, stood beside it and watched us, with curiosity, as we strode past. A Penitent Brother, called away perhaps in emergency, by his wife or his daughter. It was no use calling out. Not with the gun there.

There was a choice of two lanes. He took the darker one, always sinking, bending down through cobbled steps to the right; taking the right again when it forked to shrink to almost nothing between tall, broken houses, with netting hung in the doorways and the glimpse of a chair and a curious face, here and there, just inside.

On the right was a yard: part cobbled, part dirt, part cement. Broken tiles lined the high doorsteps, and the doors were warped and weathered pale silver, and the windows were broken, rusty, and barred. A falling building, propped up by timber, leaned across a flight of worn steps leading downward, past locked doors and blind, netted windows. The steps disappeared into darkness: only I could see a greater darkness arching over them, and I guessed that they entered a tunnel, made by two joined buildings above. A tunnel with no open doors, no prying eyes in it. The gun moved, and I was driven to the steps and down toward it.

I think, perhaps, I would have attempted to trip him. I certainly was going to scream. I knew this branch of the Cassells line had pretty well come to an end, but I didn't see why he should rat out of payment. I had my mouth open when I heard the running footsteps again far behind: spaced out, as a man runs when he is taking two, three, four steps at a time. Fast enough to overtake another man before he can disrobe. The grip on my arm propelled me suddenly again into motion, and I saw that the tunnel was just a short archway and that it stood over a perpendicular flight of black steps, whose lower reaches were flooded with clear yellow light.

It led directly into the main square of the Dalt Vila, with the Portal framing the end. And curling round the archway and up the steep cobbles on its way back to the Cathedral were the torches, the shuffling figures, the jerking, flickering litters of the Procession of Silence. The main exit to the low town and safety was closed.

The man beside me looked round. There were people in the square: quite a lot of them. There were people, too, in the steep street to the left which ran, I suddenly remembered, to another gateway, the New Port, on the west. I wondered why we didn't make for it, and then saw the lamps glittering on the folded black hats of the police. My captor moved and, then without warning, strode straight across the lit square and through the space between two houses opposite. It was wasteland and dark. I stumbled, trying to keep my footing, and was hurried across ridges of half-broken wall and piles of crumbling earth in a darkness which was almost total. Behind, over my shoulder, I caught a glimpse of the lights of the square and the gap through which we had come, empty of following figures. Ahead was a great blackness topped by a dim, irregular line: the wall of the battlements of San Juan, overlooking the town. Above it, the sky was full of stars.

It had been a mistake to look up. I missed my footing in earnest this time and, tumbling forward, fell head over heels down a steep, earthy slope, landing in blackness, all the breath knocked clean out of me.

There is no aid like cowardice in a quick-reaction alert. I got to my feet while my robed friend was still coming and made off like a hare.

I was running, I found, in a ditch. It was manmade and excessively deep, and the sides were formed by slopes of sieved, heavy, dry earth, down one of which I had just tumbled. I tried running up them again. It was like trying to climb into the top of an hourglass. I wasted time on it, while the thudding footsteps behind me got closer, and gave up and sprinted, as fast as my shaking sinews would make it, along the foot of the ditch.

It ended in a blocked tunnel. Just that. Why, I never knew. I never knew either what they were building there, or laying, or why they wanted a tunnel at all. I just knew I ran into it and turned, cornered, and stood motionless, my pent-up breath mewing with exhaustion, while he groped all over the blackness, coming closer and closer. I made a break for it in the end, running headlong for the dim mouth of the tunnel—the way I'd come in.

I fell. As he flung his full weight on me, I thought the roof of the tunnel had caved in. Then I saw his black robe fly up, and his foot came over, hard, pinning mine.

All the penitents I had seen wore black shoes. All the holiday-makers I mixed with wore light Spanish shoes in fine leather or suede. The man gripping me now, and heaving me up, breathing fast, grunting, with the gun in his hand, wore neither of these. He wore sneakers. White canvas sneakers, liberally stained with grass and with salt.

I stopped struggling, and he dragged me upward; the grip on my arm became sickening. I heard him draw breath to tell me: this is the end of the road.

"Clem, don't be silly," I said.

CHAPTER 12

I DIDN'T REALLY BELIEVE IT myself, until I felt his arm sag. I was nearly sick, then. Flo would have been sick.

I said again, "Don't be silly. We all know who you are."

"You're lying," he said. It was Clem's voice.

"I'm not," I said. Steam was coming out of my brain. "Jorge and Gregorio are in Mummy's house. Johnson took them there."

"You're lying," he said again, and his voice had got three notes higher.

"I'm not," I said. "How else do you think Johnson knew there was another replica of the Saint Hubert collar? He only wanted you to betray yourself."

I wasn't sure, even then, if what I was saying made sense. All I knew was that somehow I had to make him believe that Johnson knew who he was. That way, there was no need to kill me. That way, he needed me as a hostage for a little while yet, because he couldn't just go back to *Dolly* and pretend to have been there all night, lying faint with a bump on his head. (Who had done that? Austin?) Somehow, Clem Sainsbury had to escape.

You could see the thoughts going through his head as, automatically, he started to move once again. The hand with the gun had come down, but he hadn't released me. He had only shifted the point of the gun from my head to my back. Then we stood in the entrance of the tunnel and waited.

It was very quiet. Over the wasteland and beyond the sides of the plaza, you could hear the intermittent sounds of the procession: the tiny bugles, the flat thud of the drums, marking all the slow stages. Soon, when the Portal was clear, Clem would try to get through.

Clem. He had taken his hood off and now, maintaining his gun carefully in my ribs, he was dropping his robe. No need for concealment now: not from me. If I was telling the truth, it would make no odds with Johnson, either. And if I wasn't, he could bluff. He might even, gun pressed in my side, misdirect the hunt. So I suppose he was thinking. He didn't say anything. And in the dark I could make out almost nothing: just the humid heat of his bulk, his short hair sticking with sweat above the pale blur of his face, and the raucous sound of his breath. He said suddenly, "What a pity I can't trust you, Sarah. Damn you, why can't I trust you?" His voice was like a boy's, petulant; and he pulled me with his gun hand close, hard to his body, so that his mouth was close to my cheek. He licked my ear.

I nearly screamed. I drew in my breath with a shrieking whisper, and stopped the sound as he jerked off, groaning with anger, and brought the gun butt across the side of my head. A lot of lights sprang about in front of my eyes, and I lost my balance; when I got over it, I was leaning against the cold side of the archway with the hot, hard grip still on my arm, but there was space between us again. The drums had faded.

"The next time," said Clem, "I'll scoop your brains out like seeds from a melon." He seemed to enjoy the expression. Then we started moving again.

I had had a hope, I believe, that he would try to emerge in the square and that the police would stop him. How I thought this would save my own life, I don't know. I don't remember being concerned by much except a desire to see him under lock and key. At any rate, he didn't even look at the square. He walked instead along the ditch and back up to the wall of the battlement. He followed it, walking carefully, round all its points until it took two left-hand turns and came out, incredibly, above the roofless square of the chamber which lay just inside the Portal de las Tablas, the main gateway of Dalt Vila.

There was no float there now: jammed blazing under the balcony. There were no policemen either; these were all in the square. I saw Clem's teeth flash in a strong, healthy smile, and he said, "You managed to follow me up, darling. So you shouldn't find it too hard to get down. Just take my hand."

And the next moment we were through the low door, scrambling down that damned creeper.

The ramp down to the market was empty but for a child or two, laggard to bed, and a disbanding family party. There were plenty of lights, and in the town groups of people turning away, to catch a bus, to have a last drink, to talk with chance-met friends. White-robed penitents, having delivered their image, were gathered chatting outside their church, a litter of flowers at their feet. Inside the church, a priest was dismantling the palinquin. The lamps were unscrewed and the Virgin's gown had gone, disclosing the rusty metal of the two heavy batteries. A girl of about six, with pigtails and a frilled blouse and a round Hapsburg chin, was fooling about with a palm leaf. We hurried on.

No one looked at us: the brawny young man and the girl he was holding so closely. And yet, I supposed he had the Saint Hubert rubies in his pocket. I said, "Where are you going?"

He couldn't kill me here: not unless he were cornered. But if he were cornered, I thought, he would do it, out of sheer bravura and hate. You would have to hate people to kill as he must have killed . . . Austin. Coco. Father.

He didn't answer. But suddenly, as the silence continued, as we made our way to the quayside, I knew where he was going. He had to get out of Ibiza. No man could hide on an island. No plane would take him. But there was a boat which would take him very well . . .

Dolly. Dolly, with her powerful engine, sitting unattended in her berth, along by the yacht club.

By the quay, he found Mummy's Humber, parked

there by Dilling through the gentlemanly offices of the chief of police. The keys were still in it. Clem stopped, drew a breath, and then, flinging me in by main force, got the thing started and the gun again in my side before I recovered. Moving like a runaway hearse at a funeral, the Humber thundered across the wide space of the quayside and along to the right, on the road to the clubhouse. Clem drove all the way without changing down, with one hand on the wheel, and made the turn into the yard of the yacht club at the same speed, putting both feet on the pedals with such force that I was nearly flung through the windscreen. Then he snapped up the handbrake and motioned me out.

The gates were shut. For a moment I hoped they'd be locked and realized, then, that they wouldn't be. Men living on boats could hardly be held to a curfew. In fact, Clem heaved at one of the new, silvery leaves and, pushing his gun in my back, forced me through. Then pushing me, he began to run down the steps and along the quay toward *Dolly.*

We passed them one after the other, the beautiful boats with the yacht-club hieroglyphics: KYC; NRV; CNI, and the orange and blue nylon ropes. Boats whose owners liked swimming and sunshine and had no need to count time. Those who could leave their offices, if they had offices, to fly to the Med and take on a casual boy, the son of a friend, a student down for vacation, and float with a party of friends—a bridge four, a drinking party, a sex foursome with congenial wives—from port to port and island to island, while the weather went along with the whim. I knew all the names. I knew some of the people. Daddy, probably, had known them all. We came, running, to the bollard where *Dolly* was berthed . . .

And *Dolly* was missing.

I heard Clem's breath go in like a whistle. He looked round, heavily, like a bull. Had she changed berths? Was she out at a mooring? Was she sailing?

I looked at him. It mattered to me. Pushed to the end of his nerves, he was unpredictable. I didn't know what he might do. I couldn't see *Dolly* either, not anywhere: although we ran back along the whole frontage, desperately, and then retraced our steps. He stood gazing at the space where she'd been, his eyes black and open, as he wondered if he'd gone mad. Perhaps he had. His face was heavy and unlined, without any real stamp of living, as it had always been. I had envied him his lack of anxieties, in the simple, open-air life he had chosen. I hadn't realized that, perhaps, his brain didn't accept normal worries, that its scale of reference was quite different.

He stared at the water, and then for the last time he turned round, and I turned with him. We both saw *Dolly,* I think, at the same moment.

She wasn't in the water at all. She was lying, her masts sloping above us, in the boatyard, and she was moving slowly as the chains pulled her up: up to where a blinded horse walked in a circle, loading the core of the winch.

I think then Clem went crazy. He left me. He dropped even his gun and ran through the gate, scrambling into the boatyard past tar barrels and lumber and tarpaulined boats. Then, seizing the horse, running after it as it shook its head and tried

256

to jerk free, he tried to get it to turn, to reverse the laborious circle and unwind, so that the chains would slacken and *Dolly* would slip back into the water again—the life-giving water, where his only hope lay.

He was on the horse, urging it, when the Maserati flew down the road, and Johnson piled out, with Spry and Dilling and three Spanish police officers, hanging on by their eyebrows. A moment later, the Buick came along too, driven by Gilmore, with his father and my mother in the back. I didn't see what happened as they streamed over the weedy sand into the enclosure: I had stopped looking as soon as Clem got near the horse. In fact, I think I was crying, in horrible, great, uncouth gulps, when Mummy came over the rubble, picking her way with her flounces hitched up round her calves, and sitting down, proceeded to fish out and light a cheroot. She said, "Organized games: I never could go along with them. I didn't tell you, She-she at the time, but I got real worried when St. Tizzy's made you captain of cricket. If your body's all that healthy, I reckon there's something gone soft in your mind. Look at Derek. He was never the same after those nut cutlets."

I swallowed. I don't know why Mummy doesn't talk like other people. I said, "Oh, for Pete's sake. I suppose you'd prefer Coco."

"But that proves my point," Mummy said, taking her cheroot out of her mouth. "Think of the tennis. The fact that he was doped to the eyeballs doesn't make all that difference."

I said carefully, "I'm not sure, but I think you're saying Coco was soft in the head?"

257

"Well, he'd have to be, to let me keep him, dear, wouldn't he?" said Mummy. "He poured all the rest of himself into his concrete, poor darling. To die young is not always a sorrow. Look how fat your gym mistresses always used to become."

"But you don't want to kill off my gym mistresses?" I said. The running, the scuffling, and the subdued shouting had retired in the direction of the yacht clubhouse. "Where would we be without all those chest-developing exercises?"

"You wouldn't have had to wear your girdle under your armpits during all last year's fashion," pointed out Mummy, with justice. "The healthiest people are those who never think of their health."

"Well, Christ, they don't need to," I said, "if they're healthy. They've got leisure then to stir up trouble sticking their noses into other people's business. You don't find hypochondriacs staging a thirty-six hour sit-down protest in sleet outside the Central Iguanian Embassy. Or Olympic medalists, either."

Mummy stared at me. "There's no such place as a Central Iguanian Embassy."

Johnson's pipe glowed, suddenly, in the dark close beside us. "But there ought to be," he said. "If you've finished the cross talk, Mr. Lloyd has kindly offered to run us all back to his house for a meal."

"He *what?*" I said, straightening my knees.

"Oh, hard luck, She-she," said my mother, shaking the dust from her flounces and rising, cheroot holder extended, to touch me absently on the cheek. "I don't suppose it has struck him that you'll have to cook it. If you would bear in mind my small problem. My diet doesn't permit me to take any fat."

"Your *diet,*" I said. "Did you say your d . . . ?"
Mummy's stare would have impaled a lizard.
"Beauty," she said, "and symmetry. To have regard
for the case of one's instrument is a matter of simple
aesthetics. I believe we are summoned."

She stalked off into the darkness in the direction
of the cars. Johnson tucked his arm around mine.
"High-speed wander in the steering-unit," he said.
"But the engine's terrific. Come with us and get
drunk."

I cooked the dinner. Everyone was hollow-eyed
and sickly, except Johnson, and they kept coming
and patting me, which was sweet. They really
needed a good meal. I wasn't feeling frightfully
Spanish, so I warmed up some thick lentil soup
and fried them bacon and eggs. The bacon wasn't
fearfully appealing and the eggs were the usual, like
Ping-Pong balls filled by a fulmar, but it was something like home. I switched on all the lights in the
dining room and pulled all the blinds, and if I'd had
an LP of Elgar, I'd have put that on too. Then I
banged on the gong.

There were only seven of us: Janey and Gil and
their father, and our three guests, Derek and Johnson and Mummy. Mummy had taken off all her
flounces and was wearing a Jean Harlow thing
Janey had bought in Neiman Marcus once for a
lark: it was floor-length pink, edged with white
swansdown. She is so damned sure of herself, she
made her entrance quite straight: just glided in
puffing cheroot smoke and sat down, without being
directed, on Mr. Lloyd's right. Janey, balked of her
little amusement, glanced in Gil's direction and sat
down also, making a face. She had changed into a

259

sort of light trench-coat dressing gown, and both Gil and his father had polo-necked cashmeres and slacks. Comfort was what we all wanted. I'd had no time to refurbish at all. Gil looked at the crochet thing as I brought in the soup, and getting up, disappeared and came back with a cardigan. It was Janey's best, made of white cashmere with pearls and a mink collar, and I put it on, keeping my face straight as well. Johnson, who was wearing the same as he'd worn all day, put his pipe in his pocket and also came and sat down.

Mr. Lloyd finished handing round very large whiskeys, and sat down heavily, at the head of the table, saying "Now, Johnson," in a definite voice. Ever since he had spotted that Johnson had something basic to do with it all, he had been very hard to put off. When we'd finished exclaiming, we'd all been inclined to badger Johnson on the way home, but he had remained uncommunicative and calm. "It's a long story, and I'd rather tell it all at once and to everyone at the same time. Wait until we get in."

We'd left Dilling and Spry behind in Ibiza, with what looked like the entire Spanish police force. I gathered they were all going to Mummy's villa to take official custody of Jorge and Gregorio: Clem and the Saint Hubert rubies were already safely locked up. It hadn't dawned on me until then that Dilling, as well as Spry, was Johnson's man. Even then, I couldn't really absorb it, but just sat with my teeth chattering somewhat until the Casa Veñets came into view. We were all, I suppose, really getting over the shock.

Johnson sat, staring into his soup, and said, "Mr.

Lloyd, you are the only person here, I believe, who doesn't know that Mrs. van Costa is Sarah's mother. The deception was a perfectly innocent one and had a great deal to do with what has happened today. If the children hadn't stumbled on the fact rather by accident, they wouldn't have known either. I tell you this so that you will see there are only two families here tonight, apart from myself; and I want a promise from you both that what I am now going to tell you won't go beyond these four walls."

Mr. Lloyd's eyes, swiveling, met my mother's. She stubbed out her cheroot and absently patted his hand. "You have my word," said Mr. Lloyd to Johnson. "And you may take it I speak for my family."

"Now listen to that, She-she," said Mummy.

"*Their* family's normal," I said. "I won't tell anyone, Mr. Johnson."

"And I certainly won't," Derek said. "What are you, sir? MI 5?"

"They never gave me a number," said Johnson with regret. "I just knock around with a boat and some paints, and they call me in if anything happens to the genuine men in the field. If they go off the rails or get themselves into trouble or get murdered, for instance."

There was a short silence, as all the spoons stopped. Mummy was smiling into her plate like Mia Farrow by Leonardo da Vinci. I stared at Derek, and he stared back, going slowly red in queer patches. I said, "Daddy?"

"Yes. Schuytstraat got it wrong, Derek," said Johnson. "Your father was, as it happened, an agent. But for us, not for the wrong side."

261

"You *knew?*" I said to Mummy. It was absolute rubbish, of course. Daddy had been a charming old, liquored-up peer, and of such, secret agents are simply not made. I remembered the offer he'd made Derek of five thousand a year to leave Schuytstraat's and opened my mouth to continue, but Mummy forestalled me.

"Yeah. I knew," she said. "I guessed last time I saw him. He dropped by, you know, when he was staying with those friends in Bermuda. He looked much the same and he talked much the same, but there was a kind of difference. You wouldn't notice unless you'd gotten kind of used to him over a period. It seemed to me half of it was acting."

"Only half," said Johnson gently. "We couldn't entrust him with anything major. But he helped me once, quite unwittingly in a . . . small contretemps. He was sober at the time, and he acted with such speed and such imagination that it struck me that here was something to be salvaged. Forgive me, Lady Forsey, for putting it like that."

"Mr. Johnson, you may put it any way that you like," said my mother. "However he died, Eric owed the whole of the last part of his life to you people. We had nothing in common, Lord Forsey and I, when we parted. When we met again, I found things were quite different. Nothing was said; not at first, but we formed the habit of writing, and we arranged to meet the next year, briefly, on a friend's yacht. It was after we had become quite close again that I got out of him the cause of the change. I am telling all the rest of you this, as I have already told Mr. Johnson, so that you will understand that Lord Forsey did not regard me as an outsider when finally he told me of his new work. All the time, of course, he continued to travel and visit with friends, and present the same impecunious face to the world. It hurt him, She-she and Derek, to have to deny you some of the luxuries he felt you should have, and it hurt him even more that neither of you would ever realize he was not the man you both thought he was. I don't think it harmed either of you not to have money, although it may have been hard on you, Derek, not to have a parent whom you could respect. You placed him in a really awkward position when you accused him of betraying Schuytstraat's secrets. He didn't want either you or the firm to investigate any further, and the only way he could think of to stop you was to buy you off with a pension. He was rather proud, I may say, that you refused."

"He could have told me," said Derek. His nose had gone red.

"He was a great and good man," said Mr. Lloyd. He looked terribly struck. "And this was why he was killed? Because he was an agent?"

"He was killed," said Johnson, "because he found out the secret of Austin Mandleberg's gallery. Lady Forsey had seen some of these pieces of art in America. She is interested in artists: she knew how these exhibits should look. It struck her, seeing the exhibits a second and a third time, that they were being tampered with. Excisions had been newly made, and joins where there had been none before. She mentioned it in a note to her husband, and Lord Forsey, in Amsterdam for a trade fair, went to see for himself. Then, while he was in Holland, these highly secret items of machinery went missing from Schuytstraat's factory.

"Not only that, but they disappeared utterly, and no trace of them was ever found. No doubt he asked an unusual number of questions. At any rate, for quite the wrong reasons, he roused the company's suspicions. Meanwhile, without realizing this, he had discovered that the exhibition was going next to Ibiza. He found no difficulty in inducing Mr. Lloyd, who was a close and generous friend, to invite him to Ibiza for the duration of this exhibition. When he wrote and told Lady Forsey, she, too, on the whim of the moment, found means to rent a house in Ibiza, and taking Coco Fairley with her as cover, descended on the island as Mrs. van Costa. Her husband was perhaps a little disconcerted at finding her here, but no one knew her: even as an actress she had long been off the stage, and she had spent the last years of her life entirely in America. When she made her presence known to him, he rather enjoyed stealing off to meet her, clandestinely, at the villa. Unfortunately, Coco saw them."

"Coco," said Mummy, "was actually there uninvited. I had no wish for his company. He merely bought a plane ticket for himself, as well as for me, and threatened to kill himself if I refused to let him come with me. A silly boy," said my mother severely, "but he was right in the middle of a most valuable poem. I think it stands, still, as the best thing he has done. The letters are all formed from ten-cent New Zealand stamps with a human rights message. The impact of these words, multiplied hundreds of times was *cathartic*. He finished it, poor child, just a week or two before he died."

"Where is it?" said Gilmore. He had a doting look in his eyes.

"Oh. We posted it," Mummy said, faintly surprised. "She-she, I believe we've all finished soup."

I tore myself, with reluctance, from my seat. "Where to, for goodness' sake?"

"Let me guess," Johnson said. He contemplated the whiskey glass in his hand, the bifocals steady. "Vietnam?"

"Check," said Mummy, surprised. I shot out and came back with the bacon. Gilmore got up to help me. In the kitchen, he said, "Was she always like this?"

"Who? Mummy?" I said. "She was always bloody impossible, if that's what you mean. Well, imagine having her coming down for the Eton-Harrow match, smoking cheroots."

"I think she's marvelous," Gilmore said.

"She doesn't water-ski," I said bitingly. "How are Louie and Petra?"

"Blooming," said Gilmore. "What got into you two over your parents? They must have been quite remarkable."

"I'm glad you think so," I said, picking up a tray with the eggs. "But then, look at your taste."

When we got back, Johnson was explaining how on Daddy's death he had put into harbor with *Dolly*. It had been rigged as suicide, but he saw at once there wasn't enough blood. The body had been brought there, and death had actually taken place somewhere else. Since it was the Art in the Round Daddy had been suspicious of, there was at least a sporting chance that something had gone wrong there. He pulled strings and got the Spanish police to sit on the evidence that it was anything other than suicide. Then he went to Austin Mandleberg's gallery and started making gentle inquiries. Austin was still in Paris, and Jorge and Gregorio were most helpful. They remembered everyone who had been at the gallery during that afternoon and evening, and he was able to trace and discount every one. The only person whose visit they didn't mention was Clem Sainsbury, whom a neighbor had seen going in.

It was only a hunch, and there was no real reason then to think that Gregorio had been concealing anything. Since questioning, in any case, was quite useless and would have scared Clem off any scheme he might have, Johnson simply hired him to come and live as mate with Spry and himself on board *Dolly*.

It was then that he heard that Daddy had spoken of writing to me the day he died and that Janey had actually posted a letter. He wired London and got them to watch for it. He also got them to watch me and the flat.

I said, "Hey!"

"Your father had got himself into a dangerous business," said Johnson. "He might well have wanted to warn you, or to tell you something about it, or even to justify himself to you, after all those years, in case something went wrong. We had to know what he had written. It might even have told us his murderer."

"Well, it didn't, did it?" I said. "I should think it was the dullest letter he ever wrote in his life, probably because he was too stoned to think straight. The bit in the middle was gibberish. In any case, I've been thinking. Clem doesn't call me She-she; but Mummy does. Daddy could have picked that up from her. It *was* his letter, I expect, all the time."

"It wasn't, you know. I wrote it," said Johnson.

I gazed at him, the knife and fork limp in my hand. "You didn't," said Janey. "He gave me that letter to post himself, Mr. Johnson. And I posted it."

"But it didn't arrive," Johnson said. "And we wanted it to arrive, because it was obvious that the people who killed Lord Forsey were going to be very interested in what he might have said to his daughter. So we concocted another. I'm sorry about the slip, Sarah, over your name. It was no part of the plan that you should come haring over to Ibiza, even though you were quite right, if for the wrong reasons, in thinking your father had not killed himself. I wrote it, and I put that cockeyed section in the middle for a purpose: so that anyone hearing you speak of it would assume that it might well contain a message in code, even if you yourself did not understand it. In fact, you spoke of the incoherence in the letter in the phone call you made to Derek in Holland, reassuring him about what your father had said."

"I didn't tell you about the call," I said.

"Neither did Derek," said Johnson. "Your line was tapped. You were very well protected, you know, Sarah. We watched the flat day and night."

I thought of the one-armed bandit and the two and six for the pizza. "Oh. Big deal," I said crossly. "Pity you couldn't prevent someone from breaking in and pinching Flo's jewelry. You mean to say," I said, my voice getting high as I realized the iniquity of it, "that someone actually stood by and *watched* while a bloody spy walked in and raked through our drawers . . . ?"

"That was the point. No one broke in," Johnson said.

"They did," I said icily. "I do beg your pardon, but I have the bruises to prove it."

"All the same," Johnson said. "No one entered that flat, from the time you left to go to the film to the time you reduced the assets of the Bunting Fun Parlor."

I felt myself going scarlet. "So?"

"So there were two people in that flat all the evening," Johnson said. "Flo had no reason to invent a burglary: she could search the flat when you were out any time that she chose. That only left George."

"George?"

"You didn't see the masked man at the door: he supposedly did. George could have doped one of Flo's drinks and slapped ether about later on. He could easily have run past you in the dark, slammed the flat door without going out, and have been back in the sitting room by the time you telephoned, fixed Flo, and found him. In fact," said Johnson, "we investigated George and found quite an interesting history. He was an old ally of Clem's. He stuck close to Flo for the same reason that Clem passed so casually from girl to girl among all your crowd: to pick up tips about the houses you worked in.

"Did it never occur to you, Sarah, that you and the other girls like you are the biggest, single network of gossip about the moneyed houses of Britain that has developed today? You know the staff and the scandal and the domestic habits of every house you so casually enter for a weekend or a week. You know what jewels are kept in the bank and what goes into an old sock in the breadbin. You know what parties they go to, what they'll wear, what they're worth. And you all talk about it.

"I don't suggest Flo was a willing partner of Clem's, but he must have found her over the years a pretty valuable source of information about money and jewelry and other kinds of secrets: industrial, military. These were his business. Clem stole for a living, and like a great many other people, he used the Austin Mandleberg traveling show as a means of conveying his booty from one country into another. It was vital to him, as well as to Mandleberg, that no one should discover the secret of Art in the Round."

"So you knew about Clem?" Mr. Lloyd said.

Johnson shook his head. "Not then. We knew Sarah's flat had been bugged: we found the mechanism and left it there, so that when she got the false letter, the news of it went straight to George and his partners. We thought they would make another effort to break in and read it, when we hoped to identify them. Sarah put paid to all that by accepting your perfectly innocent invitation to come to Ibiza. It was fairly certain she'd bring the letter in question with her. That's why Austin Mandleberg was on that plane and why her luggage took so long at the airport: it was being very thoroughly searched. When they didn't find it, it seemed a fair guess that the letter must be in her handbag. Hence the rush to get it back when you dropped it, Sarah, at the edge of the road."

"You were following us?" I said. I thought of the kiss, and then didn't.

"I picked up the bag after you'd gone. Mandleberg left it behind quite deliberately, of course," Johnson said. "His face when he came back and found it had gone was a study. He raked about for the better part of an hour and then drove up and down the road inquiring at houses before he finally gave up and went home. As soon as he'd gone, I laid the letter by itself back in the ditch and brought the handbag here, to hand over to you."

"I remember," I said.

"I thought you would," he said smoothly, damn him. "It was rather a neat trick. Before I took you and Janey and Gilmore back to the ditch, I phoned up Spry at the yacht club and told him to tell Clem what had happened and that I wouldn't be long. Spry said Clem took all of three seconds to announce that he must rush out and buy something in town. He let him get a head start and then followed him. A bicycle is a wonderful thing. It was Clem whose white shoes you saw in the wood that night, Sarah. I knew it must be, but I didn't want him unmasked just yet. Spry was there, watching him. And I knew that Clem would have found and read your father's letter. He would know it was harmless. He would think, of course, that it was genuine, and the incoherence was caused, as you first thought, only by drink. And he would go ahead, as I hoped, with his plans, whatever they were."

Mr. Lloyd said, in a subdued voice, "It was Clem

who murdered Lord Forsey? But the macabre setting . . ."

"That was accident again, I believe. I don't know why Clem was at the gallery on the night Forsey went there. He may even have had his suspicions aroused. At any rate, he must have surprised him, perhaps trying to open one of the sections which Lady Forsey pressed with such effect earlier today. There was a fight, and Lord Forsey was killed.

"What then? My guess is that Clem was going to dump the body: take a dinghy out and drop it into the sea with a stone round its neck. He got it as far as the boatyard, perhaps in a wheelbarrow: it's downhill all the way, and the workshop certainly had one. At any rate, when he looked for his boat, he found she had gone. It was small wonder that what happened tonight half overturned what was left of his brain. Just like tonight, he must have looked for her, wildly, with a bloodstained body lying dead in the cart, sleeping ships beside him, and a party of late-night revelers coming along the road. Then he saw it: the classical practical joke. The boat he'd been working on, upon dry land, with the winch going round and round, and not a hope of getting the dinghy or anything else. And people approaching. So he took a desperate chance. He lifted Forsey out of the barrow and hitched him upon the horse. He was a powerful man. And he took out of his pocket the blade that had killed him, wiped it, and pressed Forsey's fingers on the handle. Then he fled to his friend's ship, the *Sheila,* and got into bed. The boy in the ship didn't even waken, and he spun him some tale in the morning; *Sheila* was leaving almost immediately anyway. As it happened, we've never traced that boy since. So still," said Johnson, "there was no real evidence, until Sarah realized she had seen a replica of the Saint Hubert rubies."

"Coffee, dear?" Mummy said.

I got up and started to collect plates. "That was after Coco died," Gilmore said thoughtfully. "I suppose Clem killed him too? Why?"

"On the evening that he died, Lord Forsey visited his wife," Johnson said. "I rather think Coco must have followed him and found that he went straight from there to Austin Mandleberg's house. It would have been fatal for him to tell anyone. Clem didn't know who Mrs. van Costa was, although Mrs. van Costa"—he smiled at Mummy—"had very kindly contacted me as soon as I arrived with *Dolly* and had made herself known. He constituted himself Sarah's bodyguard simply so that he might put a stop to any secrets Coco felt like imparting. He did, too. He waited until Dilling had gone, then doped and drowned him."

I had only got halfway to the door. "But you made Clem stay the night to guard Mummy?" I said.

Johnson smiled again, the bifocals flashing. "Your mother was safe: Clem had heard with his own ears that Coco hadn't had time to betray him. I wanted him out of the way. As it happened, it was that evening, with Sarah's help, that we were able to find the replica collar and prove that Jorge and Gregorio must somehow be in that part of the conspiracy, at least. If Clem had known that, he would have lost no time either in killing the two or getting them out of the country. Mandleberg was incapacitated, for the moment, with a gun wound.

"I let it appear that they had left the country under their own steam. We kidnaped each of them from his own house, then took them together to the salt flats and down to the anchorage. But instead of putting them on board the steamer, Spry received them on *Dolly,* which he had sailed round from her berth in Ibiza that night. They were tied up in the fo'c's'le and taken back to Ibiza while Clem was asleep in the Casa Mimosa. Then, when day dawned and we wanted Jorge and Gregorio off *Dolly,* Lady Forsey invented a reason for driving out from the villa, and of course Clem had to go as her bodyguard.

"In fact, they met you, Sarah, and went in pursuit of Derek, who was being so very energetic in his search for Jorge and Gregorio that he almost wrecked the whole thing. She found Derek and you, Mr. Lloyd, on your way to the salt flats, and managed to persuade you because of the heat, and helped for his own reasons by Clem, to cut short your inquiries. If you hadn't, you would almost certainly have heard about *Dolly.* Meanwhile, of course, Jorge and Gregorio had been safely removed to Lady Forsey's house, and Clem and Lady Forsey went on to be entertained painlessly here, at Mr. Lloyd's invitation. When the excuses for that visit ran out, Lady Forsey took Clem, on orders, to *Dolly,* where he had his unfortunate accident."

"Who hit him?" said Mr. Lloyd.

"Spry did," said Johnson. "Actually. Although when he came to, we rather gave him to believe it had been Austin."

Mummy sat up. "You told me," she said, "that someone had mistaken Clement for me."

"Well, I had to make some excuse," Johnson said cheerfully. "Couldn't have Clem blaming us for the dent on his head. As it was, we knew very soon after that that there was a second and better copy of the Saint Hubert collar in existence, and that it was therefore very likely that an attempt to steal it would be made that night. Clem, we think, was actually to encompass the robbery, with Austin presumably getting a cut for having provided the replica. Whether the stolen necklace was afterward destined for the Gallery 7 hiding place or not, I don't know. Anyway, as soon as we figured that out, our first step was to make sure that Austin believed that Clem's injury was far worse than it was. By the same token, Austin was already making himself out to be pretty feeble, whereas in fact he had every intention of nipping out as soon as you had all gone and accomplishing the theft by himself.

"You can imagine Clem's state of mind when he woke up on *Dolly* and learned that Austin had come and gone and had had every chance of delivering that blow. He lost no time, I can tell you, getting into Ibiza. He had no idea Spry was on his tail. He got to where, according to plan, two sets of penitents' clothing were waiting: one for himself and one for Austin, who was to help with the diversion. One set had gone, proving that Austin, far from being at death's door, was planning to snatch the rubies himself.

"In fact, that was precisely what Austin did, although in better faith than Clem suspected: he

274

really thought Clem was incapacitated on *Dolly*."

"Hence the punch-up?" said Gil.

"Hence the punch-up. Austin, carrying the rubies, fled for the house, with Clem hotfooting it after him. Unluckily, we were all rather close behind. Clem dropped back then and let Austin race by himself into the house, sure he knew, anyway, where Austin would hide the collar. Then he mingled, in his masked robe, with the rest of us as we all pelted past and was a spectator in all that nonsense in the gallery.

"He wasn't worried by then about Austin's fate. All he wanted was a chance to open that secret drawer and get away with the rubies. He got them out, too; only he couldn't get out of the room because I'd put a police cordon round the house with orders not to let anyone through. So when you, Gil, by sheer chance found the drawer, and when Austin, seeing that it was empty, knew Clem had taken the rubies, Clem realized that Austin would name him in a matter of seconds. So he shot him and tried to escape, with the rubies stuffed in his pocket. None of you," said Johnson gravely, "realizes even yet the full extent of Sarah's genius. To Sarah we owe the home-made bleep, or homing signal, which ensured that wherever any of you went we were able to find you."

"How?" said Mr. Lloyd sharply.

"Curry," said Johnson simply. "I followed two Pakistanis for miles. Otherwise it worked. It worked, of course, in the final resort, by allowing us to trace Sarah herself. We were with her from start to finish, although we didn't always let her know it."

Mummy said, "Not bad, She-she."

"It was my high spot," I said. "Actually, I thought Mr. Lloyd had killed Daddy."

"*I* had?" Mr. Lloyd looked amazed and then laughed. "What possible reason could I have had for doing that?"

"I don't know. But you were awfully ready with a gun in Austin Mandleberg's workshop, and you might have wanted the rubies. And then on the night of Janey's party, the night Daddy died—"

"I wasn't even—" said Mr. Lloyd, and paused. "Here."

"I know. It doesn't matter. Heavens," I said. "The coffee."

I went out and did a lot of cup rattling and came back with seven mugs and the kettle and a big jar of instant: to hell with beans in a crisis. I didn't escape it, though. The minute I got back in, I could hear Janey talking in her bright voice, the one she used after they found out her bed hadn't been slept in at St. T's. She turned it on me. "I was just going to say, I wish you'd told me your nasty suspicions. I could have set your tiny brain bells at rest. That was the night Daddy flew off to Barcelona."

"I know," I said. "Someone told me, that is. I just thought maybe he hadn't actually gone there. It was a silly idea."

"I don't suppose he did go there," said Janey languidly. "But he'd have a perfectly good alibi in Majorca. Wouldn't you, Daddy?"

Gilmore shifted in his chair and said, "Oh, shut up, Janey." But Janey went on staring at Mr. Lloyd, and her father looked back at her, without changing color or anything: just a long, steady stare. He said, without much tone, "Yes. I had."

"She sounds rather decent," said Janey. "I can't think why you don't do something about it. I mean, I can't hang around doing the flowers forever."

Mr. Lloyd got up very suddenly without touching his coffee and said to Janey, "Will you come out a minute?"

Janey got up without a word, and Gil rose at the same moment. "Can I come too?"

They were halfway to the French windows when Mr. Lloyd stopped suddenly and turning, said, "I'm so sorry. Would you excuse us?" He had gone very red now. Mummy waved graciously, and Derek said, "Of course, sir." Johnson was lighting his pipe.

There was a short silence while I poured the coffee. Then Mummy said, "You're a damned liar, She-she. You thought it was Derek. But I must say you did that rather well. Didn't she?"

"Sarah has the most delightful subconscious," said Johnson, "of any young woman I have ever met. Her conscious decisions are lousy."

"Well, goodness, if Louie's lot knew about the girl in Majorca, Janey was bound to know too. She didn't *have* to say anything. But I bet her father was relieved that she did."

Mummy put down her cup. "If Tony Lloyd marries this woman in Palma—"

"He will," said Johnson, removing his pipe from his mouth. "We checked up on that. The liaison has gone on for years: they have a child, as a matter of fact. Lloyd was afraid it would put out Gil and Janey, and the woman was afraid of cramping Lloyd's style. If things go well out there just now, I imagine he'll move her and the child in."

Mummy's face remained perfectly amiable. "It'll

throw Janey onto your market, darling. No more pouring vodka martinis for Russians."

"The Russians," said Derek suddenly. "Were they—?"

"They were," Johnson said, "in Spain on a perfectly innocent errand, but of course would hardly miss the chance of examining the goods. I'm quite sure Austin gave them a good look at the machinery while they were all in the gallery, and they were able to report back to Moscow that the exhibition should be given every possible welcome in the course of its European tour. That was all they wanted: they couldn't possibly have smuggled out anything quite so bulky. And since the real secrets were in the assembly and the content of the metal, no real harm has resulted . . . You think a good deal, don't you, of your work?"

"Yes," said Derek. "It's satisfying. I'm not a— big, forceful character. I like a quiet life."

"You haven't had much of a quiet life recently," Johnson said. "I don't see that either of your parents could have done any better than you did. Didn't you enjoy it at all?"

"Bits of it," said Derek, and his mouth gave a twitch. I didn't catch Mummy's eye. I felt, rightly or wrongly, that another problem was on its way to solution.

"And what about Sarah?" Johnson said. "Have you been casting the runes? What will you do with your money?"

"Big joke," I said, and pulled my fingernails out of my mouth. I was trying to grow them, but Lord Luck hadn't helped. *Lucky day for all money transactions,* it had said. *But you will need to take fam-*

ily matters a little more seriously. I said, with gloom, "Four pounds ten in the bank, and a week's half-rent owing to Flo."

"Daddy's money, sweetheart," said my mother. "He left you all his money. He knew Derek could earn all he needed."

I fixed my eyes on Janey's collection of woven straw skulls, and they stared back, their long black and red wigs dangling beneath them . . .

Wait. Of course. Spy money. He'd offered Derek five thou . . .

I said, "Enough for a flat?"

"Yup."

"Enough for a car? Maybe an E-type . . . ?"

"I hear these are looked on as a little bit common, She-she," said my mother. "I believe souped-up Minis are said to be groovy, if the rod doesn't snap. But anyway, you can get it. Maybe not a mink coat every year, and you can't join Annabel's, but a nice comfortable existence. You can give up your cooking."

"Oh." It had seemed to me that I could never give up cooking, except by marrying money. All the other things I was good at were unmarketable, except to a husband. And even cooking, I knew, would never bring me the income I needed, to live in the way my friends did, without cadging to do it.

I thought about it, and I made a sudden, peculiar discovery. I said, "But I like cooking, you know. I like to organize people and help them and sort of give them surprises. I'll maybe just keep it on."

"Do you suppose," Johnson said, "that you are one of the few mixed-up brats of this world whose morals will actually improve with a large gift of money? What about Gilmore?"

"I will thank you," said Mummy, rising and feeling for a cheroot, "to lay off young Gilmore. I have him in hand."

I got up, too. "What do you mean, you have him in . . ."

"I mean," said Mummy coldly, "that I am placing my business interests, such as they are, in that young man's hands, and I am going to see that he works at them. He has the makings of a real fine executive, if he would keep his mind off sex and fast cars and tennis. I don't wish him disturbed."

I stood, with my hands hanging by my sides. "You've moved over from poets?"

"You can have them," said Mummy. "You're welcome," she added.

I stared at her. "Why? A loss leader to inveigle me into the business?"

"What business?" said Mummy.

"A partnership," said Johnson mildly. "Join her, Sarah. Together, you and your mother will fell your men like a two-handed chain saw."